WHIT

CORA ROSE

CREDITS

Editor: Angela O'Connell

Copyright © 2022 by Cora Rose

All rights reserved.

No part of this book may be reproduced in any form or by any electronic or mechanical means, including information storage and retrieval systems, without written permission from the author, except for the use of brief quotations in a book review.

❦ Created with Vellum

To my sister.

PREFACE

These characters came to me in the middle of the night, and I fell in love. I had to write down their story before they disappeared. In all my life, I've never written a book so fast. The words just flew onto the pages. I hope you enjoy the story as much as I have.

Trigger Warnings: Mentions of depression and self-harm.

CHAPTER ONE

In the beginning, the gods created Whit Cristian. They also created me, Caleb van Beek. Two men, both the same age, walking around the same campus but opposites in almost every way.

Amazingly, we can cohabitate in the same space without killing one another.

Most days, I do things to try and gauge him and his responses. However, I don't find myself wanting to hurt him. In fact, I just want to get a reaction from him.

It's been futile thus far. I haven't gleaned much about him.

He's intriguing in an infuriating way. I want to crawl inside his mind and take a long ass look at what's in there.

Probably all nice and organized like his life.

I glance over at Whit from the corner of my eye and take a long sip of my beer. The cool liquid slips down my throat, and I close my eyes.

I don't know Whit well at all. Just met him, in fact, after answering a "roommate wanted" ad two weeks ago. What I do know is that he's quiet, and I can tell he's brilliant. Smarter than me, that's for sure. He's always reading, his Kindle appearing in his hand at all times of the day. He must have a hidden pocket somewhere in those signature dark jeans of his.

You know, come to think of it, I've never seen him in anything but dark clothing. Black pants, dark grey long-sleeved Henley's, and black boots. Even his pajamas are black. Yesterday, in a fit of severe curiosity, I snuck a peek in his drawers looking for any sign of color, and found none. Even his underwear is black or dark grey. This fucker has some serious color palette issues.

I have a serious urge to sneak a pair of colorful socks into his drawer and watch him lose his shit.

Not that he loses his shit. He usually just glowers.

I glance over at him, and if I squint my eyes just right, he looks a bit like Ben Barnes in that boring movie *Dorian Grey*. All mysterious and svelte.

I, on the other hand, need some serious help. My blond hair has grown too long and could use a cut. I eye my bright yellow shirt and rub at an oil stain streaked across the side. I look like a piece of dirty caution tape.

Well, hell. I'll need to go to Walmart and grab a new pack of shirts soon. Probably should grab two packages just in case. With my current job at the scrapyard my uncle owns, my clothes are trashed on a daily basis.

Running a hand through my messy hair, I lean back in my chair and take another swallow of beer. I rub at the stubble lining my jaw and note that I need to shave sometime soon.

Probably tomorrow, if I remember.

Maybe next week, once the beard settles in.

Speaking of plans...

"Hey, Whit," I say suddenly, drawing those dark eyes away from his Kindle.

He raises an eyebrow, and I feel myself blush slightly. God, this guy makes me feel like a fool for just existing. It's a fantastic talent he has. He should capitalize on it. He'd make millions.

"Going out with some people tonight."

Whit continues to stare at me, probably waiting for me to get to the point. He's probably regretting his decision to share this space with me. Since unpacking my stuff, I've felt his disappointment in selecting me as his roommate. He probably can't wait to kick me out once my lease is up.

"Want to join?" I finally ask, and Whit's eyes widen slightly, no doubt surprised I've invited him. I've never invited him anywhere. Never planned to. This just happened. I like spontaneity, and I'm pretty sure Whit has never once been spontaneous in his entire adult life.

No, spontaneity requires a bit of mess, and Whit is *not* messy.

He's not an extrovert either. One of the many other ways we are opposites. Where he collects books, I collect friends. Where he collects knowledge, I collect...well, not quite sure. Useless, random facts, maybe?

"No, thank you," he says and then turns back to his book.

"It's trivia night, my man. You may like it."

"Doubtful," he replies, not even looking up at me.

Well, hell.

I roll my eyes, finish my beer, and slam it harder than necessary on the table. I tried, at least. I made an effort with the dude. I congratulate myself on pushing past my comfort zone and then stand up, lumbering over to the trash can and tossing the glass bottle inside.

"Recycling, please," Whit says the moment the lid closes. It's one of those nice ones that shuts slowly and silently. I hate it.

I send him a glare.

This guy.

Pulling the bottle from the trashcan, I toss it into the recycling bin sitting on the far end of the kitchen. It clatters inside noisily, and I feel smug for a moment. Hope I ruined his concentration.

"Better?" I ask dryly, and Whit side-eyes me before focusing his attention back on his book.

This guy is cryptic as fuck. It's one of the reasons my cousins wanted to meet him tonight. Mainly because since moving in two weeks ago, I've mulled over him, his behavior, his attitude. Out loud. Because I *cannot* figure him out. The topic of Whit has dominated all areas of conversation. My nosy cousins are almost as invested in figuring him out as I am.

They say I have a crush.

Nah, it's an obsession.

Because straight guys don't have crushes on other dudes.

Nope.

It's just that…look, I'm not the brightest bulb, but I do have strong emotional intelligence. Usually, I can read people like a book, but I can't get a read on this guy for the life of me. He's like a sealed vault. No one in or out.

And trust me, I've tried. I've snooped. I've researched. I've stalked. I've drawn the line at asking my cousin Sem to do some digging. So, I've got nada. I've seen him around campus, walking *alone* or at home, *alone*. I've never seen him socialize with anyone, and I sure as shit haven't seen him flirting with anyone. Perhaps he just doesn't like people. He sure as shit doesn't like me.

An enigma, this one.

Everyone likes me.

"Well, I'm heading out then. For a fun night of *trivia*."

"Good," he says, without taking his eyes off his book.

I stare at him for a long, drawn-out moment before scratching at my stomach and glancing down.

Shit. Probably should change into something without oil stains on it. Have to make an impression, especially if I want to *maybe*, *possibly* get some. It's been a while.

Been a while for a lot, actually.

Haven't been touched by anyone in weeks.

Platonically too.

God, I miss my mom.

Her hugs were the best.

Probably should call my aunt and visit her. She's the next best thing.

I push the multiplying thoughts from my mind and grab the back of my shirt, pulling it over my head.

Whit's eyes dart over to me, and they linger a little too long on my abs before moving back to his book. A faint blush darkens those pale cheeks, and I find myself puffing out my chest, making sure to flex. I work hard on my body and feel proud he seems to have noticed. He usually has no glances to spare.

I make sure to walk by.

Slowly.

He peeks over at me again, and I bite back a smile before walking to the room we share and pulling on a clean shirt.

When I walk out to the living room, Whit has earbuds in his ears, and his eyes are closed.

Probably meditating.

He does that a lot when I'm around.

Well, fuck him too.

"Shit," I say, stumbling into the dark apartment. I'm still getting used to this place. It's so nice and new and expensive.

How rent is so cheap is beyond me. I got hella lucky locking this place down.

Even if I have to share a room with Whit.

"He's so…tall," I grumble, dropping my keys on the floor. I stare at them for a moment and then bend down, unable to grab them right away. The ground is spinning.

"Whoa," I mutter and then right myself.

A few minutes ago, my best friend, Mal, dropped my drunk ass off before peeling away from the curb, leaving me to maneuver my way into the apartment myself. He's usually a better friend than that. I think he's excited to get over to Bree's house. She was making eyes at him all night, and I think he knows he's getting some soon.

Unlike me.

I'm getting nothing.

Not that I couldn't have gotten anything. I could have. A few times. But I didn't want anything. Not really. I wasn't feeling it. Haven't been feeling it for a while.

Honestly, I just feel like shit tonight. My head is woozy. Everything is tilted slightly.

I just want a nice long hug. Someone to run their hands through my hair. Maybe hold my hand.

I do a pretty good job of not breaking my neck as I barrel

into the apartment and grab water from the fridge, guzzling half of it in record time.

Hell, I'm thirsty.

And hot too.

Pulling my shirt off, I fumble with the buttons of my jeans and manage to get one leg out before getting tangled in the other and crashing into the wall. Amazingly, I don't go straight through it like the Kool-Aid Man.

The lights go on, and I blink rapidly as Whit comes into my line of sight. He's like a mirage, appearing fuzzy on the edges and slowly coming into focus.

"Hey there," I slur. I know I'm a sight to behold. Half-naked, my pants hanging off my right ankle.

On the other hand, Whit's hair is slightly rumpled, and his eyes are bleary from sleep. He looks more human right now than I've ever seen him. He still looks too put together for my taste.

I'd like to mess that hair up. Maybe bite down on his neck. Leave a mark or two.

Hm.

"What are you doing?" he asks, and I find the question so ridiculous that I snort a small laugh.

"Trying to go to bed. Tripped though. And fell." I wave dramatically around and end up hitting my hand on the wall.

Ouch.

Whit rubs at his forehead before squatting down beside me. He's wearing track pants and a long-sleeved thermal. Both dark grey.

"You are so goth, emo boy."

"You're so drunk," he retorts.

"Sherlock," I say, reaching out to bop his nose but missing

and hitting his cheek instead. His skin is soft. Softer than mine. Just another way we're different.

"So fucking smart," I say.

He sighs and then tugs the wayward pants from my ankle and folds them. I don't think my pants have ever been folded so nicely before. He probably irons his clothes. Even his underwear.

Whit sets the nicely folded pants on the end table near my head. To do so, though, he has to lean over me, and I get a whiff of him.

Damn, he smells good.

I'm pretty sure I don't smell that good.

I know it, actually.

"Let's get you to bed," he says and then glances at me like he doesn't want to touch me.

Don't blame him. I'm a mess. Wouldn't want to touch me either.

"I can get up myself," I say and then use the wall to help me push myself to a standing position. My thighs bunch and flex under my weight, and when I finally manage to stand up, Whit is glancing up at me, still crouched down.

His cheeks are pink again.

"Why you always blushing around me?" I ask, my mouth unfiltered at the moment.

I blame the pitcher of beer my cousins bought, and I consumed like a champ. And the fact that everything is hazy and spinning at the moment.

"I don't blush," he bites out and then walks into the bedroom. Like I'm supposed to follow him.

Probably should.

Maybe he'll tuck me in. Run those long, delicate fingers through my hair.

I'd really fucking like that.

"You're really pretty when you blush," I say to his back. Whit stumbles slightly, and I reach out to steady him, but I miss entirely. Just end up grabbing the air like the clown I am.

"Get in," Whit snaps, holding my messy covers open for me. His bed is always neatly made while mine is, well, not. Who has time to make a bed every single fucking morning? Not me, apparently.

It probably causes him anxiety, living with me.

Probably why he hates me.

Hates my messy sheets and unfolded clothes.

He probably itches to scrub me clean.

I don't think I'd mind that all that much, to be honest.

"Tucking me in?" I ask with a small smile, and then without waiting for an answer, I slide inside the cool sheets. Probably should wash them. It's been a few weeks.

He tosses the offensive covers over my shoulders, and the corner smacks me against my cheek.

I brush it down and close my eyes with a small sigh.

"Are you going to throw up?" Whit asks, his voice echoing from above me.

He's a mile away.

"I'll be fine, man," I tell him, peeking through one eyelid. When did they get so heavy?

He's looming over me like a dark shadow. His eyes are narrowed, his bottom lip pulled between his teeth.

"What?" I ask when he doesn't move back to his side of the room like he should have.

"I don't believe you."

"Believe me, man. I've been drinking since I was thirteen. I can handle a few beers."

"A few?" he asks, obviously not believing me.

"Fine, more than a few. I'll be fine. Just go to sleep. There's only so much scowling I can take from you."

"I don't scowl."

"You scowl," I retort, and then I suddenly feel way too hot. My feet kick out, sending the sheets tumbling to the floor in a heap. My stomach churns.

Whit glances at them and then back at me.

"I'll put them on my bed tomorrow," I feel the need to tell him even though the words are thick and hard to get out.

He bends down, unable to help himself, and places them on the end of my bed, at the far corner. They're in a pile. He probably wants to fold them neatly. And iron them.

"Don't you dare fold my sheets," I say. "It's unnatural."

"There's nothing unnatural about folding sheets."

"You're a freak."

He scoffs and folds his arms across his chest. This is the most aggressive I've been toward him. We've never verbally sparred before. Usually, he just scowls at me and I tease him. I'll probably regret this in the morning.

"Ugh, I feel like shit all of a sudden," I moan, clutching my stomach. It's churning like I've been on a boat adrift at sea. Not that I've ever been on a boat. But I can imagine.

"You're going to vomit, aren't you?" he asks.

"I never *vomit*," I say just as I turn to my side and unload my stomach onto my bed.

Disgusting. It dribbles down my chin and squishes against my arm.

Whit rushes to grab the garbage can by my bed and thrusts it under my chin as I empty the rest of my stomach contents inside.

God, I'm a winner.

I glance sheepishly up at Whit when I'm done, knowing the entire room smells. I smell.

I smelled before, but I'm worse now.

"Sorry. That's never happened before."

He huffs, setting the trashcan down on the floor and then moving to the window, pulling it open to air out the stench from the room. And then he reaches out and hauls me upright, his skin cool against mine.

"You're going to take a shower."

"Probably a good idea," I mutter as he leads me to the bathroom and turns on the water.

"Will you be able to stay standing while I clean up?"

"You'll know if I can't," I say and then stumble toward the tub.

He helps me step inside, and when he's confident I won't knock myself out by crashing into the side of the tub, he shuts the door.

I stand under the warm water and force myself to push my now wet boxer briefs off and fling them onto the bathroom floor, where they land with a plop.

I'll get them later.

Quickly I brush my teeth, wash my hair, and run the bar of soap over my face and body before half-heartedly rinsing off and awkwardly reaching for a towel.

Fuck, I feel awful.

This is more than a night of too much alcohol.

I'm coming down with something.

Wasn't my cousin just saying something was going around?

"You okay in there?" Whit asks, his voice concerned.

He probably shouldn't be concerned. I just puked everywhere, and he's cleaning it up.

He should probably be hoping for my demise so he can go

back to his tidy, clean life. Without wrinkled sheets and vomit.

"Fine," I lie as I wrap a towel around my hips.

It barely covers my ass. But these towels are Whit's, so what can I expect? They probably fit nicely around his thin waist. I'm too bulky compared to him, like a bull in a china shop.

What the fuck is a china shop?

"Can I come in?" he asks when I am silent for too long.

"Yeah," I manage to croak out.

God, I'm thirsty.

He pushes the door open and those dark eyes assess me.

"You still have shampoo in your hair," he says, and I shrug.

"It's fine."

He shakes his head and then touches my arm, pulling me toward the sink.

"Lean down," he tells me, pushing my head toward the bowl.

I do as he says because I'm so tired all of a sudden.

Cool water runs through my hair, and it feels so good against my warm scalp that my hand, holding the towel around my waist, slips.

"Shit," I say as the ends disengage, leaving my ass exposed. The towel hangs on slightly. Covering my right thigh. Well done, you.

"Hold on," Whit hisses. "Stay there."

I, of course, don't listen and stand up, knocking my head against the faucet. Probably dislodged it in the process. Whit will have to call a plumber to come to fix it.

Pain ricochets through my head, and I curse. Water drips from my wet hair down my chest as Whit reaches around me and quickly rights the wayward towel. He doesn't even peek at my flaccid cock hanging impressively between my legs.

Not that I want him to.

But it *is* probably my best feature.

"I think you need bigger towels," I say.

His cheeks are bright red as I watch him in the mirror.

"Agreed."

He clears his throat and takes my hand, ensuring my fingers have grasped the towel before he steps away.

"Sorry, man," I tell him. "I think I'm sick."

Whit's eyes meet mine in the mirror, and those long fingers press against my forehead and then move to my cheek.

"You're burning up."

"Told you. I never throw up from drinking. It's a superpower."

He arches an eyebrow at me and then grabs another towel from under the sink and reaches up and dries my hair.

He's slightly taller than me, so he reaches it easily.

And damn, it feels good.

When he moves to my chest, rubbing the droplets that escaped my hair, I let my eyes flutter closed.

I let myself be taken care of for just a moment.

"Let's get you to bed," he says when he's finished.

"I don't have any extra sheets. Never got around to buying more."

"You can use some of mine," he says, and when I step into the bedroom, I notice that my bed has been made with those fancy, silky sheets he uses.

This guy is from serious money. Who has silk sheets? Mine are from the discount rack at Walmart. Very scratchy.

Once again, he folds the covers on my bed back for me,

and I drop my towel and slide inside. Naked as the day I was born.

"Smells like you," I mutter, turning my head into the pillow. I inhale deeply and crush my face into it. I can't get enough.

He gently tucks me in this time and then leaves for a moment before returning with a glass of water and Tylenol.

"Here. Take this."

I grasp the cup with a shaky hand, and he helps me pop the pills into my mouth. His thumb brushes my lips, and they positively burn from the contact. I blame the fever. I'm delusional and apparently gay when I'm sick.

Never happened before, but I guess I've developed a condition.

"Swallow," Whit says when I've made no move to do so.

I force myself to do as he says and then lean back with an exhale.

"I'll make this up to you," I tell him, and he smooths the wet hair from my forehead.

It's such a tender gesture that I find my eyes watering.

I blink back the tears because I cannot cry in front of Whit.

He'll see it as a weakness. Bring it up for years to come.

Probably not years. We won't know each other after he kicks me out. We'll both go out of our way to avoid each other.

"Just rest. I'll be right over here if you need me."

I grab onto his hand when he goes to move away and bring his hand back to my head.

I'll regret this later. Right now, I just want this.

"Don't stop," I whisper, and Whit freezes, his hand in mine.

"Okay," he says softly, and then I feel his fingers move through my hair, massaging my scalp lightly.

And through the haze of the fever, I let his hands lull me to sleep.

I wake up feverish and shivering. I'm so damn cold.

I don't ever remember having a fever before. It's the worst.

How do kids do it? They're sick all the time with this shit.

All I want is to warm up, to stop shaking so badly. My teeth chatter and clank together, and my entire body hurts from the strain of it.

Stumbling out of bed, I move toward Whit where he's sleeping on his double bed. He looks good in the shadows. Peaceful.

Until I wake him up by looming like a creeper.

"Hell," he mutters, shooting upright in bed. He presses a hand to his chest, probably to ease the heart attack I caused.

I shift before him, my entire body vibrating with the chills.

I'm pretty sure I am not wearing pants. Glancing down, I realize I'm not.

Too sick to care, though.

What's a little cock when you're dying?

"Caleb, are you okay?" Whit asks, his voice sleepy and concerned.

"I'm so...fucking cold. Can't...stop shaking."

Whit fumbles with the sheets on his bed and pulls the covers back.

"Come here."

"I'm naked," I protest half-heartedly but slide in next to him anyway.

I'll regret it all later. When I'm not sick. Then I'll dissect the fact that I was nude, cuddling with a man I'm pretty sure hates me.

"You're sick," he says, pulling the covers over us both, and I don't hesitate to wrap myself around him. Like a human candy wrapper. My leg goes over his thigh, and my arms slide around his torso. I'm half on top of him, my dick squished between us.

But I am so out of it I don't even care.

Instead, I bury my face in his neck and sigh as his warmth permeates me.

"Why do you smell so good?" I mutter, and then before he can answer, I fall fast asleep.

CHAPTER TWO

I have visions of things over the next few days. Or is it hours? I'm not sure because I'm so out of it, waking only to have Whit spoon feed me soup and then berate me into drinking water. Why is it so sexy when he scowls at me?

I'm obviously delusional.

And then I start hallucinating.

Is that my Aunt Del? Luke? Mal? Did he come over too? Mom?

Hands are on my scalp, rubbing, gently pulling at my hair. On my back, my face.

I lean into it. Purr like a fucking cat because I'm an animal now, apparently.

But it feels so good, so right, that I just go with it.

When I finally wake from my mini-coma, Whit is asleep beneath me. I'm wrapped around him like a koala on a tree.

I don't even want to tell him I'm awake because he feels so nice underneath me.

But I should move. I don't even know how long I've been

suffocating him. He probably wants me out of here. Wants me out of his life.

God.

I grunt, and Whit shifts beneath me.

"You're awake," he says softly, his eyes blinking rapidly as his pupils dilate.

His lean body bunches and stretches beneath me, and I realize my cock is half-hard against his hip.

Oh, kill me now.

"Sorry, man," I grunt, shifting off him.

I'm naked as the day I was born. And suddenly feel *very* ashamed about it.

I wasn't ashamed when this all started, but I sure as fuck am now.

"It's fine, Caleb," Whit says, pulling at his shirt.

He's sweated through it. Probably from me stifling him to death.

I have been told I'm a human heater.

"How long have I been out?" I ask, running a hand over my now very bearded face.

"Three days."

"Shit."

"Your friends and family were worried about you."

"So, I didn't hallucinate that then?"

"No, they were texting and seemed worried so I replied. And then they showed up. En masse. I hope you're not upset."

"Nah. Not upset. There's no stopping them anyway," I mutter. "Thanks, man."

"No problem," he says, pushing himself up and lunging off the bed, not touching me. He's probably over me in general.

I don't blame him.

"Probably want your bed back, huh?"

He shrugs and then eyes me through those thick lashes. "I gave up on that about three days ago when you wouldn't leave."

I close my eyes and huff. "I can get a little clingy. I have attachment issues."

"It's fine."

I lift my arms and catch a whiff of myself. "Fuck, I smell. I can't believe you let me sleep with you like this. I need to shower."

Whit peeks over at me but doesn't say anything. Just sucks his lips between his teeth and fiddles with my bed.

"Go on," I say, pushing myself upright. "I know you have things to say. You're practically bursting at the seams."

Whit hesitates before glancing back at me. "Just go shower, Caleb. Then come lie back down while I wash my sheets."

I want to argue, but how can I when he took care of me for three whole fucking days. When he let me smother him night after night? Day in and day out.

I stand up and move toward the bathroom with shaky legs, stumbling only once. Whit keeps his back to me, probably not wanting to see my dick waving between my legs.

Probably saw enough of it the past few days.

"Why am I still naked?" I ask before entering the bathroom.

"You complained the fabric was too itchy. I gave up trying to clothe you after the first day."

I stare at his back and then close the bathroom door. But I don't lock it. Just in case I topple over and need to be rescued again.

When I'm done showering, I feel slightly better and move

toward my bed, just wanting to lie down for a little longer. Damn, I'm tired. This is surprising since I slept away the past three days.

My bed is, of course, nicely made with freshly laundered sheets. The covers are turned down, so I pull on some boxers before slipping inside.

I don't see Whit, but his bed is stripped, and new sheets are on it. I hear the shower turn on and ten minutes later, he reappears wearing something clean, his hair brushed and his face shaven.

"Are you hungry?" he asks, shifting on his feet, his hands in his pockets.

"Yeah, but I can get it when I get up. You've done enough."

Whit clears his throat and adds, "I don't mind."

I push myself up on my elbows, the sheets falling down my chest, exposing my entire abdomen. Whit glances at it and then moves his eyes to study his desk.

"Why you being so nice, huh?" I ask.

"Why wouldn't I be nice?" he responds, his eyes flashing to mine and then looking away again.

"Because you dislike me."

Whit inhales sharply. "I don't dislike you, Caleb."

God, I like it when he says my name. He rasps it. His voice getting all husky.

Apparently, I'm still suffering from the effects of the fever.

"Could have fooled me," I say and then let my head fall back on the pillow and cover my eyes with my forearm.

"I'll make you toast," he says after a moment and then disappears into the kitchen.

Fucking, Whit. He's so damn confusing.

Especially when he returns with the toast and helps me eat it.

And what's more confusing is I let him do it.

And I really fucking like it when he brushes the crumbs from my lips.

I'm apparently starved for affection because my body lights up like the night sky on the Fourth of July.

My bewildering thoughts are placed on hold when my phone rings. Whit and I glance over at it, and he reaches for it first, swiping at my screen and putting it on speaker.

"Hello, Aunt Del," he says, and my eyebrows lift.

"Hey there, sweet pea," she drawls. "How's Caleb?"

"I'm fine," I manage and then add. "Since when is Whit your *sweet pea*."

Sue me. I'm jealous.

"Since he took care of you for three whole days. Without complaining. Have you thanked him yet, Caleb?"

I glance over at Whit, and his lips are twitching.

"Yeah, I did."

"Good, I'm sending Sem and Luke over with food for you both."

"No, don't send them," I protest, but my aunt ignores me.

"They'll be there in a few hours."

I roll my eyes as she asks Whit some questions about how I'm *really* doing and then hangs up with the promise to call him later.

Since when do they chat?

Are they best friends now?

"How well did you get to know my aunt and cousins while I was out of it?" I ask, dreading the answer.

My cousins are nosy fuckers and can't hold onto a secret if their lives depended on it.

"As well as I could with you wrapped around me," he responds, his face betraying nothing.

"And Sem and Luke were here? Liam and Anne too?"

"I did say they came en masse."

"Oh, fuck me," I mutter and then ask. "When you say *wrapped around me*, what do you mean by that?"

He bites the bottom of his lip, and my eyes are drawn to it. He has a really lovely mouth. Soft, pink, and kissable.

"It means that I got up *once* to let them in, and you were moaning for me to get my ass back to bed. And when I did, you...."

"Out with it," I mutter, not liking where this is headed.

"You crawled on top of me."

"On top?"

"Yes."

"They saw everything?"

"Everything," he confirms, and his eyes twinkle.

"It's not fucking funny, man. They won't let me live it down. They saw me needy as fuck."

"You *were* needy," he adds, and I poke his side.

He jerks away and rubs where I touched him, but I don't apologize. My life just got one hundred times harder, and he's partially the reason behind it.

"You shouldn't have cuddled with me in front of them," I say.

"I wasn't cuddling with you. You were cuddling with me."

I groan and then place both my arms over my face, imagining the ribbing I'll get from my cousins. It's inevitable. They probably volunteered to come over and deliver the food to see it all. Maybe even get a repeat performance. What a shit show.

"Tell me what else I did while they were here?"

"Do you really want to know?"

Oh, Jesus.

I peer out from between my arms and manage to say "Yeah, I do".

Whit hesitates and then says, "You said a few things."

"Just tell me, Whit."

"You said I smelled good and didn't know why. You kept on sniffing me." He clears his throat and then adds, "You also said my skin was soft and ran your hands up and down my face."

"Shit."

"You also rambled some and said you were gay from the fever. Not sure what that means, but your cousins latched onto that one word and now think we're together."

"Oh, damn it all to hell," I say and then turn over, not facing him.

This is damn humiliating is what it is.

Fingers trail across my skin, just light enough. I wonder if I'm imagining it. But no, I'm not. He's touching me, and I don't say anything because I don't want it to stop.

"It's okay. There's nothing to be ashamed of. You were really out of it."

I don't say anything, just stare at the blank white wall in front of me. Should probably paint it or hang up a picture.

"You don't know my family. There's a reason I needed a place to live this year."

"I spent a lot of time with them the past three days. I know enough."

I look at him, and he offers me a small smile.

"You didn't sign up for this, for my family and me," I tell him. "I'm sorry."

"It's okay," he says, and then he pushes some hair off my forehead, and my eyes flutter. "You still hungry?"

"I'm good," I say and then face the wall again.

"You're lucky you have a family who loves you."

"Yeah, I know, man. They're just a little much. It'll die down soon enough."

Whit sits on my bed for a few moments longer and then stands up, leaving me to my thoughts.

It did not die down. Not that I expected it to. Sem and Luke are in my living room playing video games when I wake up from dozing, while Whit reads his Kindle in his chair.

Like it's all perfectly normal, having them here.

"Ah, you're up," Sem says, towering over me. He slaps my back roughly, and I stumble slightly. I'm a big guy, but Sem is even bigger. He hulks like a Viking.

"Your boyfriend here almost didn't let us in. Said you'd be sleeping a while," Luke adds, not taking his eyes off the TV, his fingers smashing into the controller, his tongue sticking out of his mouth. "But you know how persuasive we can be."

"Plus, we had food to deliver," Sem adds.

"Ah," I reply and then shift awkwardly on my feet and scratch at my stomach.

Sem lowers himself down onto the couch, leaving me nowhere to plant my ass.

Why is there only one small couch in this apartment again?

"Don't stand there fidgeting, Caleb. You're making this damn awkward. You know we're accepting motherfuckers. You're gay. No big deal. Sit on your boyfriend's lap, for god's sake," Luke adds, cussing when his character online is shot and dies. "Well, hell. I suck at this game."

"Go on," Sem says, staring at me intensely and gesturing toward Whit.

Whit makes no move to help me. He just watches this all unfold like it's no big deal.

"You're seriously going along with this," I say to Whit, who just arches an eyebrow at me.

Gah, that look he gives me.

"I'm going to smother you with your pillow later. I'm stronger than you."

Whit's lips twitch. He's getting me back for the past three days. I'm sure of it.

I turn to my cousins and say, "He's not my boyfriend. I'm not gay. You delivered the food. Now go away."

"That rhymed. Good one," Luke says before whooping loudly.

"He's ashamed," Sem says, and I want to smack my face. And then his. And then Luke's and Whit's as well.

"Nothing to be ashamed of, cuz," Luke says, folding his arms and leaning back. He smiles crookedly at me.

"Oh, for fucks sake," I mutter. I know they won't let up on it. They will harp about it incessantly. The best thing is to just give them what they want. So, I make up my mind, walk over to Whit, and lower myself roughly onto his lap. He grunts from the impact of my ass on his thighs.

Good.

Sem and Luke watch it unfold and look pleased by this new development. I'm seriously not sure if they really think Whit and I are together or if they're just messing with me.

I can never tell with them.

Whit's hand cups my hip, and he pushes lightly, trying to get me to move to my left.

"What? Not comfortable?" I say, wriggling around on him. "That's what you get."

I outweigh him by at least fifty pounds. He cannot be comfortable.

Though he let me sleep on top of him for three days, so he's got to be okay with it.

He sighs heavily, and then in an impressive move, he lifts me up just enough to shift me where he wants me.

Holy shit.

I glance back and look at him, my eyes wide.

"For reals?"

He smirks softly and then goes back to reading his Kindle like it's no big deal that he just lifted my heavy ass up.

"They're cute, right?" Sem asks Luke, who just nods.

"This is not a matinee performance. There's no popcorn here. You both need to leave."

"So rude," Luke comments. "How Whit puts up with you is a mystery."

"A huge mystery," Sem agrees, rubbing his chin, and then adds, "How do you put up with him, Whit?"

"He grows on you," Whit says, and I elbow him lightly in annoyance.

Luke watches this and then tilts his head, "You haven't been home since you moved out. You avoiding us?"

I know how offended they all are that I moved out my senior year of college, but I just needed my space. They're all just too overwhelming. In the best way possible, but still.

I needed a minute to breathe.

"Jesus, I will see you all next weekend. We can catch up then."

The two of them stare at each other, wordlessly conversing before nodding.

"Fine. Bring Whit. Aunt Del's request."

"It's like I'm in the mafia," I mutter. "The only way out is death."

"So dramatic, this one," Sem says, ruffling my hair while Luke lightly punches my shoulder.

"No need to get up for us. You two look comfy," Luke adds before moving to the door, and then the two of them disappear behind it without a goodbye.

Thank the gods.

"Oh, Jesus fuck. How is this my life," I say, turning around slightly and glancing at Whit, who is biting his bottom lip, his eyes twinkling with something.

Mirth perhaps.

"What?" I ask, annoyed with this whole thing. "It's not funny."

"It's a little funny," he says and then moves his eyes back to his Kindle.

"Put that down and tell me something," I say, grabbing it from his hand and setting it on the arm of the chair.

"What would you like to know?" he asks, those long fingers of his tracing patterns on the cushion beneath us. His nails are short, almost bitten down to the quick. I've never seen him bite his nails before.

What a weird observation to have right now.

"How are you okay with this?"

He shrugs. "It's harmless."

I meet his eyes, and he looks away quickly.

"Harmless? I am *never* going to live this down. My family is insane. No matter what I tell them, they will stubbornly believe we're together."

"It's sweet."

"It's obnoxious. Next thing you know, you'll be marrying me and wondering what happened!"

He bites down on his bottom lip, and my eyes slip down to stare at his mouth.

He probably tastes good too.

He clears his throat, and I shift on his lap. Right, what was I saying?

"Um...now do you see why I had to move out?"

He moves his legs underneath me, and his hands go to my hips again, pushing me slightly to the right.

"Can I have my Kindle back now?"

I huff in annoyance. "For real, man?"

"Yeah, there's nothing to be done about it."

"You'll have to spend your weekend with my family. There's a chance we'll burn something down, or someone'll end up in jail."

"Are you saying you have a record?"

"Not yet," I mutter and then yawn.

Shit, I'm pooped. What the hell did I get sick with?

This is no joke.

Suddenly the door opens, and I stare as Sem and Luke reappear. My worst fucking nightmare. Right in front of me.

"Aw, so cute. Look at those two," Sem says to Luke, noting that I'm still firmly planted on Whit's lap.

Not that I feel like moving. He's comfortable. Like a nice, soft blanket.

"Did you give them a key?" I ask, and Whit shrugs like it's no big deal. He has no idea what he's asking for.

"Give me the key," I say, holding out my hand and wiggling my fingers.

"No need to be aggressive," Sem says as he slaps the metal

in my palm, a manic smile on his face. "That's why we were coming back. Didn't mean to interrupt."

And then they're gone again, the door shutting on a quiet snick.

"We need to get the locks changed."

"Why?"

"They made copies. They'll show up unannounced at all hours. Believe me. They have no boundaries."

Whit's unconcerned. He's back to reading, and I want to poke him. But instead, I just lean into him and rest the back of my head on his shoulder.

He doesn't say anything, just goes back to reading. Like two guys chillin' on an overstuffed chair is totally normal. I've never sat on a man's lap in my entire adult life, but I really fucking like it.

Usually, I'm the one being sat on because I'm bigger, and I can't very well plant my muscular frame on some petite girl.

Not that Whit is bigger than me. He's not. But for some reason, he doesn't seem to mind it.

"I have to be crushing you," I say, and Whit peeks at me.

"I'm used to it."

"That so?"

"Feel free to move if you're concerned."

"Is that a passive way of asking me to move?" I ask.

"No."

Okay then, I think, and then reach over to the end table, grab the remote, turn on the TV, and put on some obscure cooking show.

Good enough.

I should probably get up and move to the couch, but I don't want to. Nah, I'll just stay here for a while longer.

We sit like that for two hours, me half watching the cooking show and half dozing while Whit continues to read. He's a smart cookie. I peeked at what he was reading, and it was something about the Civil War. Who would read that for fun?

Not me.

Or anyone I know, really.

But I do know he's going to school to be a lawyer or something fancy like that. I found that out from my internet stalking. Told you he was brilliant.

I'm in college for a business degree. Not that I want to end up in a suit and sit in an office all day, but one day I'll be running the scrap yards my uncle owns with my cousins, and I want to know what I'm doing. I don't want to run them into the ground.

Whit moves his legs again. In the past two hours, we shifted a few times. Whit ended up with his legs sprawled in front of him and me curled into his torso. His left hand rested on my waist, his fingers stroking absently against my side. My face was tucked into his neck, and my palm rested against his chest. I could feel the constant beat of his heart against it. It was soothing.

I didn't think too hard about it.

I just went with it.

Why couldn't guys cuddle or hold hands? Who came up with that shit rule? Maybe we'd all be happier if we were able to show some affection every once in a while.

"You're hungry," Whit says when my stomach rumbles loudly.

"Meh," I say.

"Let me heat you up the soup your aunt made," Whit says, his hand moving up to squeeze the back of my neck.

"If you insist," I mutter and then roll off of him. Very reluctantly.

I plant myself on the couch and feel lonelier than I should.

This was becoming a problem. One I would examine more later.

Whit stretches, arching his back, and a pop resounds from it. Then he stands up, moves to the kitchen, and opens the fridge.

A few minutes later, a bowl of steaming soup is set on the table.

"Come on, Caleb. Time to eat."

I sigh, push myself up, and amble over to the chair, and after I sit down, I stick the spoon into the liquid. It does smell delicious. My aunt is a fantastic cook. So is Liam. I live for his culinary treats.

"You having some?" I ask, taking a heaping spoonful.

"Yeah. Your aunt insisted. I don't want to report back that I didn't do as she commanded."

I snort. "Good man."

We finish the soup in silence, and then something occurs to me.

"Did you miss class or work these past three days?" I ask, as Whit grabs our empty bowls and places them in the sink. He rinses them out and puts them in the dishwasher. Always the good little cleaner.

"It's fine."

"Shit. I'm sorry, man."

"It's fine. I emailed our professors and let them know

what was going on. I don't work right now, so that isn't a concern."

"Thanks. Thanks for doing that."

He begins wiping down the counter, his eyes not meeting mine.

"You're welcome."

I watch him for a moment, how he moves around a space, picking up things, and putting them back where they belong.

Living with me must cause him so much anxiety.

Still doesn't stop me from asking, "Want to watch a movie?"

"I actually have plans tonight."

"Oh," I say, sounding more clingy and whiney than I should. He owes me nothing. We aren't even friends.

I just slept on him for three days and then sat on him for a few hours.

"I'll be back in a bit."

"Okay."

He stops near me, those dark eyes meeting mine. "Will you be okay while I'm gone?"

"Yep," I say, leaning back like I'm totally fine with him doing who knows what. When deep down, I'm not. Don't want to analyze that too much. My brain is still working out of this fog I've been in for the past three days. I'll get over this infatuation with my roommate soon.

"Okay, well, text me if you need me."

"I won't. Have fun, man," I tell him, and he nods before grabbing his keys and leaving the apartment.

I walk over to the couch and pull a blanket over me, putting on another mindless show and counting the minutes until he's back. It's an incredibly long time. Forever, really.

He returns a few hours later and walks straight to me, bending down and pressing his hand against my forehead.

"I'm fine," I grouch, and he tilts his head slightly, watching me.

"I'm fine," I say once more and then ask, "How was your thing?"

"Fine," he says.

It's fucking awkward. I'm acting like a jilted lover, but I can't help but ask, "And who did you meet up with?"

He lowers himself into the chair opposite me, and I force my eyes to the TV.

"I'm part of the speech and debate club here. We have a tournament coming up soon, so I had to meet with my team to go over a few things."

I look over, and he's staring at me.

"You're a smart dude."

"At times," he replies and then shifts his eyes to the TV.

"Nah, man. You're like super smart. Always reading and shit. I see you. We would have kicked ass at trivia if you'd have come."

He doesn't reply, just sits there and rubs those fingers over the chair's fabric.

"Don't feel like you need to watch this. You can watch whatever you want." I gesture toward the remote, and he shakes his head.

"This is fine."

"Is it, though?" I ask, getting the impression he's uncomfortable for some reason.

Probably because I'm needy, and he can tell I want him to come over here so I can snuggle.

I've never snuggled in my entire life until this dude.

For reals.

I'm slightly addicted to it.

"It's fine."

Oh, for fuck's sake, I think and then say, louder than I mean to, "Get over here, Whit."

He glances over at me, and I push myself into a seated position.

"Come on. Don't make me beg."

He taps his fingers on the chair and inhales and exhales slowly like he's debating if this is a good idea or not. It's insulting, but I get it. Kind of. Mostly.

He pushes off the chair on his second deep breath and moves toward me. He lowers himself down next to me, and then I'm moving on top of him. I don't even hesitate. Probably should make myself seem less desperate. But I've always been an open book. What you see is what you get.

"No need to get weird about this," I mutter as I tuck my forehead into the side of his neck and fling a leg across his thighs. "We'll just get it out of our systems today and then go back to normal tomorrow."

Whit sighs beneath me and begins fiddling with my hair.

"What is normal?" he asks, ever the philosopher.

"Don't ask me. My entire life has been weirder than a *Dr. Who* episode."

He chuckles at that and then shifts slightly so that our hips are now connected.

I rest my hand on his chest and move my eyes to the TV, not really watching what's happening, and instead listen to his heart thump against my ear.

It's calm and steady, and it slowly lulls me to sleep.

CHAPTER THREE

I said I'd get it out of my system, but I don't. Not really. We don't cuddle the rest of the week. In fact, I barely see him. It's like he's avoiding me.

Don't blame him. He's probably had enough. My desperation was off-putting, apparently.

I can tell because he's been on a cleaning spree. The apartment shines. I'm scared to even brew a cup of coffee for fear he'll lose his mind if I make a mess. And don't even get me started on my bed. He's made it for me the past four days. Don't know what's up with that, but it's an issue.

I make sure to rumple it just to irritate him.

If he starts ironing my socks, I might lose my shit entirely.

"You're heading home this weekend?" Mal, my best friend, asks as he begins to lift two dumbbells, straining his already straining muscles. He's a big dude, about my size, with dark brown hair matching his eyes and tattoos covering his arms. He looks like he's from a motorcycle club when in fact, he was raised in a middle-class home with a mother who is an elementary school teacher and a father who likes to garden.

His life growing up was relatively average compared to mine.

Mine was a shit show in the best possible way.

It's my first day back in the gym since getting sick. I'd felt too weak to do anything but lie down and go for short walks until today.

But enough is enough. It's time to get back to my life.

"Can't escape it. I've been summoned," I say from the bench. My arms are screaming at me for skipping an entire week.

"Your family's wild, man."

"Don't remind me. You coming with me?"

"Nah, next time. I have plans with Bree this weekend."

"Sem'll be disappointed," I tell him, and he shrugs.

"He'll live. I just saw him two days ago. Broke into my apartment and was chillin' on my bed and watching a movie."

"Yeah?" I ask, knowing that the two of them grew close last year when my mom passed but didn't realize how often they actually hung out. My family had really pulled through for me when I was grieving, and Mal stepped up. At the end of my mom's life, he'd practically moved in with my aunt and uncle and took charge of all the funeral arrangements for me.

I couldn't ask for a better best friend.

"Yeah, he's a needy asshole," he smirks, and I force a smile because apparently, that's a trait that runs in our family.

I'm feeling a little needy myself.

I should probably get laid soon.

Preferably today.

"You taking Whit with you still?" Mal asks, and I sigh, moving to do sit-ups.

"No clue. Haven't had a chance to talk to him. It would be easier if he didn't come, to be honest. It'll just fan the flames if he does."

"Sem couldn't shut up about it," Mal tells me, and I roll my eyes.

"Oh, for fucks sake."

"He said how cute you two were. And I have to admit, man. You two *were* cute together."

"Oh, shut up," I grit through my teeth as I begin a set of crunches.

"You were all over him, and he looked like he was *loving* it."

"Okay, asshole. Whatever. He's harder to read than an Egyptian hieroglyph. That's how I know you're so full of it."

Mal chuckles and then sets his weights down. "I am, but he didn't look miserable holding you, that's for sure. Probably why Sem and everyone thinks you're together."

"Despite telling them otherwise."

"You know how they get."

"Yeah, I do."

We're silent for a while, and then Mal asks, "So, you into him?"

I nearly fall out of my plank position and smash my head on the ground. "What?"

"You into dudes or what?"

"Why would you ask that?"

Mal wipes a towel across his face and shrugs. "Just curious."

"Well, I'm not. I like pussy and boobs. Lots of them."

I do. I like them very much. They're non-negotiable. But I also like cuddling with Whit and having those strong legs underneath me and his hands in my hair.

So, what the hell is up with that?

Not something I have time to contemplate right now.

Mal watches me for a moment and then slaps my back lightly. "Alright, dude. Whatever you say, yeah? Whatever floats your boat. Want to go eat? I'm starving."

"Yep," I say as we head to the showers to wash the sweat off.

We make it to the cafeteria in record time and stack our trays with food. When I go to sit down, Mal nudges me.

"Look who it is. Your elusive roommate."

I glance behind me and see Whit sitting at a table with two other girls and a guy. He's leaning forward, his mouth moving as he discusses something with them. He's wearing his usual dark grey pants and a black long-sleeved shirt. His hair is neatly combed, his face clean-shaven.

He looks intense, his eyebrows drawn down, his eyes flashing.

"He's a serious guy," Mal says, drawing my gaze back to my best friend.

"Yeah." I take a large mouthful of food and then swallow it down quickly. I don't taste it. I just consume it like a vacuum.

"He did well with your family, though."

"I know. My aunt was calling him sweet pea."

Mal guffaws loudly at that and then shakes his head. "You should just marry him, man. When has your aunt ever liked any of your girlfriends."

"She's never met any of them."

"Exactly."

I mull that one over and then sigh.

"Maybe I should go say hello," I tell Mal as I shovel more food into my mouth. I just want to get the chewing and swallowing over with. Why does eating take so long?

"Nah, he's busy. Looks like it's something important."

I glance over my shoulder and see Whit talking to the guy next to him, who happens to be entirely too pretty. Is he wearing suspenders?

I glance down at my track pants and loose tank top.

Tugging my ball cap, I pull it off and put it on backward. I definitely don't look anything like the guy currently fawning all over him.

Maybe this pretty boy's the reason Whit's been avoiding me. Maybe they're a couple?

In between bites of food, I turn around and watch Whit some more, because I can't help myself, and catch him furiously texting on his phone and then shoving it back into his pocket like he wants to be done with whatever conversation he's having. I also see the pretty boy running his hands along Whit's arm.

Too much touching going on here.

"You want to trade places?" Mal asks when I can't tear my eyes away from the two of them.

"Huh?"

"You're basically craning your neck like a giraffe over here. If we trade spots, you can watch Whit comfortably."

I snort but don't deny it. Just go to move next to Mal, bumping his hip with mine and then grabbing his drink and taking a large swig.

"Seriously?" he asks me, and I smile widely at him.

"You love me."

"Pfft," he says, and then a moment later, "Oh shit."

My eyes fly up to Whit, and I see the tiny guy next to him lean over and press a kiss on Whit's cheek.

"Huh," I grumble, grabbing Mal's drink and taking another large gulp. It goes down the wrong pipe, and I end up choking. Coke dribbles down my chest as I wipe at my chin with the back of my hand.

"Classy," Mal says as I peek up at Whit, who is now looking at me. Those dark eyes flash as his eyebrows lower slightly.

I raise an eyebrow at him, and he shrugs the guy away. Don't know what that was about, but it bothers me. Is he into guys? Sure looks like it. Not that I care, but I wonder. Or maybe he isn't, and this dude is making Whit feel uncomfortable. Either way, I don't like it. At all.

Pushing my tray of food away, I look at Mal. "I think I should go say hello. You know me, friendly, yeah?"

"Good idea. I'll join. Scare that ghost-looking-fucker away. I'll flex my muscles. Oh, and how about this," Mal adds with a crazy smile. "I'll call Sem too. He could show up and really freak that guy out. Grunt, throw him around the cafeteria for a bit."

"Do *not* call Sem."

Mal has his phone out, his fingers tapping on the screen, and I smack it out of his hand without warning. It falls dramatically to the floor with a crack.

"You did not just do that," Mal gasps, and I ignore him, knowing that he has a nice case for this very reason. He's constantly dropping his phone. It's been fine then, and it'll be fine now.

"Let's go," I say and then stalk toward Whit, whose eyes haven't moved from me as I traverse the room toward him.

As we grow closer, Whit's tablemates turn to watch me approach. Their eyes widen, especially the pretty guy next to Whit, who seems to pale at the sight of Mal.

I turn to glance at my best friend and see that Mal is scowling dramatically.

He looks like a serial killer.

I say, "Cut the shit, Mal," out of the corner of my mouth. "You're scaring them."

He smacks the back of my head, and I resist the urge to smack him back. Instead, I stop next to Whit and stare down at him.

He shifts in his seat and taps his fingers against his knee.

"Hey, roomie."

"Hello, Caleb."

"You've been avoiding me," I say, tucking my hands in my pockets lest I grab onto the back of his neck and squeeze.

"I've been busy," Whit replies, and I arch an eyebrow at him.

"That so?"

Mal moves toward where the pale guy is sitting and crouches down next to him, staring at him intently. Pale guy just shakes in his...is he wearing a bowtie with pigs on it. For reals? Who is this kid?

"You're frightening him," Whit tells Mal, who ignores him.

Whit then turns to me. "Call off your pet."

"Mal's not my pet. He is feral, though," I respond, and Mal snaps his teeth at pale dude.

But I'm a nice guy, so I take pity on him.

"Look, Mal, leave Casper alone. You're scaring him."

Whit bites his bottom lip at my quip, and I see his knuckles whiten as he grips his thighs.

"Alright," Mal says and then stands up to his full height. His muscles bunch under his shirt as he flexes them.

"Apologize," I tell Mal, and he tilts his head, considering this before he says, "Sorry, Casper."

"My name's not Casper," not-Casper says softly.

"My bad," Mal says flippantly. "You making my boy, Whit, feel uncomfortable? Got a little handsy for a bit there."

Casper holds up his hands, his ears turning pink.

Are his nails painted? Yep, yep they are.

"I...meant no harm."

"Keep your hands to yourself, hm," Mal says, and Casper turns to glance at Whit, who is silent through the entire thing.

Interesting.

Mal studies the boy and then moves to stand near Whit and me.

"Welp, my job here is done. See you later?"

"Yep," I say and watch as Mal fist bumps Whit and then struts away.

Whit watches him go and then turns his stare to me. Casper is scooting farther away from Whit, putting space between them.

"Did you need something, Caleb?" he asks after a moment of silence.

I shift on my feet and shrug. "You've been making my bed."

It's not why I'm here, to discuss my sheets, but I don't know what else to say. I feel slightly crazy. I don't like how not-Casper looks at Whit and then at me.

I narrow my eyes at him before moving them back to Whit.

"Does it bother you?" he asks.

"Nah, you do you."

"Anything else?" Whit asks.

I look over and see the two girls staring at me, their eyes wide and confused.

Yeah, girls, me too.

"You going to Houdini on me for much longer?"

Whit taps his fingers on his thighs. "I should be home soon."

"Fine," I say and then rock forward on my feet. "I'll see you then."

"Good," he says with a nod.

We stare at each other for a moment longer before not-Casper interrupts.

"My name's Magnus."

I narrow my eyes at him and then force myself to smile. "Magnus. Cool, nice to meet you, man."

I reach out, and he reluctantly shakes my hand. I resist the urge to crush his nail-painted hand in mine. I could, easily. He's much smaller than me. Smaller than Whit too. I could probably throw him out the window right now, just shot-put him right out there into the bushes.

"And you are?" I ask the two girls, forcing my gaze away from Magnus.

The girl on the right with light brown hair reaches out her hand. "Kate." And then she nudges the girl on her right, who has freckles and bright red hair. "This is Bev. We're on the debate team with Whit.

"Nice to meet you both. I'm Caleb. Whit's roommate."

"We know. We've heard *all* about you," Kate says, and Whit scowls at them.

I feel my chest puff up a bit, and I give into temptation and cradle the back of Whit's neck. He's tense at my touch.

"That so?" I squeeze.

"He won't shut up about you," Kate says, and Whit stands up so fast his chair topples backward onto the floor.

"I think we should go now," he says quickly, shooting his friends a scathing look.

The girls don't seem bothered by it, though, just shrug as he turns to walk away. Magnus, on the other hand, watches us with wide eyes.

When I don't follow right away, Whit grabs onto my wrist and pulls me along with him.

"No shame in being obsessed with me," I tell Whit, who just stares straight ahead, pulling me along with him, his fingers still wrapped around my naked wrist.

I like the feeling entirely too much, so I don't try to struggle out of his hold. I just let him pull me outside the cafeteria.

When we're safely outside, his hand flops back to his side, and when I glance over at him, his cheeks are pink.

"You're blushing again," I say, and Whit mutters under his breath as we walk side by side toward the parking lot.

"You giving me a ride home?" I ask when we reach his Audi.

He unlocks it with a beep and then slips inside. I do the same, and when the door closes, I run my hands across the leather interior. It looks expensive and entirely too clean.

"Nice car," I tell him.

It sure beats my old Jeep Cherokee.

He doesn't respond, just starts it up with a roar and then glances over at me.

"Seatbelt," he utters, and I roll my eyes.

"Sure thing, daddy-o."

He clears his throat, and once I'm snapped in, he peels out of the parking lot. To be honest, it's a turn on watching him maneuver this slick car through the campus and onto the road. And when he accelerates, my dick twitches in my pants.

I'm having a serious identity crisis around this dude.

Shifting in my seat, I adjust my growing cock.

"So," I begin because I need to fill this silence. "You talk to your friends about me?"

Whit swerves around a slower car and then looks over at me. "They exaggerate."

"Nothing to be ashamed of. I've told my cousins all about you."

"I know," he says, his hands tightening on the steering wheel.

"That so?"

"Yes. It was a deduction I made when they arrived at our place. They knew far too much about me. Also, Sem told me I was the main topic of conversation whenever you were around."

I lean my head against the headrest and stare at him. That dark hair, those plump lips.

"Yeah, well, can you blame me? You're hard as fuck to figure out."

Whit whips into his assigned parking spot and cuts the engine. He turns toward me, one hand still on the steering wheel, the other tapping on his knee.

"I don't open up to many people. It's nothing to do with you."

"You open up to that pretty boy back there?"

Whit licks his lips and then pushes out of the car.

"Hey, what's that supposed to mean?" I ask indignantly, following him into the apartment.

He hangs his keys up nicely and squats down, unlacing his boots.

"Look, you're pissed…Because you're damn hard to read, I can't really tell."

Whit stands up and meets my gaze. His dark brown eyes flash as he pushes past me into the kitchen. He grabs a glass from the cabinet and fills it with water. I watch his Adam's apple bob as he swallows.

I shift on my feet because hell...

"I'm not pissed," he interrupts and then sets the cup in the sink and turns toward me. "Let's just...watch a movie. That's what you wanted, right?"

He moves to the couch and sits down, fiddling with the remote.

I grab two beers and follow him, sitting down right next to him. Our thighs brush, and I scoot even closer. He looks at me as if to say, *Do you mind?* but I ignore him, just pop the cap off my beer. It falls to the floor with a clatter, and Whit huffs.

"What are we watching?" I ask, and Whit begins scrolling through Netflix while tapping his fingers against his knee.

It's driving me insane, this nervous habit. And I hate that it's always around me too. I must stress him the fuck out.

So, I do the only rational thing. I thread my fingers through his and rest our hands on my knee.

He has really soft hands.

Whit's cheeks pinken as he eyes our entwined fingers, my large hand nearly engulfing his.

"What are you doing?" he asks, his voice husky.

"Holding your hand," I say like it's no big deal. In reality, it is because I've never held another man's hand in my entire life. I've also never cuddled with a man before. Whit seems to be the exception in both of these situations.

"Why?" he asks, his eyes flicking up and meeting mine.

"Because you're tapping them all the time, and it's driving me up a wall."

That's the only reason I can give that makes any sense.

"I apologize. I'll stop," he says, but I make no move to let him go, just lean back further, spreading my legs and taking another swig of beer. My track pants are worn, and my tank is wrinkled. The armholes are stretched, and my pierced right nipple is exposed. I glance down at it but don't move to cover it up.

I catch Whit looking at it, and I want to tease him about it, but I don't. Just lean a little closer to him instead.

"Cool, cool," I reply and then gesture to the screen. "How about that one?" I suggest.

The screen has stopped on a new sci-fi series that I've heard good things about. Worth a try.

"Okay," he says, clicking on it, and it begins to play in the background.

And I should be focusing on what's happening on the TV, but now Whit's right hand is tapping a rhythm on the couch.

I stare at it.

"You're doing it again," I tell him as the opening credits roll.

He clenches his fist, and I sigh.

This guy.

"You're a nervous wreck," I tell him and then finish off my beer and open the next one, the top joining the other on the floor.

Whit glowers at the two caps littering his perfect space.

Well, tough titties, dude.

"You want to get those, huh? Put them in the garbage. It's killing you not to."

Whit's lips form a straight line, and he tucks his hair behind his ear.

"I'm fine."

Scoffing, I finish my second beer as the TV show plays on. I don't watch all that hard, probably because Whit is moving his eyes from the bottle caps to the TV and occasionally looking at our intertwined hands. Sometimes he even checks out my exposed nipple.

His nervous energy is interrupting my concentration on top of other things.

But at this point, I have a nice little buzz going, so instead of letting it get to me, I nuzzle in closer to him, resting my head on his shoulder. Our locked hands are now cradled in my lap, and I start stroking a thumb over the back of his hand.

"You coming with me this weekend?" I ask him when the first episode concludes.

Whit tenses slightly next to me. "Do you need me to?"

"To be honest, man," I begin, "I'm not sure you'd get away with not showing up. I'm pretty sure if I arrive alone, there is a good chance my cousins will come looking for you. You'll probably be dragged there despite wanting to come or not."

Whit sighs next to me and says, "Then it's best I go."

"Alright," I say as the second episode begins playing. "They're going to act like we're together. No matter what we tell them, they won't believe it. Just be ready for the harassment. You sure you're okay with that?"

"I'll be fine."

I hum under my breath and then release his hand, pull off my ball cap, and swipe my hand through my hair. Then I stand up and stretch, my tank riding up and exposing my lower belly.

Whit's eyes flash to it, and then he looks away.

I see that slight flush on his cheeks, but don't say anything. Instead, I just say, "If you say so," and then I point to the opposite side of the couch. "Alright, man. Move over there. My back is killing me."

Whit glances to where I'm pointing, and he arches an eyebrow at me.

"Why?"

"Why do you think?" I say.

"I'd like to hear you say it," he says, and I frown at him. This fucker.

"You for real?" I ask, placing my hands on my hips.

"Yes. Why do you want me to move, Caleb?"

I know what he's trying to do. Humiliate me, make me feel ashamed because straight guys don't do this. We don't spoon on couches, but I don't feel ashamed. Not really.

"Fine. I want to cuddle. With you. Now move."

Whit's lips twitch, but he doesn't say anything. He just moves to the opposite side and spreads his legs open across the chaise.

It's slightly obscene, in a very mild way, but instead of thinking too hard on *that*, I just follow, sliding between his legs. My back hits the front of his chest, and the back of my head rests on his shoulder. I can feel the smooth skin of his cheek against my stubble, can smell his familiar fragrance, and I sigh.

Whit doesn't touch me anywhere else, his hands resting on the couch beside me.

"This how you cuddle?" I ask, turning my head slightly, so I can see him. "Girls must be lining up to fuck you."

His eyes flick and meet mine.

"If you want my hands somewhere, put them there."

I sigh and then grab his left hand and bring it to my stomach. He spreads his fingers, and my muscles bunch under his touch.

"Better," I say and then turn my gaze toward the TV, but I'm distracted by Whit's right hand clenching the fabric of the couch tightly.

I reach over, pry it off, and then place it on my chest, right over my heart. It thumps wildly at his touch, but he doesn't comment on it. Instead, he tenses slightly before relaxing under me.

The rest of the evening passes like this, Whit holding me as I doze. In moments of consciousness, I feel his hands drifting across my abdomen. They don't stray far from their initial resting place, but they explore in their own way. His fingers trace my abs, up to my exposed nipple ring, across my collarbone, and down my sternum. It's subtle, his touch, but it's there.

And I like it, the feeling of his hands on me. More than any straight guy should. My dick is half-mast the entire time I'm in between his legs, and I wonder if he notices.

I'm not exactly small.

And these track pants hide nothing.

Whit's phone buzzes in his pants pocket, and he shifts up to pull it out. When he does, I can feel a hard bump against my lower back, and I bite back a smile.

Looks like I'm not the only one.

That fucker, trying to act all nonchalant about it.

Pfft.

"I have to take this," he says. "Da?"

I can hear a deep voice on the other end, and my ears strain to make out the conversation, but then the two of them begin conversing in some different language. Russian? Slavic? I don't know. I have no idea what those languages sound like, but it sounds Eastern European.

But gods, that's hot.

I shift between his legs and adjust my growing hard-on.

What the hell is wrong with me?

His tone turns icy, and his words grow louder before he

hangs up and tosses his phone to the opposite side of the couch.

"I didn't know you spoke another language," I say when the silence grows too unbearable.

"I do."

"Come on, man. Give me something. What language was that?"

"Romanian," he says, and then his fingers are tapping against the couch again.

"Who was that?" I ask as I grab his hands and place them back on my abdomen. His fingers flex against me and then relax.

"My father."

"Ah. Not a fan?"

"No," he says, and then he leans his head back and sighs heavily.

I give him a few minutes and then say, "You sounded angry."

"I am."

Welp, he's not much of a talker when he's pissed. Not much of a talker in general, to be honest.

"You going to be okay?" I ask, and Whit huffs a bitter laugh.

"I always am."

I glance up at him, my lips level with his jaw, and I nuzzle him with my nose. It's the gayest thing I've ever done, but I can't help myself. And fuck if he doesn't smell good.

"Hey," I say when his eyes flash down to me. "Snap out of it, man."

He licks his lips and then moves one of his hands from my abdomen to my hair, fisting it and tugging it roughly. My neck's now exposed, my Adam's apple bobbing in my throat. I can see his eyes, his pupils blown out as he watches me intently.

The alpha move is so surprising that my entire body lights up, and my dick thickens. If I were to look down, my shorts would be tented.

"Snap out of it?" Whit asks, his lips hovering over mine, his hand clutching my abdomen to keep me in place.

Not that I'm moving. Nope, I'm glue on this couch. You couldn't move me if you tried.

"Do you know how I snap out of it, Caleb?" he asks, and I swallow roughly.

"Nah," I mutter, and then he exhales shakily.

His hands flex once more, and then he's letting me go.

"I need to go study," he says, pushing at me to get me to move.

I'm like cooked spaghetti, though, and struggle to get my body in motion. But as soon as I scoot up a few inches, he's up and moving into our bedroom.

"So studying is how you snap out of it?" I call to his retreating back, but he doesn't answer.

And I'm on the couch with a hard cock and a muddled brain because I do not know what just happened. Maybe Whit leaving's a good thing. Because it looked like he wanted to kiss me, but that can't be right?

Right?

Because he's not into me.

I'm straight.

I think.

Shit.

Whit reappears, his messenger bag slung over his shoulder as he swipes his phone off the couch.

"You're for reals heading out?" I ask, staring at him, a pillow over my lap. Because that's not obvious at all.

He glances down at it and then stares at the door. "Yes."

And then he's gone, the door closing with a loud thump.

I remove the pillow and stare at my crotch in apology.

Well, hell, what am I supposed to do now?

CHAPTER FOUR

I spend the night tossing and turning in bed, and when I wake up, it's Friday, and I'm in a foul mood. Mainly because I was hard most of the night but refused to jack off. While I've come to terms with the fact that I enjoy cuddling with another man *and* holding hands, making myself come to thoughts of Whit was just a little too queer for me.

So, I refused.

But shit, I'm tired right now. And horny. And just miserable in general because Whit didn't come home last night. Now I'm wondering if he was really just studying or if he was out fucking someone.

I should have been out fucking someone, but I stayed home like a loser. Fighting my aggravating erection and trying not to think of Whit's lips next to mine.

What is it about this guy that makes me crazy?

And how the hell am I supposed to spend the weekend with him when I feel like this?

Oh shit, now I'm hard again.

I press the palm of my hand against my straining cock and will it to go away, but it doesn't. It just gets harder.

"Well, hell," I mutter as I pull on my pants.

Maybe some fresh air will get it to go down. It's definitely more of an introvert. Displaying itself in public isn't something it enjoys.

I tug on my sweatshirt and a beanie, open the front door to leave and nearly barrel into Whit, who's just coming home.

He looks rumpled, like he spent the night *not* sleeping, and I resist the urge to ask.

Because I do *not* want to know, nor do I need to.

Shit.

I want to know.

"Heading out," I mutter as I quickly push past him.

"Okay," I hear as I disappear down the hallway and head to my Jeep.

I sit in the parking lot for a few minutes, debating where I should go to clear my head and decide to go to the local coffee shop. Thankfully, by the time I arrive, my cock is flaccid.

I order a large mocha with extra whipped cream and sit next to the window, scrolling through my phone, when a text pops up.

Whit: When will we leave today?

Oh shit.

I *should* respond, but I don't.

I'll text him later.

This is *not* me being passive-aggressive. I'm momentarily putting this entire weekend on hold because just thinking of him spending a few days with me is making my cock twitch in my pants. This whole thing is getting uncomfortable.

"Hi," a quiet voice says behind me, and I see a familiar pale-faced guy standing awkwardly next to me.

"Casper," I say, much too friendly, and then narrow my eyes. Right. This guy was touching Whit the other day. "What's up?"

"I..." he clears his throat. "It's Magnus. Anyways, I just wanted to say hi. You know because, well, any friend of Whit's is a friend of mine."

Whit's not my friend, but I don't say that. I just eyeball Magnus, wondering if *he* was with Whit last night. Is he the reason why Whit looked so deliciously rumpled?

Then again, is Whit even into guys?

I don't know.

I don't know much about my roommate, it seems.

Magnus looks at me, shuffling on his feet. He's wearing a button-down shirt, plaid pants, and suspenders.

Who is this kid?

"You here alone?" he asks, and I nod.

"Why?"

"Just thought maybe Whit was with you."

Of course, he'd want to know.

"Nope, just me."

Magnus gestures to the seat next to mine, and I see his nails are painted a different color today. They're bright blue and match his shirt.

I raise an eyebrow at him.

"Can I sit?" he asks, kind of nervously.

"I don't own it," I reply, and he nods, biting his lip and sliding onto the stool. His legs dangle off the ground like a damn child.

"So..." he says, and I interrupt him.

"What's up? Just spit it out. I'm in a shit mood this morning and in no mood to guess."

Magnus nods vigorously. "Sure. I just...um...."

"Aren't you supposed to be on the debate team with Whit? From what I can see, you're shit at speaking, little dude."

Magnus straightens his shoulders for a moment, feigning confidence. "I happen to be amazing at debates. Now talking to the Hulk is another matter."

"The Hulk?" I ask, and then I add, "Never mind. Just tell me what you want to say."

Magnus clears his throat. "Are you and Whit...you know... like, together?"

He whispers the last word, so I ask, "Together?"

"It's just, well, you know.... You seemed kind of possessive of him the other day, but you're not really his type, so I was just wondering."

I bristle. "And what type might that be?"

Magnus waves his hand around nervously, accidentally slapping me in the arm a little too hard and pales even more. "You're too...big."

I sit a little taller, pissed that this tiny little guy is making me feel like shit about my genetics.

"So?"

"So, Whit..." he clears his throat, and I lean closer to intimidate him. "He's a top, okay? You think you'll be bending over for him? A guy like you?"

"Do *you* bend over for him?" I ask, nearly growling the last part.

Look, I'm mostly a passive guy, but this little shit is making me mad.

"I..." Magnus' face is beet red, and he's shaking a little.

"Look, it's none of your business. None of this is."

"I know..." Magnus whispers and blinks rapidly.

So, this is the kind of guy Whit goes for. Whiny and small and weak. The kind that wears suspenders and bowties.

Shit, I'm totally not his type.

Not that I care. I don't.

"Don't cry," I tell Magnus, who just sniffles next to me. "Look, Whit and I aren't fucking. I'm not even gay."

That gets Magnus to stop blubbering. He blinks some more, and then a shocked laugh comes out of him.

"Are you...are you serious?"

"Do I look like I'm making a joke?"

He shakes his head vigorously. "No. No. You look very serious. I...well, I'm sorry I assumed."

"You should be."

Magnus brightens after that, his pale face gaining some color, his head bobbing as he sits next to me.

"Why are you still here?" I ask him, and he stops moving.

"I don't know. Guess I'm just lonely."

His honesty is something I can admire. Most men can't admit that kind of thing.

I side-eye this little dweeb and then do something I probably shouldn't.

"Want to come hang out?"

This gets Magnus sputtering for a few seconds.

"Hang out...you mean...." His voice trails off, and I roll my eyes.

"I do not want to fuck you, little dude. I'd split you in half."

His eyes widen, and then he shakes his head before nodding. "I'm...okay, yes, we can hang out, but just so you know...I'm very insulted."

I raise an eyebrow, "Why?"

"Because I'm a size queen."

"What the hell is that?" I grumble, and he turns beet red.

"I...well, I prefer large...you know."

My mouth opens and shuts, and then a loud laugh erupts out of me, and people turn to stare.

"Well, shit. Maybe we *should* go at it then. You could be my first," I joke.

Magnus shakes his head and then shakes it some more. "I..."

"Just kidding," I say, playfully nudging him, and he almost tumbles out of his chair. "We can just hang out and play some video games. Maybe have a beer."

Magnus considers my offer and then nods, sliding out of his chair and following me to the door of the coffee shop. He stands at least a foot shorter than me, and I have the urge to throw him over my shoulder just to mess with him.

"What's he doing here?" Whit asks, his eyes narrowed as I come through the front door with Magnus slung over my shoulder like a sack of potatoes.

He was squealing a moment ago, pinching my sides and swatting at my ass, trying to get me to put him down. But he chokes it back when he hears Whit's disapproval.

"I made a new friend," I tell him as I set Magnus down on the floor. He smooths out his wrinkled clothes and messy hair and clears his throat.

"Hi, Whit."

Whit glances at Magnus and nods. Then turns those dark eyes toward me. "Caleb, I'd like to speak to you."

He nods toward the bedroom, but I ignore him, walking to the fridge instead and grabbing two beers. I'm a little salty at the moment, mainly because Whit didn't come home last night and because I'm apparently not his type.

I hand a beer to Magnus, who holds it awkwardly in his hands, and when he doesn't uncap it, I do it for him, letting the cap sail to the floor with a satisfying clink.

Whit arches an eyebrow, and I sigh heavily.

"Okay, Mag, just get a game started. I'll be right back."

Magnus nods, looking between Whit and me before moving to the couch and plopping down. His feet barely touch the floor.

I follow Whit to the bedroom, where he shuts the door and leans against it. I move to open my beer, and Whit says, "If you drop that cap on the floor...."

"You'll what?" I ask my fingers on the cap.

He narrows his eyes at me, and I smirk, twisting it off and holding it between my fingers, dangling it over the floor.

That look he's giving me, like he'd like to paddle my ass, is causing problems down south. I shift on my feet, pocket the cap, and then take a swig of my beer.

"What's going on?" he asks.

Shrugging, I reply, "I invited Magnus over to hang."

"Why?"

"Because we ran into each other."

Fuck this guy with his questions, I think, as anger boils up inside of me.

"And where did you run into each other?" he asks.

"The coffee shop. You interrogating me now, Sherlock?"

Whit folds his arms across his chest and narrows his eyes at me. "And you just happened to have a conversation with the guy who is terrified of you and then invited him over to hang out?"

It does seem a little ridiculous when he puts it that way.

I scratch at my jaw and shrug. "He came up to me. Started

sniffling and looking like a lost puppy. I felt sorry for him. He's so...fragile."

Whit huffs a disbelieving laugh. "Are you being serious right now?"

"Um, yeah. I am."

He eyes me, his cheeks slightly flushed, so I decide to push him a little more.

"He told me some things too," I add, and Whit freezes.

"What did he tell you?"

I smirk and then take another swig of beer. "Interesting things."

Whit begins tapping his fingers against his thighs, and when he catches me staring at them, he shoves his hands into his pockets.

"Tell me," he demands.

I pretend to mull over it before I shake my head. "Nah."

Whit stands completely still, his eyes blinking before he steps toward me.

"Tell me, *Caleb*."

Nng, when he says my name. It gets me going. I feel myself start to chub up even more and I hate myself just a little.

"You gonna make me? Heard you like to be in control."

Whit mutters under his breath. Then before I can even blink, he's on me, his hand at my throat pushing me back against the wall, and his body pressed up against mine. I could easily throw him off. I know I could, but I don't. I just let him maneuver me wherever he wants.

And I am so into it. I love being thrown around, apparently. My cock is rock hard now, straining against my pants, begging to be touched.

"I do like being in control," he says, his lips near my ear.

His warm breath against my skin makes me shudder beneath him.

He moves one of his thighs between my legs and presses forward with it, right into my aching dick, and I huff out a breath.

"Oh fuck," I whisper, and he chuckles darkly.

"Magnus has a big mouth and a nonexistent filter. Did he tell you I like to fuck men?"

"Yeah," I say, my hands moving up to grip his biceps. He's stronger than he looks.

"Do you like to fuck men, Caleb?"

I exhale shakily and don't answer because I don't fucking know.

"Or do you like to be fucked?"

Oh shit.

He shifts his leg against my hard length as his hand squeezes against my throat. I should have jacked off last night *and* this morning, so I wouldn't seem like such a desperate motherfucker right now. It's humiliating.

But I'm into it because I allow myself to be held against the wall and tormented.

"Did he also tell you, you're not my type?" he asks, and I force myself to look at him.

"I'm everyone's type, asshole," I grit out before my breath catches.

"Not mine," he says, and then he's pushing away from me.

He runs his hands through his hair, and he inhales and exhales deeply a few times like he's trying to get himself under control. And all I can do is just stand there and try and not come in my pants like a pathetic thirteen-year-old boy after his first sexual experience.

He pinches the bridge of his nose as he calms down. "I am going to ask him to leave."

"No," I manage to say, irritated that I'm so turned on and pissed that he's leaving me hanging.

Whit's eyes flash up to meet mine. "Why?"

And just because I'm a dick, I say, "Apparently, he likes to be torn up during sex with big cocks. Sounds like fun."

Whit's nostrils flare, and his eyes flash with anger.

"I thought you were straight," he says through clenched teeth.

"Apparently not as straight as I thought," I mutter and then adjust my cock in my pants.

It's painful.

Whit whips his eyes from my crotch, and his cheeks flush.

"Don't have sex with him," he says, and I push myself off the wall, stalking toward him.

He stumbles back slightly, and I reach out and steady him.

"We'll see," I lie, because I'm not fucking anyone, least of all Magnus.

Now *being* fucked sounded pretty fantastic mere minutes ago, so there's that.

I adjust myself once more and then open the door and see Magnus sitting there, fidgeting with a bracelet he has around his wrist. His eyes move from Whit to me and then flash to my tented pants.

There's nothing I can do about it, so I plop down next to Magnus and sigh.

"Sorry about that, Mag," I say and rub at my chest. "Whit was feeling a little possessive."

Whit shifts on his feet and stares daggers at me.

"We need to pack for the weekend," Whit says. "You can't stay long, Magnus."

"Oh, um, where are you going?" Magnus asks as I hand him a controller for the Xbox.

"We are spending the weekend with his family," Whit responds. "And we need to leave soon."

"Nah," I reply and turn on the Xbox and queue up a game. "We can leave in a few hours. Don't want to get there too early."

"You still need to pack," Whit says, irritated.

"It'll take me two minutes to pack my shit," I tell him and then nudge Mag, whose eyes are ping-ponging between me, Whit, and the TV.

"Relax. We have time," I reassure Whit and then nudge Mag too hard. He hisses, and I pat his head in apology. "Now, little dude, I'm going to kick your ass."

Magnus' eyebrows lower, and he squints at me. "I'm fantastic at this game, I'll have you know."

"We'll see," I reply.

Whit stands there for a minute, watching us before he huffs and disappears into the bedroom without a word.

"He seems upset," Magnus whispers, not tearing his gaze from the TV.

He *is* pretty damn good at this game. Not that I'd admit anything to this little dweeb.

"He doesn't want us fucking," I reply as I take a critical hit from Magnus, who preens next to me on the couch.

I glower at him, and he clears his throat. "Told you I was good at this game. And to address the other comment. I have no shame, so I probably would let you fuck me."

"That so?" I ask, and he blushes.

"That's so. But I would probably regret it."

"Why's that?" I ask, starting a new game.

"Because you're scary."

I peek over at him and roll my eyes. "I'm a nice guy."

"You sicced your friend on me."

"Ah, Mal. You think *I'm* scary," I reply and then chuckle. Before it's cut off when my character dies again.

"You little..." I say, and Magnus scoots a little farther away from me.

"Don't hurt me."

I glower at him and then turn all my attention to the game.

"No more chatting, you little shit. You're distracting me."

Magnus clears his throat. "I'll still kick your ass, you big...oaf."

And he does. Over and over.

CHAPTER FIVE

Whit's eager to hit the road. He moves in and out of the bedroom, tapping those fingers and glowering at me. When I lean back in defeat, Whit practically shoves Magnus out of the apartment.

"So rude, man," I say with a small smile.

Whit points to the bedroom, and I give him a small salute.

"Yes, sir," I tease.

I manage to pack my stuff in under two minutes. Whit secretly times me, trying to prove a point. I see the timer on his phone, so I just shove my shit into a plastic bag. He watches it all, mouth slightly agape.

"You are a barbarian," he mutters as he places his small suitcase into the trunk next to my half-spilled bag and then slides into his car.

I shrug, sprawling my large frame in the passenger seat.

Despite a small pep talk, my cock is hard again because Whit in this expensive car apparently does things to me.

Filthy, pornographic things.

"Who bought you this car, fancy man?" I ask, fiddling with the window.

He puts the child locks on, and I roll my eyes.

"My parents," he says as he pulls out onto the road.

Dark clouds gather in the sky, and the smell of petrichor permeates the air. God, I love the rain. We don't get enough of it out here.

"Your parents rich?" I ask, placing my arm on the center console and bumping his. He doesn't move it, though, just lets our arms rub against one another.

"Define rich."

"Shit, man," I say, absently letting my finger trace the vein across the back of his hand.

He doesn't mention it and doesn't move away from me. He just keeps those eyes on the road.

"If you have to ask to define your wealth, you've got to be filthy rich."

"I suppose."

I snort as my fingers continue to caress the back of his hand. "You do realize you're hanging out with a redneck this weekend, yeah?"

"And why does that matter?"

"We do things differently," I reply.

"I assumed so, after meeting your family."

"Got that right," I say, and then he turns his palm up. I slide my fingers between his, like its totally fucking normal to hold hands with some dude while he drives me to my house for the weekend.

Yeah, totally straight. That's me.

We drive in silence for the next hour, me flipping through songs on his playlists, searching for something we'd both like.

Apparently, the one thing we have in common is music.

"You like EDM? I thought you'd like classical music or something."

"And I thought you'd like country music or heavy metal."

I shrug. "I could go for both, but EDM is cool too. Now, Sem and Luke like classic rock."

"You have better taste then."

Whit's mouth turns up in a small smile and I preen.

"Turn here," I say, pointing to an unlit, unpaved road. It's begun to sprinkle, and Whit turns his windshield wipers on and then sits forward a little more, slowing the car a bit because there are no streetlights out here. It's just rocky hills, shrubs, and a few native trees.

Whit steers the car, and we bump along, rocks pinging the outside of his vehicle as he maneuvers down the dirt path.

"How much longer?" he asks, and I snicker.

"Told you I should've driven," I say, but he just sends me a look.

"I was not driving in that death trap for over an hour. I'm amazed it still runs."

"Serves you right, then," I say, squeezing his hand. "You're such a snob."

Yeah, I haven't let go of him. Don't fucking judge. His hand feels nice in mine.

"Right here," I say, and Whit drives down a long driveway. A moment later, an old two-story house appears before us. A little worn, but it's home. To the right is an oversized, detached garage that houses all the toys my aunt and uncle have collected over the years, and to the left are a few of the trucks we play with.

I should come home more often. But being here reminds me of my mom. Of watching her slowly wither away to nothing.

I rub at my chest and swallow roughly.

I've got this. I've got Whit here as a distraction, and my cousins will keep me busy. Or get me into trouble. Could go either way, really.

When Whit parks and I finally let go of his hand, I turn to look at him.

"You were warned."

"I'll be fine," he says, then pushes open the driver's side door as my aunt opens the front door and rushes out, a kitchen towel thrown over her arm. She's a woman in her fifties with greying hair and a stocky build. My aunt is the shortest one here. All of us tower over her. And yet she manages us all.

She's an impressive woman.

My heart swells, and I beam at her. I talk shit about my family, and yeah, they're wild and slightly insane, but they're mine.

"The boys are here," Aunt Del shouts and then rushes over to Whit, pulling him into a hug. He has to bend over to accommodate their height differences.

It's so damn cute.

"Geez," I say. "Feelin' the love."

She smacks me on my shoulder because she can't reach my head and then pulls me into a hug. Instead of crouching like Whit did, I lift her off her feet and spin her around.

She shrieks and then smacks me again as Sem and Luke appear on the porch along with my uncle.

"You drove *that* out here?" Luke says, whistling. "That car's like a hundred grand, cuz," he adds.

Sem, Luke, and my uncle move toward Whit's car and stare at it. It is sleek. Dark grey too. Shocker.

"How's she drive?" my uncle asks Whit.

"Smooth," Whit replies.

"I expect to drive it tomorrow," Luke says, and my uncle frowns at him.

"It's polite to ask, Luke. I raised you better than that."

Luke walks around to the other side of the car and then meets Whit's eyes. "Let me drive it tomorrow, please?"

Whit taps his fingers and peeks over at me, and when he sees me watching them, he nods. "Sure."

Luke whoops, and Sem opens the passenger side door, looking inside.

"Warned ya," I tell Whit and then squeeze the nape of his neck and follow my aunt into the house.

My aunt turns toward me in the kitchen and asks, "How you doing, sweetheart? Really, be honest with me."

"Fine," I say with a shrug.

She stares at me, trying to read my mind.

"Okay, I believe you. I know its...hard being here. You going to be okay?"

I pull her into me and give her a good squeeze. "I'll be fine, Aunt Del." It's partially true. I *will* be fine. But my aunt still thinks I moved away my senior year because I hated living with them.

I didn't. I practically grew up here, but I just needed space to breathe after my mom passed.

That and the commute was killer.

"Whit's a good distraction."

"He's something," I mutter, and my aunt watches me a moment before slapping her hand onto the counter.

"Okay, enough of that. On to other things. I want to be as accommodating as possible because there is *no* judgment in this house. So, you and Whit will sleep in your old room."

"Sounds good," I reply and then snag a cookie from a plate on the counter and shove it in my mouth.

"There's only one bed," she adds, and I shrug, like that fact doesn't thrill me.

"You saw us. Don't need a lot of space."

I grab a second cookie, and she moves the plate out of my way. "Save some for Whit."

I roll my eyes as the man of the hour appears with my uncle and two cousins trailing behind him. They're slightly damp from the mist outside. Whit's shirt clings to his lean frame and I shift on my feet at the sight.

In his hands are his suitcase and my torn plastic bag.

"Aw, babe," I say with a smirk. "Thanks."

I grab my bag full of crumpled clothes and press a kiss on his cheek. He blushes and shoots me a scowl.

Sem and Luke reach for a cookie, but Aunt Del smacks their hands away and then hisses, "They're for Whit."

"Hey, why the fuck is he so special, huh?" Luke asks.

"Because," Aunt Del says. "Caleb has never brought someone home. We're trying to get him to *stay*."

"Aw," I reply, slinging my arm over Whit's shoulder and pulling him into me.

My aunt stares at me and then adds, "We have to entice Whit in any way possible."

"Damn," Sem says with a chuckle.

"Are you saying I can't keep my man?" I ask my aunt, who just raises an eyebrow at me.

"Oh, fuck off," I mutter, letting my arm fall from Whit and grabbing a cookie so quickly my aunt doesn't have time to smack it out of my hand. I shove it in my mouth.

Crumbs fall down the front of my shirt, and I turn to smile at Whit.

It's his turn to look at me like I've just crawled out of a dumpster.

"He adores me," I say around a mouthful of food.

"Looks like it," Luke hoots, and I look at Whit, who looks horror-struck. "You can sleep with me tonight if you want," Luke tells Whit, and I shoulder my way past my cousin, linking my hand with Whit's.

"He's mine, asshole," I say. "I keep him very satisfied."

"Keep it down in there tonight," Luke says.

Whit huffs a laugh as I glower at my cousin.

"I bet he's a screamer, huh?" Luke adds lowly, and I sock him in the chest.

He curses, and then my aunt is shooing everyone out of the kitchen. Bless her.

"Go settle in," she says, and Whit and I make our way upstairs and into the guest room. I close and lock the door, lest Sem barrel in.

"That was...."

I hold up a hand, halting whatever words were about to escape his mouth. Then brush the crumbs off the front of my shirt and wipe my face.

"Do you have siblings?" I ask, satisfied I no longer look like the Cookie Monster.

Whit shakes his head.

"Then just know that they can be overbearing, but I love 'em."

Whit leans against the door as I upend my plastic bag on the bed and the crumpled contents fall out.

"I wasn't insulting them," he says.

I glance over at him. "I know. It just must be a culture shock."

"It's different. I like it."

I look at him skeptically but decide to let it go. He's a big boy. He can handle himself around them.

"I'm going to shower and then go downstairs and chill for a bit. Want to join?"

"Join you in the shower?" Whit asks with a slight smirk.

"Fuck you," I mutter and grab my sweats and boxers. Trying to pretend that the idea of him wet and naked doesn't do things to me.

"And just so you know, when you fuck me, I will not scream."

"When?" Whit asks, and I flush, stalking past him.

What the hell was I thinking saying that?

"See you downstairs," Whit calls out as I disappear into the bathroom.

When I'm done, I find Whit downstairs sipping on a beer. He's changed into black pajama bottoms but kept his dark grey Henley on. On the other hand, I'm clad only in my grey sweats and nothing else. Even my feet are bare.

"Started without me?" I ask, rubbing at my stomach and looking around the room.

My uncle is nearly lying down in his recliner. Sem and Luke lounge side by side on the couch, leaving me nowhere to sit.

"One of you should move onto the floor," I say, and they ignore me.

"Just sit on his lap like before," Sem says, handing me a beer.

I grab it and then look at Whit, who slightly spreads his legs.

Oh, fuck it all.

"Fine," I mutter and then lower myself onto his lap. I open the beer and set the cap on the end table.

"I see you respect your aunt's space," Whit says softly, and I nudge him with my elbow.

He huffs at the contact, and I settle against him. I take a long sip of the cool beer, and it slides down my throat as I try and ignore how good his thighs feel against mine.

But it's impossible. And then, to top it off, Whit's hand moves onto my stomach, and his dry, warm palm just rests there. Against my bare skin.

Oh shit.

My cock perks up, and I shift slightly in his lap. Sem and Luke will not let me live this down if they see me standing at attention.

"So, Del tells me you two have been together a while," my uncle says, and I glance at Whit, who just rolls his lips between teeth.

"I don't know where you're getting this information," I mutter.

My uncle eyes the two of us and then says, "Just didn't know you were gay, son. Though, I did wonder."

"Wonder about what?" I ask.

My uncle shrugs, glancing at the TV. "Just if you weren't interested in girls. Makes sense now. You're interested in men."

I sigh. "I'm not gay."

Sem and Luke laugh at this like it's the funniest thing. Like I'd ever joke about something like this. Assholes.

Whit's thumb is now rubbing small circles across my skin, and I see my cock growing in my pants. This is a horror show.

"No shame in it, Caleb. Don't understand it, but that doesn't mean it's wrong," my uncle says.

I roll my eyes and then place my hand over Whit's, stopping him from moving those insufferable fingers.

"Not in public," I hiss at him.

When I remove my hand, his is frozen against my belly.

"They're meant for each other, don't you think," my aunt says, appearing in the doorway and observing the room. She smiles sweetly at me when she sees where I'm sitting.

Sem moves to the floor and pats the seat he just vacated. "Come on, ma. Take a seat."

"Asshole," I mutter, and Sem chuckles.

"You two are so cute," my aunt croons and reaches over and pats my leg.

Holy fuck, she almost touched the erection that's snaking down my thigh.

The thought of her hand on it shrivels me slightly.

"You two just seem so different from each other. Opposites do attract, but tell me again, Whit, what drew you to each other?"

"Again?" I ask, and Whit's thumb starts drawing circles against my skin, and I'm going fucking insane. "When did you two talk?"

"She calls me sometimes," he says, and I scowl at him.

"I'm going to kill you," I mutter, stilling his hand with mine once more and then turning to my aunt. "None of you should be talking to him without me knowing."

"Why?" Luke asks.

"Because."

"Not a good reason," Sem says, and I flip him off.

My aunt is beaming next to me, and I shift on top of Whit, so she won't see what's happening below my waist. Because it's back to growing, and her noticing it would be mortifying.

The only problem is, now I'm curled up on Whit's lap, looking ridiculous, but I'm not sure I can stand up because I'm fully hard.

Should have jerked off before I left. I should probably jerk off all the time before I'm around this dude.

My aunt turns to Luke. "I want you to find someone like Whit."

"I'm not gay, ma."

"I know that, but I think you should find someone classy like Whit."

"I'm classy," I tell my aunt, but she just ignores me. Which is fine because Whit's hand is now sprawled across my happy trail.

And he's fucking playing with it.

Those nervous fingers. I want to do things to them.

I shiver, and Whit's other hand threads into my hair.

"You cold?" he asks against my ear, and I roll my eyes.

"No."

Just trying not to traumatize my aunt by coming in my pants while sitting next to her. That's all. Simple.

My aunt must have heard Whit's question because she hands him a blanket, and he spreads it over the two of us.

Well, good. At least now my dick is covered, but now Whit's fingers start to go crazy.

He's playing with the string of my sweats, and I bite back a groan as I close my eyes and will myself to stop being so weird.

"I hope you'll stay with us for Thanksgiving," my aunt tells Whit.

His fingers still against me before starting up again.

"What makes you think we'll be together then?" I ask, kind of grumpily.

"Oh, shut up, you," my aunt tells me and then says to Whit, "You're welcome to come."

"That sounds very nice, Mrs. van Beek."

She blushes. "Call me Del, please."

I roll my eyes and shift on top of Whit. I cannot get comfortable.

"How can you stand him on top of you all the time?" Sem asks, his long, thick legs sprawled out in front of him, picking at the label of his beer.

Whit is tracing his finger over my happy trail again. "I enjoy it."

"He enjoys it," I say snidely and then place my head on his shoulder, shifting my body down a little, moving his fingers up to my chest.

Now he's running that thumb aimlessly over my nipple ring. Back and forth. Tugging, rubbing. My eyes nearly cross as bolts of desire shoot down to my cock. I can't stand it anymore. I'm too wound up, and I need some relief. Like yesterday. I cannot sit here another minute.

"I need to go to bed," I blurt, realizing that I had just interrupted my uncle.

I have no idea what he was saying or if it was important. All I know is I need Whit's hands off me.

I jump up, clutching the blanket around my waist, and jog up the stairs two at a time.

I hear footsteps behind me, but I don't stop. I enter the room and kick the door shut. Only it doesn't close, just hits something and swings back open.

"Are you okay?" Whit asks, and I glower at him as I drop the blanket.

"Do I look okay to you?" I hiss, and his eyes widen slightly when he sees the tent in the front of my pants. It's enormous. "Shut the fucking door before they get an eyeful."

Whit steps inside and closes it, locking it.

And then we are staring at each other in the dimly lit room.

"That looks painful, Caleb," Whit finally says, and I groan.

"Your fingers are infuriating. You shouldn't have touched me like that back there," I say as I adjust myself and turn around.

It's one thing to lie on top of this guy and occasionally snuggle, but it's another thing entirely to do *other* things.

But currently, I'm forgetting the reason why it matters so much.

Whit clears his throat and then gestures to the bathroom.

"Perhaps you should take care of it."

I snort. "You should be the one taking care of it, asshole. You caused it."

He stares at me and then shifts on his feet, those fingers tapping a rhythm on his thighs.

And then he's stalking toward me, and I stumble back, the back of my legs hitting the end of the bed.

"What are you doing?" I ask, and he doesn't say a word, just cups me.

That hand of his is *cupping my junk*, and I nearly pass out.

And then he squeezes, and I can't breathe.

"I always take responsibility for the problems I create," he says, and then his thumbs hook into the waistband of my sweats, and he tugs them out and down until my cock is bobbing and straining between us

"Oh fuck," I hiss as he wraps those long, soft fingers around my thick length.

The sight of it, his hand on my weeping cock is obscene. I've never had a guy touch me there. Never. And for some reason, I can't tear my eyes away from the sight.

He slowly moves his hand, and I have to grip something

before I topple over. Sparks shoot up through my abdomen, and my nipples harden painfully. My hands scramble to find something to hold onto so I don't fall over, and I grab onto Whit's shoulder, holding onto it for dear life.

And he works me expertly, that hand sliding up and down, fucking me with his fist.

Once. Twice. Three times.

I can't tear my eyes away. I'm just watching him move his wrist up and down.

How is this so good? This shouldn't be so good. It's a guy...Whit....

His eyes meet mine, and then without warning, my hips jerk, my balls draw up, and I'm coming, shooting my load all over him.

It's an obscene amount of come. It goes on for ages and coats his hand and the bottom of his shirt. There's so much it drips onto the floor. I can hear it splattering between us.

And when it's finally over, I feel my entire body heat.

"That was...fast," Whit says, still gripping my softening cock.

"Don't say another word," I grumble. "It's been a while, okay?" I close my eyes and inhale deeply through my nose. "Let go of me, Whit."

Those long fingers unwrap from around me, and he takes a step back. He's coated in me. He smells like my release.

My cock twitches. My eyes slide up and down his rigid body, and I see the front of his pants are tighter than usual. Oh fuck. *He liked that*.

"Thought I wasn't your type," I rasp, and he narrows his eyes at me.

"I'm going to go wash."

Then Whit disappears into the bathroom, and I'm left to clean up the mess I made.

He returns a little while later, a new shirt on but wearing the same pajama pants he had on earlier.

I'm sprawled out on the little bed, feeling slightly embarrassed that I came so quickly and more relaxed than I have any right to be.

I should be freaking out over the fact that a guy just got me off, but I don't honestly care.

That was the best hand job of my life.

And apparently, just seeing Whit again is making my cock ready for a second round.

Would he go for it? I know I'm not his type, but he wouldn't have done that unless he wanted to, right?

"I usually last a lot longer," I manage to say as he climbs in next to me and turns out the light. Our legs brush, but he pulls his away from mine and stares at the ceiling.

"You don't believe me?" I ask.

He sighs heavily. "I believe you, Caleb."

I don't believe him, though, and I turn on my side and look at his silhouette.

"I'm very good at sex."

He fiddles with the sheets.

"Go to bed, Caleb."

"Whatever," I mumble and then roll onto my other side and close my eyes.

He doesn't want to talk. Fine. I'll leave him alone then.

———

I wake up to the sound of gunshots. They sound like they're right next to us like someone is aiming right through our window. The sound vibrates the glass.

Stupid asshole, I think with a smile.

"What's that?" Whit asks, his hands clutching my back. I'm sprawled half on top of him.

Huh, must have made my way over to him in the night. I was peeved when I fell asleep, but apparently, my body didn't care about his irritating silence earlier. All it seems to remember is how good his hand felt on me.

I nuzzle my face into Whit's neck. He smells so damn good. My cock is hard against his hip.

"That's the sound of freedom, babe," I mutter.

Whit pinches my side. "I'm serious. What *is that, Caleb?*"

"Probably Sem unloading out there," I say, rolling my hips slightly.

"Why would he do that in the middle of the night? Is he insane?"

"Because he can and I told you. This is like a whole other world for someone like you. Have you ever even heard a gunshot in your entire life?"

He ignores my comment and relaxes slightly until the gunshots start up again.

"It's a good thing your family lives out in the middle of nowhere," he mutters, his hands tightening against me again.

"Heh. And you wonder why I moved out," I reply, and then I nip at that tendon in his neck.

I'm not close enough to him. I want to crawl inside of him, to put up permanent residence.

Caleb lives here.

Pushing myself up, I move on top of him, so I'm entirely sprawled across him. He grunts under my weight but doesn't push me off. I can feel his semi against my belly. It's a major turn-on, and I can't help but rut against it.

"Stay still," Whit hisses.

I do it once more and then force myself to stop.

"Sorry. My dick is desperate for you, apparently. You should have never given me a handy, dude."

He huffs underneath me. Probably in disbelief.

I know. This whole thing is ridiculous.

"I liked it too much. You've created a monster."

I arch into him, and he pinches my side. Hard. A curse slips from my lips, and I rut against him once more in retaliation.

"You started this," I whisper. "You need to fix it."

Whit pinches me again and then says, "I can't just give you hand jobs all the time."

"Uh, yeah. You can."

He pushes at my chest, and I cling onto him like a koala, my hips gyrating against him. And I can feel him growing hard against me.

Oh hell. That's intoxicating. Whit is getting hard for me.

"Caleb," he chastises, but I'm chasing a second orgasm, and I'm having a hard time telling myself this is a bad idea.

"Just give me a minute. Probably just ten seconds," I mumble, burying my face in his neck. "It's your fault for smelling so fantastic."

Whit's hand is in my hair, and he pulls on it roughly until I blink down at him.

"Stop," he says, his chest expanding beneath me.

"Shit. Oh fuck," I mutter and roll off him. What the hell am I doing?

I rub at my face and sit up. I was rutting against him like

some kind of animal, and he didn't want it. I'm a terrible, terrible person. My mom would be ashamed of me.

"I'm sorry. I'll...sleep on the floor," I mutter. "But first, I need to...."

I move to stand up and find some relief, but Whit's on me, pulling me back until I'm sprawled across the bed.

"I didn't say you could go," he says, straddling my hips, and then he tugs down my sweats and palms me.

"Fuuuuuck," I groan as he wraps his fingers around me and pumps. "Yes."

Whit squeezes me and asks, "How soon will this be over?"

"Screw you," I mutter as he reaches over and cradles my balls with his other hand.

And I nearly come undone right then.

"Caleb, I think we both know that *I'd* be the one screwing *you*."

My eyes roll back in my head at those words, and I arch my hips into his hand. I cannot believe this is happening right now. Can't believe that I'm letting him get me off a second time tonight. It's wrong because I'm straight. Sort of.

Probably not.

Probably not at all.

Whit tugs on my balls, and I explode all over his hand and my chest once more.

And when I come down from it, he lets me go, sliding off my thighs, and disappears into the bathroom.

And when he reappears five minutes later, I ask, "You want me to...uh...."

"No," he says, climbing in beside me and pulling the covers up to his chin.

I puff out a breath, sort of thankful he didn't ask that of me but annoyed he didn't at least offer me the option.

Maybe I wanted to touch him, to watch him come undone.

"Want me to sleep on the floor?" I ask him because I don't know. I molested him moments ago, and then he got me off. And now he's being all cold towards me.

Maybe it grossed him out. I should ask him about it, but I can't find the words.

"No," Whit says and then sighs. "Come here."

I shouldn't. I should stay far, far away, but I climb on top of him despite my concerns and fall asleep in his arms.

The following morning, after waking up hard as hell, Whit arches an eyebrow at me as if to say, *Really, again?* Then he pushes me onto my back and jerks me off.

I'm able to regain some of my dignity by lasting at least one minute this time.

He goes to the bathroom when I've finished, and I hear the shower turn on. I can't move. My entire body is jelly, so I just lie there, come on my stomach, cock out, and doze.

Whit is standing over me when I wake up.

"Your aunt is asking us to come down for breakfast," he says.

I rub at my stomach and feel the wetness still there. My cock twitches at the memory of Whit over me, his hand working me so good, and when I grow hard again, he rolls his eyes and exhales.

"I told you," I whine, and Whit reaches down and jerks me off again.

Like it's totally normal for roommates to do this.

For coming a short while ago, I bust a nut way too fast.

"Shower," Whit tells me after washing his hands and eyeing my come-soaked abdomen. "I'll be downstairs."

I groan and throw an arm over my eyes. "Don't make me. Let's just stay in bed all day."

Liam is pounding on the door before Whit can respond to that ludicrous suggestion. "Up assholes. Time to get up!"

My eyes widen, and I sit up, the wetness slipping down my abs and onto the sheets.

"You better not be fucking!" Liam adds with an evil chuckle.

He's the worst of them all.

"Go away," I shout back and then shoot out of bed.

Whit's watching me, his eyebrows raised. He must think the lot of us are such heathens.

Liam's still outside our door because he shouts, "It rained last night, so get your ass downstairs so we can go out. I didn't drive all the way here for you to fuck all day!"

"You live ten minutes away!" I reply.

"Hurry up, you ass eater!!"

Liam thumps on the door once more, and I groan even louder.

"You did this," I blame Whit, who just points to the bathroom.

"Shower, Caleb."

CHAPTER SIX

I grumble my way through breakfast as Liam ribs me endlessly. I haven't seen him in ages, and I growl at him when he flicks my ballcap off my head. I look ridiculous this morning, having forgotten an extra shirt.

So now I'm wearing a borrowed shirt from Sem that says, *All Trash, No Trailer,* ripped jeans, and a Texaco hat. On the other hand, Whit is wearing what he usually does, looking way too good for being up earlier than me.

Sem and Luke are outside getting the trucks ready. I can hear them laughing and talking through the open front door.

"Where's Anne?" I ask Liam. "I prefer her over you, you know."

"She couldn't make it today."

I sigh. "She's my favorite sister-in-law."

"She's your only sister-in-law," Liam says and then shoves the rest of the eggs into his mouth and heads outside. "Be out in five. We got shit to do!" he shouts.

"What are we doing?" Whit asks a minute later when we

step onto the porch. There's a mist in the air, and the ground is soaked. It's not too cold yet, but the rain seems to wash the usual haze away. This is my favorite time of year.

"You'll see," I say and then smile inwardly because Whit has no clue what he's getting into.

I lead him to where Sem, Luke, and Liam are all chatting.

"We're getting into this?" Whit asks, eyeing the monstrous truck in front of him. It's the Frankenstein monster of trucks. Different parts from the scrapyard have been clobbered together to create it. It's my baby, and I cannot wait to have Whit next to me as I take it out.

"Yep."

"And you're driving?" he asks, looking unsure.

"Yep."

"There are no doors."

"Nope."

"And no roof."

"Nope. Say hello to Betsy." I pat the truck and add, "Betsy, this is Whit."

"You've named it?"

"Yep."

I chuckle and crowd into him, pushing against his back until he's forced to climb up into the truck.

I shamelessly watch his ass as he pulls himself up.

"Stop checking him out and let's go," Liam says right before starting up his Jeep. It rumbles low and loud.

Whit clicks on his seatbelt and then sends me a stern look.

"This is not what I thought I'd be doing on my Saturday morning."

I pull myself into the driver's seat. "Wish you were still jerking me off instead?"

Whit flushes and then taps his hands against his legs. "I think getting into this truck with you was a bad idea."

I smile widely, flip my hat backward and twist the key in the ignition. The truck sputters and coughs but then roars to life. Whit winces at the sound and turns to stare at me.

"Oh, Whit, you have no idea."

I rev the engine a few times, being a general asshole, and then I'm peeling out of the gravel driveway and chasing Liam, Sem, and Luke. Liam's in his own Jeep, and Sem and Luke are in another large truck that they've been working on together.

"Why are we going off the road?" Whit asks loudly when I steer us over some bushes. We bump and bounce over some holes in the ground, and he grabs onto the oh-shit bar in front of him so tightly his knuckles turn white.

Mud kicks up against the truck's sides, and some flings onto my jeans as we continue to move away from the house.

"It's called off-roading, babe. Well, technically..." I say as we bounce over a small hill and splash into a muddy puddle. It flings onto Whit's clean pants, and he stares at it before turning toward me. "It's called mudding," I add and then rev the engine again, lurching us forward. Whit curses under his breath, but it's all drowned out by the sound of the truck engines.

"You did good for your first time," Liam says, slapping Whit roughly on the shoulder. "Wouldn't have guessed you were a virgin."

Whit flicks his hands down toward the ground, and mud slaps onto it.

I chuckle and pull him into me. He scowls at me. He's been giving me the evil eye all morning.

"Laugh all you want," he grumbles.

We're a mess. My entire lower half is covered in mud, but Whit, well, he got the worst of it when I purposefully hauled ass through a mud puddle on his side.

He's covered in mud. From head to toe.

He looks fucking adorable.

I pluck at his muddy shirt, and my smile widens.

"You look good messy," I say, swiping at a smear on his face.

He smacks my hand away, then pulls his shirt away from his skin. It makes a sucking sound.

"I am going to kill you in your sleep."

"Nah, then who would cuddle with you, huh?"

"I have my pick," he mutters, but I ignore him. I'm sure he does, but all that matters is that I'm the one who is all up on him at night.

And the one he's wrapping that hand around.

"Let's go shower," I say and then tug him toward the back of the house.

"Clothes off!" My aunt shouts. "I will not be cleaning up your muddy mess. Off and put it in the laundry bin."

Liam, Luke, and Sem begin undressing, and I follow suit, leaving Whit to stand awkwardly in front of us.

"Come on, man," I tell him, peeling my shirt off. "Clothes off."

Whit stares at me and then shakes his head. "I—no, I...."

I tilt my head. I've never seen Whit at a loss for words before.

"Why not?" I ask when my cousins crash through the door, each fighting who will get a shower first.

"I...please just get me a towel."

My eyebrows meet, but I don't question him. He seems almost embarrassed. So, I disappear inside the house and then reappear a moment later with a large beach towel.

"You going to tell me what the deal is?" I ask, and Whit shakes his head.

"You got issues with your body? 'Cause from what I can tell, it's nice."

Whit grips the towel tightly in his hands and then whispers. "Please leave, Caleb."

Well, fuck when he says it like that.

"Okay, man. I'll go shower."

Whit nods, not looking at me. When I exit the bathroom five minutes later, Whit's standing in the room, the towel wrapped around his shoulders, hiding his body from my eyes.

"All yours," I say, and he nods, pushing past me and locking the door behind him.

What the hell is that about?

I try and shrug it off but can't quite let it go.

So, when he appears ten minutes later, fully clothed, I'm on him.

"You seriously not going to talk to me about what that was back there?"

"Not about this, no."

I rub the back of my neck. "You mad at me for taking you out?"

Whit shoves his hands in his pockets and shakes his head. "It has nothing to do with that."

I sigh, hate being in the dark. Still can't get a read on this guy, and it bugs me. It's like a mosquito bite that won't stop itching.

"You seriously not going to share?"

"No, can we just go downstairs?" he asks, and I sigh heavily, not wanting to give this up but not quite sure if I should push.

Whit and I are still practically strangers. I don't know much about him. He's as much of a mystery as he was a month ago.

"Sandwiches are ready," Liam says when we go downstairs. He's made an ordinary turkey sandwich look like it should cost a hundred dollars. My mouth begins to water as I grab onto the plate.

Whit and I take a seat at the kitchen table, and I try and keep my distance but end up scooting so that our legs are at least touching. My thigh presses against his, and only then do I dig into the sandwich Liam made, groaning on the first bite.

"This is amazing," I say, consuming half the sandwich in about ten seconds.

Whit nods in agreement, taking smaller bites and wiping his mouth every so often.

He looks good when he eats. He must think I look like a garbage disposal.

"Anne's going to be pissed she missed this," Liam says, waving a hand between us.

I chug a cup of water. "Yeah, well, maybe Whit and I'll entice her out of her hidey-hole next time."

Whit peeks over at me, and I explain, "His wife's an artist and goes through these phases where she just paints. We don't see her for weeks."

Liam glugs down a soda and then wipes his mouth with the back of his hand. He burps loudly and then pats his belly.

"Well, as much as I'd like to stay and chat, I've got to go set shit on fire. I'll be back tomorrow morning for more fun.

I'll see if Anne can come. She'll want to see your boyfriend again."

"We can't wait," I tell him and nudge Whit when he just chews silently.

When Liam lumbers out of the house, Whit says softly, "So we're boyfriends now?"

"Apparently," I reply and then scoot closer and hook my ankle around his. "You good with that?"

Whit takes a long sip of his water and then says, "For now."

Not sure what he means by that, but I let it go. I can dissect his reluctance later.

"What are we going to do the rest of the day?"

"Well, thought we'd go shooting."

"Shooting?"

"Yeah."

Whit side-eyes me. "I have a moral qualm against guns."

"Shut the fuck up," I tell him and then stand up. "Finish that sandwich. You eat like you're the Queen of England."

"Better that than a two year old," Whit replies, and I lean down and bite the back of his neck. He hisses loudly and rubs at the sting.

"Let's go. Enough of your weird moral dilemmas. The real world awaits."

He finishes a short time later, and then the four of us go to a makeshift range on my parents' property, where we take turns shooting our guns.

"Why does it look like there was a fire here?" Whit asks, and I smile widely.

"Ah, yeah, we blew shit up last time I was here."

"Seriously?"

"It was epic. I'm sure we can recreate it if you want to watch."

"No. I'm...no, thank you."

He's at a loss for words.

Sem and Luke use their AK-47s to shoot up the rusty car and wooden targets in the distance while they laugh maniacally like they're Scarface or some shit. Seeing it for the first time through Whit's eyes, I realize we seem slightly insane. Especially for a guy who has probably lived a very sheltered life.

What did Whit do while growing up? I know he traveled. Did he sit around in a ginormous home library and read? Eat with fancy silverware? Go to golf clubs? Learn how to fold napkins? I glance once more at my cousins. Damn, I don't even know what's going through his head right now.

Oh well. Life is all about having new experiences, right?

Whit watches my cousins for a while before Luke coerces him into trying it. He uses some backward logic to convince Whit, but all I know is that I get to wrap my arms around his waist to keep him steady while he fires a few rounds.

"You're terrible," I laugh, my hands resting on Whit's hips.

He glowers at me and lowers the gun to the ground.

"I've never shot a gun in my life. Of course, I'm terrible."

"Well, there's nowhere to go but up. You can come with me to the shooting range near school, and then when we come back, you can kick ass."

Whit shakes his head, ignoring my comment about the future. "I think this is the last time I'll handle one of these."

I roll my eyes and then load his gun again and place it back in his hands. Then I press myself against his delicious backside and place my palms on his thighs. The muscles flex and bunch under my palms, and I knead them lightly.

"Stop distracting me, Caleb," he says.

"Something about you, yeah?"

He huffs, and I whisper, "You got this."

He unloads the clip, hitting the target once.

Everyone whoops, and Whit cracks a smile at me.

He looks so fucking cute with that rare smile that I grab the gun and set it down before pulling him into me and nuzzling his neck. He smells like Whit, but with a hint of gunpowder and rain. It's hot.

"Get a room," Sem shouts before unloading his gun into the targets. He cackles like a nutcase.

"Had enough?" I ask, and Whit nods. And because I can, I grab his hand, and we walk back to the house in silence.

When we end up in the bedroom, we stare at each other.

Something crackles between us, and then he's on me, roughly pushing me against the wall.

"Damn," I mutter as he peels my shirt off and tosses it onto the floor.

"Not going to fold that?" I tease, and he cups me roughly, my smile fading into a gasp.

"I shot a gun today," he tells me, unbuttoning my pants.

"No one forced you. That was all you," I say, and he pushes my pants and boxers down in one fell swoop. I kick them off my ankles and stand before him, my cock straining toward him, my balls swinging between my thighs. I'm entirely naked except for my backward ballcap.

He eyes me, taking me in, and then his eyes shoot up to meet mine.

"There are many things I'm doing with you that I've never done before," he admits, wrapping his hand around me, one finger at a time, and I arch into him when he finally makes a fist.

"That so?" I manage to gasp as he works me quickly to the edge.

Those magic fucking hands, twisting and squeezing me just right.

"Yes, Caleb. That's so."

I'm panting, my hands grasping onto his shoulders, holding myself steady while he works me to a crescendo.

"Whit," I moan. I'm so close, so ready to burst. "Please."

And then he reaches and cradles my balls, and I burst into his hand. He catches it all, and then his phone rings as I'm coming down from my post-orgasmic haze. It ruins the moment. Shatters it really. Gone is the Whit with blown out pupils and reddened cheeks. Instead, he's glowering, annoyed with this entire situation. Was he hoping to let me return the favor and the ringing phone ruined his plans?

Damn, I hope so. I have been dying to get my hands on him.

"Ignore it," I tell him as he wipes his hand off with some tissue.

"I can't," he tells me, his shoulders tense, his breathing stilted. And then he grabs his phone and begins to speak in Romanian.

So, it's his parents, I think as I watch him tap his fingers against his thigh.

If it's possible, his shoulders rise even more. They're almost at his ears now. He turns away from me, his voice clipped, almost angry.

I tug on my boxers, sit on the edge of the bed, and listen. Part of me wants to go and wrap my arms around him because he just seems so agitated, but I don't know if that will make it worse. Does he even want me touching him when he's annoyed? Guess I could try, yeah? I'll never know unless I try.

So, I push up from the bed and walk up behind him, wrapping my arms around him and resting my chin on his shoulder.

He stiffens for a moment but then melts into me. And I love that's he's letting me do this. I like it more than I probably should.

He continues to speak into the phone and then listens for a moment. The man on the other end does not sound happy or kind. I don't like his dad. He sounds like a shithead.

My hands spread across his chest, and I press him into me, wanting to ease some of the frustration his tone denotes. Wanting to soothe him. It helps a little. His shoulders lower slightly, his body not as stiff against mine.

This tense conversation goes on for a few more minutes, and then he's hanging up and sagging against me.

"I hate him," he admits, and I press my face into his neck.

"I hate him too. He sounds like a dick," I say, and Whit huffs a laugh at that.

"He's not the best father."

"I've never had a dad, but even I know yours can do better."

"You have your uncle. He loves you. That's more than I have."

"Yeah," I say, and then press my lips into his neck and don't kiss him exactly, but let my mouth linger there, just breathing on him.

It should be creepy, but he arches his neck slightly to give me more room.

So, I keep my mouth there for a few more seconds before nuzzling him.

"We should go downstairs," he says, and I squeeze him tightly.

"Why?" I ask. "We could just stay up here for a while."

"Your aunt's missed you. She wants to spend time with you. I'm sure your uncle does too."

"You guilting me into this, Whit?" I ask and then add. "You think that you can tell me what to do just because I let you jack me off?"

Whit turns his face slightly and meets my eyes.

"Yes."

I roll my eyes and then let him go. "Alright, fine. Let's go."

We spend the rest of the evening playing cards, and I'm surprised when Whit kicks our ass multiple times.

Makes me horny as hell. But then again, everything he does seems to set me off.

It's getting a little ridiculous.

When we sit outside that night, my body curled up against his under a blanket as we watch the stars and just listen to the wind whip through the trees, I feel so at peace.

Whit seems happy too. He hasn't pulled his Kindle out once, and I'm feeling flattered.

"You like it out here?" I ask, and Whit nods, tracing the shell of my ear.

"It's been a while since I've disconnected."

"You should do it more. Maybe disconnect that phone of yours too."

Whit leans his head back and sighs. "Yeah, I should."

"Ever feel like just running away?" I ask.

Whit turns to look at me, pressing his face into my hair, sighing.

"All the time."

And when we crawl into bed that night, I don't even bother to pretend. I just crawl up on top of him and bury my face in his neck.

WHIT

"Tomorrow, we are going on the ATVs. Just wanted to warn you," Caleb tells me, and I can't help but shudder at the thought.

Today in that truck was *awful*. All that mess, but if I'm being honest, being with Caleb is...I can't think about it. I don't know what I'm doing with him.

I always promised myself I'd never be with a straight guy again, but I can't quite seem to get rid of him.

This is a recipe for heartbreak.

"I'll stay back and help your aunt cook dinner," I tell Caleb, threading my fingers through his hair, and he almost purrs against me.

He's a big guy, muscular and tall, and he nearly crushes me when he crawls on top of me, but I...well, *like* it is one word for it.

"Loser," he mutters into my neck. "You're coming with me, or we'll drag you out there."

"Please don't," I say.

He lifts his head, and our eyes meet. Those blue eyes twinkle. "You begging, baby."

The term of endearment slips out of his mouth, and I feel my cheeks heating. I've never blushed so much in my adult life.

But I like how that word sounds coming from him.

"I never beg," I say.

"I bet," he mutters and then arches his hips into mine, his cock dragging against me. It's delicious in the worst possible way.

"I have no problem begging," he adds, licking those full lips of his. "I'm a complete slut, apparently."

He's good-looking in a rugged way. He's not my type at all. I like petite men, pretty men. Caleb is not pretty or petite. Not at all. No, it's worse. He's sex. All-consuming sex.

What am I even doing? I cannot be entertaining this. There is too much waiting for me once this year is up. I can't start something with a guy who is totally wrong for me.

He doesn't recycle. He packs his clothes in plastic bags.

His clothes are stained and wrinkled.

He has a nipple piercing.

There's a good chance he'd want me to bend over for him, and I never do that.

No, I'm always in control. I like to be the one fucking.

I'd never give anyone so much power over me.

I need to end this, put a stop to it.

But instead of doing what I should, I say, "Roll over."

He does as I ask, and I'm on him, pulling those pants down, pulling out his enormous cock, and stroking him.

He makes the most delicious noises when he's turned on. Whimpering, moaning, and saying my name. It's addictive.

"We shouldn't be doing this," I tell him, my hand twisting up and over his drooling head.

"Fuck that. Why stop when this feels so good?" he replies, panting.

He's lasting longer than before, and my cock is straining against my pajama pants. This whole weekend has been torture. I should pull myself out and find relief too.

But I won't. I have more self-control than that. I always have control around Caleb...most of the time.

He's chanting my name now, and I feel like a god. It's disconcerting.

I run my free hand over his muscular abdomen, feeling those muscles flex under my fingers. I tell myself that all this muscle is uncivilized, but I like it.

I want to spend the rest of the night mapping the ridges and grooves of his body.

It's a work of art.

Caleb's panting and arching his hips up into my hand, and then he's coming, his seed warm against my fingers.

"Holy shit. How is this still so damn good?" he asks me.

And I rub my fingers together, feeling his release between them, and then force myself off the bed. It's that, or I'll do something I shouldn't. This arrangement, whatever it is, is already too precarious.

I need to end this.

I will, as soon as we get back to the apartment. I'll tell Caleb that this cannot happen anymore.

And then, in a matter of months, I'll never see him again.

I should feel relieved that I have a plan, but when I slide back into bed with Caleb, and he scoots over to me, wrapping himself around me, I feel…

Melancholy.

CHAPTER SEVEN

I don't know if there is anything better than having Whit wrapped around me. His thighs are pressed against mine, his hands clutching my chest, his face pressed into my shoulders.

I need to ride ATVs with him more often. Or maybe I'll buy a motorcycle and take him for rides.

"You good, man?" I shout as I maneuver us down a long hill.

His hands clutch me tighter in response, and I laugh loudly. This was the best idea my cousins had all day.

Luke and Sem are ahead of us as we traverse the hilly terrain. In the distance, I can make out a large water tower and some electrical poles.

I rev the engine, and we barrel up to the top of a hill, the tires spinning for a moment before we crest the top, and I stop abruptly.

"Why are we stopping?" Whit asks, and I turn to face him. His hair is wind-swept, eyes sparkling, and our lips nearly touch. I can feel his breath against my mouth, and I meet his dark gaze.

"Why you lookin' at me like that?" I ask.

Whit licks his lips. "I'm not looking at you in any particular way."

"Yeah, you are," I say softly. "Thought I wasn't your type."

"You're not," he replies, but his eyes flick down to my lips, and I can't help but wet them. Because I think kissing Whit would be life-changing.

But before I can close the distance, Sem whoops loudly and flies through the air on his ATV. He actually lifts his legs off the back of the machine like some kind of stunt devil, and Whit watches him with raised eyebrows.

"He should be wearing a helmet," Whit utters, and I laugh loudly.

"Probably. Not wearing one explains a lot, actually," I reply and then ask, "Wanna drive?"

Whit shakes his head. "I think it's best if you do this."

"You sayin' I'm better than you at something?" I ask.

Whit rolls his lips between his teeth, and I want him again. It's getting a little ridiculous. I've never wanted anyone the way I want this dude. Never had this insatiable need to be consumed by someone.

"I never thought you were lacking," he tells me, and I resist the urge to turn the ATV off and straddle him.

This guy.

"Ready for more?" I ask and rev the engine.

Whit sighs behind me but doesn't reply, just tucks himself against me.

When we get back home an hour later, Whit dismounts the ATV on unsteady legs. I wrap an arm around him, helping him into the house. He probably doesn't need it, but he lets me do it anyway.

We spend the rest of the day lounging outside, me drinking beer, my legs propped over Whit's while we shoot the shit with my cousins, aunt, and uncle. Anne makes a brief appearance, her clothes spattered with paint, her hair pulled up into a messy bun. She pulls us both into a long hug and then asks all the obligatory questions about our relationship before disappearing a short while later. Anne gets like this sometimes when her creativity is at a peak. I'm surprised she even showed up at all.

Whit reluctantly lets Luke and Sem drive his car, insisting on riding along with them and returns home a little too pale.

But then he looks at me, and his cheeks redden. Probably because I was making heart eyes at him. But how could I not? He just made my cousins extremely happy, and he did it despite being uncomfortable. But wasn't what this whole weekend was about? Whit pushing past his comfort zone and doing things with me that he wouldn't normally do?

God, my mom would have loved him.

When the sun has set and it's time to finally leave and head back to our apartment, I don't want to leave. Things will most likely go back to the way they were, Whit and I coexisting as friends. At least here, we could at least pretend to be together. Back at school, there's a slight chance Whit will go out of his way to ignore me. Maybe even avoid me altogether.

As I shove my clothes into my plastic bag, I glance over at Whit who is zipping up his suitcase.

"This wasn't too painful?" I ask him, and he glances over at me.

"No. It was nice."

I nod, rubbing at my stomach before clutching my plastic bag in my hand.

"You going to be weird when we get home?" I ask him, and Whit grasps his suitcase and moves toward the door.

"Nothing needs to be weird about this."

I'm not quite sure what that means, but I follow him downstairs and then out to his car, where my aunt, uncle, Sem, and Luke hug us goodbye.

Then we're alone in the car again, and I'm hard because he's driving. Duh.

I adjust myself, and Whit snaps his gaze to my crotch before moving it back to the road ahead of him. A slight smirk lines his lips, and I roll my eyes but don't say anything.

He already knows what he does to me. It's blatantly obvious. No need to pretend.

Plus, he already jerked me off after we got back from going out on the ATVs. I admit I'd begged until he'd spun me around, forcing my hands against the wall. And then he reached around and pumped me until I spilled onto the floor.

He's never once found release with me, but I know he's usually hard when he's getting me off. I don't understand why he doesn't let me touch him, but I never push. I'm not entirely sure he actually likes doing what he does to me.

Maybe he hates it, just does it to get me to shut up.

Oh shit.

That sudden thought sours my stomach, and I glance out the window at the passing cars.

What the hell am I doing? Why am I even messing around with this guy? Most of the time, he seems to put up with me, but other times I'm not entirely sure he's not disgusted with me. But then there are times when he looks at me with those dark eyes, and I wonder....

"What's wrong?" he asks after a few moments of silence.

"Who says something's wrong?"

He arches an eyebrow. "You're not talking or fiddling with the music or...." His voice trails off.

"Or what?" I ask.

"Touching me," he adds, those fingers tapping on the steering wheel.

I scoff and then lean my head back against the headrest.

"Just trying to give you a break," I tell him, and he clasps onto the steering wheel tightly with both hands, those fingers of his flexing.

"Who said I wanted a break?" Whit finally says, and I peer over at him.

"Just never sure how you feel. You're not exactly easy to read, and you never open up."

He loosens one hand and lays his arm across the center console. His palm is up, inviting me to link my fingers with his. God, my heart aches with the small gesture, knowing it's his way of conveying what he wants without saying it.

"Want me to hold your hand, Whit?"

He scoffs and starts to move it away, but I grab it before he can escape and wrap his palm in mine.

He glances down at it and then sucks his bottom lip into his mouth. Like, he's not sure what the hell he's doing. Yeah, buddy, me too. I was straight a few months ago.

"So, Whit," I say, rubbing my thumb across the back of his hand, "since you're trying to be more open with me, tell me something about you that I don't know."

He glances over at me, and I smile at him. "And really, that could be anything because I know next to nothing about you."

"What would you like to know, Caleb?"

I shift in my seat because when he says my name like that, all serious and unsmiling. I want him to *do* things to me.

"Alright, how old are you?"

He blinks at me. "Twenty-two, you?"

"Twenty-one."

"Middle name?"

"Stafford."

"Really, you sound so distinguished. Mine's Carter."

"Caleb Carter," Whit says, and I'm at full mast right now. I'll come within seconds if he says that while he's pumping me in his fist. I'm sure of it. Good thing that's already happened. No reason to be embarrassed about how easy I am.

"Could you refrain from saying my name until we get home?" I groan, and Whit side-eyes me.

"I'll try."

I clear my throat, pressing the palm of my hand against my erection, needing some relief.

"Okay," I begin. "Um, tell me where you grew up."

"Romania for the first five years and then moved to New York. You?"

"Grew up right here, my whole life."

"Have you ever traveled?" Whit asks.

"Nah, but I'd like to visit all fifty states one day, you know? Maybe travel overseas."

Whit nods.

"Bet you're well-traveled," I say, and Whit shrugs.

"I have traveled, but most of it wasn't for leisure."

"That so?" I ask, and Whit nods.

"My parents would drag me to events all over the world. I rarely had time to explore like I wanted to."

"Oh, how you suffered," I joke, and Whit glances at me in all seriousness.

"I did, Caleb. My childhood was not...ideal."

I blink at him. What the hell. What does that mean?

"Care to elaborate?" I ask.

"No."

Silence engulfs the car's cabin, and I stare out the window. After a few minutes, Whit removes his hand from mine, wipes it on his pants, and places it back on the steering wheel. And I feel like shit.

Why did he wipe his hand? Am I grossing him out? Jesus, my mind is a mess.

"Sorry, man," I mutter. "I just want to know you."

Whit's silent and then, "I don't want to be known, Caleb."

Well, no shit.

I snort and cross my arms, pissed that he's so closed off. Not that he owes me anything, but I can get a hint. He doesn't want to be known by *me*. I get it.

When we arrive back at the apartment, I'm in a terrible mood. I try to keep it civil, but I'm too silent, and Whit is watching me with wary eyes.

As soon as the door closes and the lock engages, Whit says, "I think we should end this before you get hurt."

I scoff. "Oh, only I'd get hurt?"

Whit taps his fingers on his thighs and nods. "Yes, it's for the best. You're straight. This isn't you. It's a phase and...experimentation."

"That so?" I ask, and I can tell my questions about his statements are starting to annoy him because the rhythm he's creating with his fingers is gaining speed.

"You're not my type, as we've established. And I'm clearly not yours."

"You sure?" I ask, and Whit's fingers stop moving.

"Stop it, Caleb. We should remain roommates, that's all. This whole thing was a bit of a mistake."

I arch an eyebrow at him and then shrug, pretending like I'm not totally disappointed. Like I hadn't envisioned crawling into bed with him tonight and pressing my face against his neck.

Of him saying my name while I came.

"Whatever you want, dude."

I pull my shirt over my head and toss it onto the floor. It's immature, I know, but I smirk when his eyes flare in annoyance. Makes me feel a little better.

That's what you get, asshole.

Unbuttoning my pants, I fling them off with a kick, leaving them draped in the hall.

"I'm going to shower," I tell him.

He stares at me.

"Pick up your clothes."

"Nah," I say. "I'll do it later, roomie."

Whit's hands clench into fists, and he flexes them slowly. His cheeks are flushed, his eyes flicking from my discarded clothing on the floor to my nearly naked body.

I brush past him, letting my hand trail across his hand that hangs by his side, and a shock of lust travels up my arm.

And then he's grabbing onto my wrist, stopping my forward momentum.

"It's for the best," he says tightly.

"Is it?"

"You'll see." He lets me go, and I disappear into the bathroom, not quite sure what just happened or why, but feeling like shit, nonetheless.

I don't see him for the next few days. Our schedules don't overlap. I work long hours at the scrapyard, trading shifts with Sem and Luke, and then when I'm not in class, I spend time at Mal's place. I'm sure Whit is doing something similar. Because when I'm at the apartment, he's not there.

I see him *once* when I'm leaving the apartment. I'm walking down the stairs, my cap pulled low over my head when he's coming up.

He meets my eyes, and I just nod at him, not quite sure what to do at this moment.

He brushes past me, and my arm tingles when he touches me.

I pretend it doesn't bother me, but I miss the fucker. Miss sleeping with him at night, miss holding his hand. Whatever, best to get over it now. He was right. Better to nip this in the bud before things get out of control.

I'm back to being straight, I think.

Not sure if I can swing from one end of the spectrum to the other at the drop of a hat. Is that a thing?

I don't know what I'm doing.

Other guys don't really do it for me. Objectively, they're okay to look at, but I don't ever get hard from thinking about a dude's dick. I just have a thing for Whit, I think.

He's still the star in all my fantasies.

Asshole.

On Friday, things come to a head when I'm getting ready to head out with Mal and Bree. I'm going to be a third wheel, but I need to do something fun to help me stop obsessing about my roommate.

I'm going to get some tonight.

And by some, I mean sex. Hopefully by a very willing and enthusiastic *woman*.

I'm grabbing my wallet and phone and am about to head out when the apartment door opens, and Whit appears.

His eyes meet mine before sweeping over the rest of me.

I look damn good tonight, not my usual laid-back self. I'm wearing a clean white t-shirt, a flannel long-sleeved shirt, and new blue jeans. My hair is styled, and my face is sporting nicely trimmed stubble. The only thing not quite clean is my work boots.

Where we're going, this outfit will be a hit with the ladies.

"Won't get in your way," I mutter, about to move past Whit when he stops me.

"Where are you going?"

"Out."

He clears his throat. "Obviously. *Where* are you going?"

"What's it to you?" I ask, leaning against the door, crossing my ankles, and folding my arms across my chest. My eyes take him in, his dark jeans, his long-sleeved shirt. He looks good. Better than I've ever seen him look, actually. Not sure if I'm imagining things or if he's blooming when he's not around me.

That thought pisses me off.

"I haven't seen you."

I narrow my eyes at him. "That wasn't by design?"

Whit shoves his hands into his pockets and looks...I dunno...lost or something.

"Look, you don't need to pretend to care, alright? We can just avoid each other like we've been doing, yeah? Better to be roommates like you said."

Whit shifts on his feet but doesn't say anything.

"I need to go, man. Got to get some."

I'm halfway out the door when Whit says, "Wait. Can I..." He clears his throat. "Can I join you?"

My eyebrows rise, and I look over my shoulder at him. "For reals?"

He gives a clipped nod, and I shrug. "If you want."

Damn it, my heart is galloping at a hundred miles an hour. Why does he want to hang out? Does he miss me? If he has, why has he been avoiding me? Shit, men say women are confusing, but they sure haven't met Whit. He's a mindfuck.

He sets his messenger bag down and follows me outside to my Jeep.

"This bar we're going to is probably not your scene," I tell him as he slides into the passenger seat.

His foot hits a few empty soda cans and a few discarded receipts as he buckles in, but he doesn't comment on the mess. Just stares at it for a moment before he looks out the windshield.

I don't say anything, I just put the truck in gear and shift it into first.

His eyes move from the passing scenery outside to my hand on the gear shift, and I catch him watching me a few times. He glances away quickly when our eyes meet, but his fingers aren't moving, probably because he's sitting on them.

Is he nervous?

We drive for about ten minutes, and after I park, we walk into the crowded bar together.

Mal towers over everyone, so he's easy to see over the throng of people, and we make our way over to where he and Bree are waiting at the bar. One of his tattooed arms is slung around her shoulder when we approach. Those grey eyes of his narrow when he sees who I'm with.

"Hey, man," I say, giving him a one-armed hug and then pulling Bree off her feet as I crush her to me and press a kiss to her temple.

"Hey, Whit," Mal says and then eyes me in confusion.

Yeah, me too, dude. I don't know what's going on.

"Hello," Whit tells him and then shifts closer to me, our arms bumping. I resist the urge to pull him into me. Nah, if he wants anything from me, he needs to initiate it. I'm not going down that road right now.

Mal leans toward me and whispers into my ear, "Why the hell you bring him? Didn't you want to find someone to bring home tonight?"

I sigh. Yeah, Mal. I did, but what the hell was I supposed to do when he looked so lonely.

And to be honest, I like him here, even though I know nothing'll come from it.

"Won't stop me," I tell Mal even though it feels like a lie.

I look over at Whit, who is talking with Bree, and when our eyes meet, he flushes.

Oh hell.

"Alright, well, let's grab our drinks and then find a table. Then we can get to work," Mal says, eyeballing Whit.

Whit looks at him and then me and then back at Bree, continuing their conversation like he hadn't just overheard us making plans.

He has to know why I'm here.

We all order beers, except Whit, who orders a gin and tonic, and we make our way over to a table and slide in. Mal and Bree, then Whit and me.

If this had been before, I would've slid closer to him, hooked our ankles together, maybe even slung one of my legs over his, but he made it clear he wasn't interested in continuing anything, so I give him a healthy distance.

And by healthy, I mean a few inches because this booth is tiny.

"Alright, bro," Mal says, stretching his arm around Bree. "Let's see who we can find for ya."

They begin looking around the bar, and I take a sip of my beer, doing my best to ignore Whit, who is sitting stiffly beside me, his long fingers turning his drink around and around and around.

"What about her?" Bree asks, pointing to a brown-haired woman leaning up against the wall. She's wearing cowboy boots and a short white dress.

"She's pretty," I say.

"Looks like she's here alone," Mal says and then asks, "What you think, Whit? She look good enough for my boy?"

Whit stops spinning the glass in his hand and looks up at my best friend, who may or may not be a little salty about how Whit left things with me. Mal's been the one who's listened to me process this entire thing. He's slightly overprotective and very loyal.

Whit swallows. "I'm not sure what his type is, so I can't objectively say."

I roll my eyes and lean back in my seat, and my thigh bumps Whit's leg. On accident. Still, a tingle spreads through me at the contact.

"How about her?" Bree offers, pointing to a redhead on the opposite side of the bar. She's laughing with her friends and seems like the life of the party.

"She looks fun," I say, and Whit takes a long sip of his drink.

"Want to get out and chat them up? See which one sticks?" Mal asks.

I shrug. "Yeah, give me a minute to finish my beer."

"You mind if we go dance while you do that? Love this song," Bree says, and I wave them away.

Mal looks reluctant to go but is ultimately swayed by Bree's hands moving all over him. He's a total sucker for her. Has had a crush on her for ages. The fact that she's now giving him the time of day has made his entire life.

When Whit and I are finally alone, we sit there in silence until Whit leans toward me. "I didn't realize you were coming here to pick someone up."

"Yep. That's the plan," I tell him, not sure what to say. "That bother you?"

Whit spins the glass around in his hand and takes another sip but doesn't answer me.

I swallow down the rest of my beer and slap the table, startling Whit a bit.

"Welp, off I go. Wish me luck," I tell him and scoot out of the booth. I can feel Whit's eyes on me as I stride across the floor. Good. He did this. We could have been fucking around this whole week, but he made it weird. He can lie in the bed he made. Without me.

I make my way over to the brown-haired woman, who smiles at me sweetly. She looks like she'd be nice to take to bed. Maybe she'd even hold me after.

She tells me her name, and we shake hands. She has soft skin, kind of like....

"Excuse me. Can I talk to you, Caleb?" a voice says in my ear, and I turn around and see Whit standing behind me, his lips set in a thin line.

I turn back to the brown-haired girl, whose name I don't even remember, and tell her I'll be right back. Then follow Whit outside. All the way to my Jeep.

"Get in," he tells me.

"Um, I was kind of in the middle of something, man," I say.

"I think we can reasonably say that she wouldn't have gone for you."

"Oh, you're so full of shit, Whit," I say and then fold my arms across my chest.

Whit huffs. "Please, get in the car."

"Why?"

"We're going home."

"Uh, no. We're not," I reply and then dangle my keys in front of him. "In case you forgot, I'm driving. And I'm here for a chick, man. Don't kill my vibe."

Whit flexes his hands and then shakes his head, muttering something under his breath.

"I would rather you not," he says.

"Rather I not what?" I ask, my heart picking up its pace. Not sure what he's going on about, but I'm getting a vibe. It's a vibe that I like more than I should.

Whit runs a hand through his hair and says, "I'd rather you not take one of those women home."

"And what's it to you?" I ask, widening my stance and puffing my chest out.

Whit clears his throat. "I'm happy to continue our previous arrangement if that's what you'd like."

I arch an eyebrow. "Arrangement?"

"Yes," Whit says, and I can't help the small chuckle that escapes me.

"You for real? You were the one to call it off. Think I recall you saying it was *for the best*," I say using air quotes.

This guy. Who the fuck does he think he is? Showing up here, killing my vibe, and then wanting to go back to our *arrangement*.

Who calls it that anyway?

"I was mistaken."

"Oh, is that so?" I reply sardonically.

"Yes."

When I don't respond because I don't even know what to say, he points to the Jeep, "So can we please just go home now?"

"And just leave Mal and Bree here?"

"You can text them."

"We just got here."

"I'm sure they will understand."

"What if I don't want to go home with you?" I ask.

Whit's eyes meet mine, and he tilts his head slightly, and then he takes a few steps toward me until he's pressed up against me, and despite not wanting to, my half-hard cock plumps up to full mast.

Because I apparently have no control when I'm around this guy.

He reaches down and gently presses his palm against it, and my eyes flutter closed.

"I think you do," he says softly, and then he steps away from me, leaving me extremely flustered.

I was never in a winning position with Whit. Might as well roll over now before it gets embarrassing.

"Fine," I grumble and adjust myself before hopping into my Jeep.

It roars to life, and I pull out my phone and text Mal and Bree, letting them know that I took Whit home.

And then we're on our way home. I'm not sure what the plan is once we arrive, but when we step inside the quiet apartment, and the door locks behind us, Whit and I just stare at each other.

"So, what now, huh?" I ask.

Whit's eyes move across my body. "What would you like, Caleb?"

Oh, that's a loaded question, but I'm not about to beg. My feelings are still hurt, and I've felt like shit for the past five days.

I run a hand through my hair and scoff. "I cannot believe this. I'm so stupid."

Whit takes a step toward me. "You are not."

"I am. I ditched my friends and my plans to *come home with you*, and you won't even say what *you* want," I reply and then run a hand down my face. "I'm going back. What the hell am I doing here with you?"

I turn to leave, and Whit grabs me, his fingers tight around my wrist.

"Stay."

"Nah," I reply, but I don't budge, just let him hold me in place with his hand.

"Let's watch a movie," he says. "You pick. Anything."

He tugs on my arm, leads me to the couch, and places the remote in my hand. Then he sits down next to me and slides his hands under his thighs.

I turn on the first movie I see and then look at Whit, sitting stiffly next to me.

"Why you sitting like that?" I ask, and Whit tries to loosen his posture, but he's just as rigid as he was a moment ago.

"Why you look like you want to escape? You were the one who wanted me here," I remind him.

"I want to be here. I don't want to escape. I'm just...nervous."

"Nervous?"

"Yes, because...I don't know what I should do at this

moment. I realize I've messed up, and I don't know what to do. I don't know what you want. But being only roommates isn't what I want."

I watch him the whole time he utters this, his eyes never leaving the TV.

"What do you want, Caleb? Tell me, please," he pleads, and I swallow.

He looks so vulnerable right now, laying himself out for me to see, that I feel no need to stretch this torment out any longer.

"Well, I have missed being held," I offer.

Whit turns toward me, and before I can blink, he's pulling me into him, shifting our bodies until I'm lying on top of him. His fingers in my hair, pulling lightly on the strands, his other hand moving under my shirt, rubbing up and down the bumps of my spine.

"I missed this too," he admits shakily, and I let myself nuzzle my face into his neck, inhaling his scent.

"Thought you were annoyed with how clingy I am."

"You're not clingy."

"I am just a bit. I warned you, though."

"I don't mind it."

I hear his heart thudding in his chest, and I reach one hand up and trace the outline of his collarbone. All feels right in the world. Later I'll dissect this moment and wonder if I made the right decision, letting him in again, but right now, all I can think about is how good this feels.

"What else did you miss?" he asks.

"You fishing for answers?" I tease.

He tugs roughly on my hair, and I bury my face further into his neck, rubbing my nose against his earlobe.

"I think I'll keep some secrets," I whisper, and he shudders beneath me.

We lay like that, his hands in my hair and on my skin until my shirt is halfway up my torso.

So, I sit up and pull my flannel off and then my white shirt. I drop them onto the floor, and Whit glances at the pile before moving his eyes to my bare chest.

"You looked good tonight," Whit says as I lower myself down on top of him.

"I always look good," I say, and Whit scoffs.

His fingers are sliding across my back again, and I'm vibrating with pleasure at the contact. How did I go a whole five days without this? How did I go my entire life without it?

"Why am I always the one naked, huh?" I ask. "When do I get to see you?"

Whit tenses beneath me, and I lift my head up, and our eyes meet. His dark eyes flash, and I tilt my head slightly.

"What are you hiding?" I whisper.

He opens his mouth and then closes it, then his eyes shut tightly.

"Hey," I say softly, cupping his face with my hands and running my thumbs over the smooth skin of his cheeks.

His eyes flutter open, and he stares at me with something I can't read. I can't ever fucking read this guy.

I rub my nose against his, and he exhales shakily.

"Caleb," he whispers, and my heart cracks a little.

My lips graze his because how can they not. When his mouth is *right there*. Those soft, plump lips just begging to be kissed.

I move my mouth against his, and his fingertips dig into my back, his hips arching slightly into mine. I've kissed plenty of people, but never a man.

I'm not sure that matters anymore.

I'm so far past straight that I can't turn back now.

"Can I kiss you?" I ask, and Whit blinks up at me before he pulls my mouth down onto his in response.

Our lips collide, and he holds me there for a moment, the two of us just breathing into each other. And then our lips begin to move, sucking, licking, and biting. My entire body vibrates with nervous energy because this feels so damn good. And when he opens for me, and his tongue sneaks into my mouth, I groan loudly.

Because Whit's *tongue is in my fucking mouth*, and he tastes like candy. Sweet and addictive. I'm having a sugar rush as he tilts his head and sweeps inside, licking slowly from one corner of my mouth to the other. He's tasting me, feasting on me. Moaning softly as he does, like he's never tasted anything so good. And that sound, the sound of Whit letting go, makes me go nuclear.

I run my hands through his hair and arch my hips, pressing our hard cocks against each other as I begin to rut against him.

"Caleb," he says, pulling away, biting down on my lip, and then sucking it back into his mouth. Trying to kiss away the sting. Soothing the ache building within me.

"Jesus," I exhale as he swallows my words and arches his hips up, meeting my thrusts. We're losing control. The two of us are just bodies trying to find release.

Holy fuck, this is so beyond hot. Why didn't I just kiss him the first day we met. We could have been doing this the whole time. I've been missing out.

Whit whips his mouth from mine, and he pants heavily.

"Wait," he breathes. "Wait."

I pause, my entire body frozen on top of him. I can feel the vein in my cock throbbing with my heartbeat.

"What's wrong?" I ask, and he shakes his head, trying to catch his breath.

"I...if we keep doing this, I'm going to come."

"Isn't that the point?"

"In my pants."

I press my nose against his and exhale sharply.

"And that's a problem because?" I arch my hips into him, and his dark cheeks flush even more. "You worried you're going to get a little messy, Whit?" I arch my hips again.

"Caleb," he moans, and then he's meeting my thrusts, and our lips are on each other again. Plundering. Pushing us farther and farther to the point of no return. Not that I ever want to go back. Nah, I want to be right here, my body pressed up against this guy.

I'm groaning now, he's panting, and our hips are moving just right, our cocks sliding against each other perfectly. Just fucking right.

We should have done this ages ago.

Ages ago.

"Oh fuck," I mutter as I feel my orgasm begin to crest.

Whit is right there with me, his eyelids heavy, his lips swollen from my kisses. Then I'm coming, my entire body shaking with release, my boxers growing wet from how much I'm spilling into them.

Whit slips over the edge right after me, his mouth open on a silent gasp, his head thrown back, his cheeks red, and I can't help but bite down on his neck and suck on his Adam's apple as he comes because it's so fucking sexy. Watching him come undone by me.

When we're spent, when the last bit of come is wrung

from our bodies, we lie there panting as we try and regain our breath. My heart is going a million miles an hour, and my entire body is limp against his.

"I'm not moving," I mutter, too boneless to clean myself up. I'll just live like this forever.

"You better move, Caleb. I need a shower," Whit says, one arm hanging loosely against the floor, the other still tangled in my hair. He's as out of it as I am.

That does something to my insides.

"Let's just strip down and do it again," I tell him. "I'd love to see you filthy and wrecked with my come all over you."

Whit's fingers tighten in my hair, and he tugs at it until my mouth is over his. And then he kisses me again, roughly before he breaks it and shoves at my shoulders.

"Time to get up."

I huff my frustration but let him roll out from underneath me and disappear into the bathroom.

I was hoping for an offer to join him in the shower, but I know I won't get one. So instead, I just whip off my pants, using my boxers to clean myself up and toss them back onto the floor.

That's how he finds me, sprawled naked on the couch, with a heap of clothes littering the ground.

"We should finish the movie," I tell him, and he glances down at my half-hard cock.

"You should put more clothes on."

"Nah," I say as I rub at my chest. "One of us should be naked all the time, and since it won't be you, then it will have to be me. I'll take one for the team."

Whit glances at me and then walks over and sprawls on the other end of the chaise. I'm not far behind because if this asshole thinks that I'm going to just let him put some distance between us after *that*, he's sorely mistaken.

"You do realize," I say as I press a kiss to his lips and then slip between his legs, "I was clingy before, but you've just opened a whole other can of worms."

I lean my back against his chest and then tilt my head up and press my lips against his, sweeping my tongue into his to get another taste. Why does he taste so damn good?

I finally pull away and melt against him, my head on his shoulder. His hands are sprawled across my lower abdomen, his fingers playing with the hair of my happy trail, and my cock is half awake from the feeling of him touching me.

"There's no getting rid of me now, man," I say.

"Are you sure?" Whit asks.

"I'm sure."

Whit is silent for a moment, those fingers tracing the rim of my belly button, and then he asks, "What is this to you, Caleb?"

I turn to glance up at him. "What do you mean?"

"You were straight before, so what is this?"

"You mean am I experimenting with you, like you said earlier?"

Whit swallows and nods.

"I dunno, man, I just like being with you. We gotta label it?"

"I'm not asking for a label, just want to try and avoid the fallout if you realize this isn't what you want."

"What I want?"

"If you realize that being with a man isn't what you want."

I thread my hand through his hair and tug his lips down to mine, kissing him for a long moment before pulling away. His lips are swollen from mine, his cheeks a little roughed up from my stubble.

"I have no issue being with a man as long as that man is you."

And isn't that the truth? Something about this guy...

A gasp exits my mouth when Whit's hand surrounds my cock, tugging it until it's throbbing in his hand.

"You sure?" he asks, and I arch into him.

"As long as *you* can be with a guy like *me*."

"And what guy is that?" he asks, pumping me slowly, toying with me. That fucker.

"A guy who isn't your type."

Whit tilts his head and takes my ear into his mouth. "I was wrong."

I moan as he cups my balls in his other hand and rolls them in his palm.

"Wrong about what?"

"About my type. You happen to be something I didn't expect to want. But now that I have you...."

I'm fucking into his hand now as he sucks on my neck and licks at my ear. His voice trails off, but I don't even notice. He has a way of distracting me from things I should pay attention to.

CHAPTER EIGHT

We never make it back to the bedroom. I fall asleep against Whit, my naked body sprawled across his fully clothed one. That's how Sem and Luke find me the following morning.

They barrel in. The door whips against the wall and has the two of us startling awake.

"Oh shit," Sem says as Luke slaps a hand over his eyes.

"Could have gone my whole life without seeing this," Luke adds.

They both start laughing, and I glower at them, making no attempt to cover myself. If they hadn't entered like assholes, they wouldn't be staring at my naked butt.

"Go away," I grumble, and they turn away slightly, giving us some privacy.

"Nah, we drove all the way here. And we *did* text you."

"Ugh," I grumble and bury my face into Whit's neck, and his hands slide through my hair. This is not how I wanted to spend my morning, with my two oafish cousins hanging around. I had other things in mind. Had dreams about it, in fact. In explicit detail.

"You're both assholes to the tenth degree. Why won't you just go away?"

They blink at me, and I mutter, "Ugh, fine. Just give us thirty minutes. And you owe us both coffee and breakfast."

They agree and disappear through the apartment door. I can hear them thundering down the stairs.

I mutter, pressing myself into Whit, "Told you to change the locks, but you didn't believe me. This is all your fault."

"Do you really think being locked out would stop them from showing up? They would most likely just pound on the door until we opened up."

I bite down on his neck and then roll my hips. "Fine, you're right, but I'm still annoyed."

"Let's shower and get you dressed before they come back."

"Don't wanna," I say and roll my hips again.

Whit chuckles, and then his hand slaps my ass. My cheeks flame, and I glance up at him.

"You for reals?" I ask, the sting on my ass doing *nothing* to help abate my desire for him. It only escalates it.

He slaps my ass again, and my eyes widen. "You're only making it worse."

I roll my hips into him again, and Whit arches an eyebrow at me. "We can work with that."

He slaps my ass again, and it hurts like a motherfucker this time.

"Damn, you and those hands," I say, moving off him, rubbing my sore butt. "And what do you mean we can work with that? What's that mean?"

Whit stands up and glances at my red ass, then moves into the bedroom without a word.

I, of course, follow because now I'm curious. And wild animals couldn't keep me away.

"You going to explain?" I ask, folding my arms across my chest and watching as Whit gathers his clothes and sets them on top of his dresser.

He turns toward me and says, "You should shower before they come back."

"You and your showers. What if I want to smell like sex for the rest of the day? Would that gross you out?" I ask him with a smirk.

His cheeks redden slightly, and then he rolls his eyes.

"Fine, you asked for it, Caleb. On the bed. Ass up."

I arch an eyebrow, but I do as he says because why wouldn't I? I'm curious. And horny.

"What you going to do?" I ask, glancing back at him, and he runs a hand across my ass slowly. Tantalizingly slow, like he has all the time in the....

Without warning, he smacks it. Hard. Harder than he had on the couch.

I grunt as I lurch forward.

"What the hell, Whit?" I say, narrowing my eyes at him, but he ignores me and does the same to the other cheek.

I grunt at the stinging sensation, knowing my ass will be sore and red when we're done.

The thought of it causes my cock to ache. I like this way too much. I should be embarrassed, but I've crossed so many lines over the past two weeks that I'm beyond caring.

"You look good submissive like this," he says softly, and then his hand smacks down again. And again, and again, until I'm thrusting my hips into the air, seeking relief from the throbbing in my groin. He doesn't let up, not until the skin on my ass has begun to tingle.

I'm begging at this point. Like a whore. I have no shame, apparently.

"Turn over," he says after a few minutes, taking pity on me. I *am* a sad sack at this point. Whining, moaning, and begging.

I flip over, and he straddles me and takes me into his hand. And after that, I lose track of time. It's just Whit on top of me, those fingers doing things to my cock that they have *no* business doing. His hand sweeps up and down, twisting deliciously at the top while his other hand rolls my balls in his palm. Pretty sure I pass out for a moment as I crest the peak and come tumbling down.

His hands, those *fingers*, are life-changing. No joke.

And after *that*, I have no desire to get up, move from my bed, or do anything in general. But Whit makes sure to get me in the shower, and I grumble the entire time.

My ass is sore, and it chafes against my jeans when I pull them on.

"You're evil," I tell Whit as I tug my shirt on. "You could have warned me that my ass would be red from that."

"And yet, curiously, you didn't ask me to stop." He steps up to me and runs a finger over my lips.

I snap at him, biting down, and his eyes flare. I was out of it when he got me off, but I *do* know he didn't come. How is this guy so in control of stuff like this? I'm practically a slut for it, but it's like he could go without. Or maybe he's just shy? I don't understand him at all.

"When you going to let me see your…?" I wave my hand at his crotch, and Whit opens his mouth to respond, but Sem and Luke pound on the door before he can say anything.

"Open up, you fucking fuckers," they say, and Whit arches an eyebrow as if to say *I told you so*.

Reluctantly, I open the door and my cousins stride in, holding onto two coffees and a brown bag that better contain breakfast, or I'm going to be pissed.

I grab a coffee and the bag and pull out a breakfast sandwich.

Fantastic, I think, as I take a large bite. I'm famished. Haven't had so much sex in my entire life.

"So, what do you two want?" I ask as Whit takes a sip of his coffee and watches my cousins as they sit at the table.

"Did you not read your texts?" Luke asks.

I roll my eyes, shoving more of the sandwich into my mouth.

"Been busy."

I shift on my chair, and my ass smarts. Throwing Whit a glower, which he ignores, I turn back to my cousins.

"What's the plan then?"

"We're going to the aquarium," Sem says, and I shake my head.

"What are you twelve? I'm not going to the aquarium. I have other things to do."

"Like what?" Luke asks.

"Like..." Like messing around with Whit, that's what.

Luke rolls his eyes to the ceiling, "Yeah, you got nothing. Now I know you want to mess around with your boyfriend all weekend, but you've been talking about going to this aquarium for months, so here we are."

"That wasn't me. That was Mal," I roll my eyes.

"Yeah, well, he's coming too. Meeting us there. So, get your ass up and let's get a move on before traffic hits," Sem says.

I groan and stand up, rubbing at my backside as I do. Whit smirks.

"I'm so going to get you back for this later," I tell him quietly, and he flushes prettily.

God, this guy. I want to kiss him but refrain. If I start, I won't want to stop.

We make it to the aquarium in record time because traffic is light. I obviously couldn't keep my hands to myself in the car when Whit looked so good behind the wheel. I might have slightly taken advantage of the fact that he needed to focus on the road. My hands traveled over his thighs, up to his stomach, and I spent an exorbitant amount of time playing with his nipples.

I could see his arousal from where I sat, straining against his pants, but he wouldn't let me touch it. Just arched that eyebrow at me when I tried.

So, I avoided it, but kept on touching him relentlessly until he parked the car.

Joke's on me, though, because he just slides out of the car like *no big deal* while I'm aching.

Fuck this guy.

I take several deep breaths and then step out of the car. I stretch, and my shirt lifts a bit, showing off the bottom of my stomach. Whit takes a quick look and then glances away. His bottom lip rolls between his teeth.

"Caught you looking," I say to him as I bump his shoulder.

He clears his throat but admits nothing, just nudges me back. I don't understand this guy. How he can be so controlling in the bedroom and yet blushes like a schoolgirl when he sees just a bit of my stomach? It's confusing and yet so endearing.

I want to hold his hand, but his are stuffed inside his jeans, so I leave it. For a second, I wonder if maybe he doesn't want to publicly claim me. Maybe he's embarrassed by me. I glance down at my grey t-shirt, torn jeans, and boots. I tug my hat down slightly lower on my head, and Whit glances at the movement.

"What?" I ask as we move toward the ticket booth.

"Nothing," he replies, moving into line. I nudge him again, and he huffs. "You're like an overeager puppy."

"Didn't hear you complain earlier."

Whit grins as we slowly move up to the front of the line. "If you must know," he says softly, "I was thinking how handsome you look today."

I preen and feel myself puff up. "That so, Mr. Cristian?"

"Yes, that's so."

"You know," I say, leaning over so I can say this quietly into his ear. "Always thought you'd like someone who dressed more like Magnus."

Whit hums under his breath and then says back, "I like the hat. It...does things to me."

My eyebrows rise at that nugget. "That so? Tell me more."

He glances away from me and then says, "I think you should wear it next time we're alone." Then he leans over and mutters. "Backwards and with you completely nude."

Welp, there goes my self-restraint. It was already hanging on by a thread. I'm straining against my pants again. I covertly adjust myself as we step up to the ticket booth, and Whit pays for both of our admissions. I argue, saying I'll Venmo him the money, but he scowls at me.

"I have more money than I know what to do with. It's my treat."

"Does this make me your sugar baby then? Should I call you daddy?"

Whit rolls his eyes and then slaps a ticket into my palm. I let my fingers slide against his as I take it from him, and he huffs.

We walk into the park side by side, catching up with Sem, Luke, Mal, and Bree, all conversing in the lobby.

"Alright, they made it," Sem says and slaps me on the back before fist-bumping Whit. "Where to, Mal?"

Mal lights up like a child on Christmas, and I chuckle at how excited he is. He's been wanting to come here for ages. Weirdo.

We make our way through a few exhibits, stopping to look at the colorful sea life. I keep my hands to myself, not wanting to make Whit uncomfortable. But damn, I want to hold his hand but can't because he keeps them out of reach.

It bugs me, wondering why.

It's me, I think. Totally me. He's embarrassed. He just likes me when we are alone. He doesn't want to admit he's with this redneck asshole.

"Why the scowl," Bree asks, her pretty, blue eyes meeting mine.

"Uh," I mutter, looking forward at Whit's back. He's staring up at a swarm of jellyfish. His body is illuminated by a soft blue glow. "Nothing."

Bree pokes me in the side. "I don't think it's nothing. You keep scowling and peering over at Whit."

I groan and then run a hand down my face, and it all comes blurting out. "I want to hold his hand, but he's keeping them away from me. Like he doesn't want to be seen with me. You know? I think he's embarrassed by me."

Bree's eyebrows meet. "Really? He keeps looking over at you. I think he's trying not to pressure you into anything."

"Really?" I ask.

"He probably doesn't want you to feel pressured into coming out."

I snort. "Too late for that."

"Yes, but that was with your family. What about the world?" She gestures to the people standing around, and realization dawns. Bree's explanation makes more sense than mine.

Whit's not trying to pressure me. He's being considerate.

This guy, seriously.

My mind made up, I thank Bree and stalk over to Whit, wrapping my arms around his waist and pulling him into me. Resting my head on his shoulder, I kiss his neck.

He stiffens in my hold, and for a second, just a moment, I wonder if Bree was wrong, but then he relaxes into me and places his hands over mine.

"I want to hold your hand," I tell him softly.

Whit glances over at me, his dark eyes flashing. "You can. If you want."

He looks unsure, but I just press another kiss to his neck and then move to his side and hold out my hand, palm up.

He looks down at it and threads those long fingers I'm obsessed with through mine.

We stand there looking at the jellyfish moving around us, and I wonder what everyone around us thinks. Two men holding hands in a public place. A place with families and children running around. But when I look around, no one's paying us any attention.

Huh.

No one gives a shit.

"Just so there's no confusion in the future, I always want to hold your hand, Whit," I tell him, and he meets my gaze, those eyes sparkling.

"Okay."

I tug him forward, following our group out of the jellyfish exhibit and to a place where we can pet stingrays. There's a shallow pool in the middle of a large room with sea anemones, two giant stingrays, and many colorful fish. A group of children is leaning forward, their hands trailing in the water. How cool is this? Mal had every reason to be excited to come here.

"Come on," I tell Whit. "You going to pet one?"

"No," he says, shuddering at the fish swimming through the shallow pool.

"Why not?" I ask.

"They're slimy. I'd prefer not to."

"Come on. New experiences stretch you." When Whit still doesn't budge, I add, "For me, yeah?"

He watches me for a moment and then sighs. He bends down, reaches his hand into the water, slides his fingers across the back of a stingray, and then pulls his hand out, flexing it.

"Good enough?" he asks, looking annoyed, but I just beam at him.

"Yeah, babe, that's good."

He flushes and then moves to the sink to wash his hands.

I snort and spend the next ten minutes running my hands through the water, touching everything. Mal finally has to pull me away. I could stay here all day. Apparently, I'm a ten-year-old child when it comes to this stuff.

I wash my hands and see Whit standing on the periphery of the exhibit, his thumbs quickly tapping out a message on his phone.

"Your dad?" I ask, and Whit fumbles with this phone and shoves it in his pocket.

"Um...yes."

He clears his throat and then points to the sink. "Did you wash your hands?"

"Yeah, I did. What did your dad want?" I ask, not letting him divert the conversation.

His brows furrow. "The same thing he always wants."

"And that would be?" I ask.

"I have...commitments, and he's making sure I'm following up on them."

"What kind of commitments?"

Whit doesn't meet my eyes. "There are things that I just can't divulge at the moment."

"Why? They top secret or some shit?"

Whit glances at the ground and then closes his eyes. "Caleb, there are things in motion that I just don't want to talk about. I'm sorry."

I want to know what these *things in motion* are, but I don't press him on it. In time, I hope he'll be able to open up to me about his life. Past, present, and future.

"Okay. I'll let it go for now."

He gives me a clipped nod, and I reach out, running my fingers down his arm and linking mine with his.

We spend the rest of the morning walking through exhibits, Whit's hand in mine, and then leave to eat lunch at the beach. We purchase sandwiches from a beachside deli and carry them onto the sand. I sit between Whit's legs, his hands wrapped around my waist as we watch Sem, Luke, and Mal race into the water, shedding clothes as they go.

"They're going to get arrested," Whit says to me.

I chuckle. "Told you people go to jail when they hang out

with them. But nah, they're keeping their boxers on. No public nudity. Not here. We do have standards."

Whit presses his cold lips to my temple. Not quite a kiss, but more like a brush of his lips against me. I *love* it.

"You can join them. If you want."

I look up at him. "I see what you're doing, yeah? You want to watch me strip. Dive under a wave and walk out wet. Probably a fantasy of yours."

Whit huffs. "I just don't want to hold you back, Caleb."

"Nah. You aren't. I'm fine right here. With you."

It's late afternoon when we arrive home, and I'm exhausted. Had too much fun.

Flopping down on the couch, I unbutton my jeans and kick off my boots. My legs are sprawled out in front of me when Whit steps between them.

"What?" I ask, seeing the serious look on his face.

He seemed thoughtful after our time on the beach. The drive home had been quieter than usual, as if he was contemplating something. I didn't pry either, even though I wanted to. Just let him have his silence.

"I like you," he blurts and then tucks his hair behind his ear, his cheeks red.

"Aw. I like you too, Whit," I say with a wide smile.

"You...you force me out of my comfort zone in more ways than one."

"Good."

"I just," he sighs. "I'm gay."

"I got that."

"And you're...."

"Didn't we just discuss this? I don't know what I am. I just know that I like being with you."

Whit rubs a hand across the back of his neck and then shoves his hands in his jeans.

"I don't let people in. Ever."

"I got that."

"I never meant to go so far with you, but...it got out of hand. You're just irresistible. It's obnoxious, really."

"Thanks?" I say, biting back a smile. Whit ignores me, just barrels on. Like he's rehearsed this. Probably had while we were driving home earlier. To be a fly on the wall of his brain.

"When we first met and you decided to move in, I thought it would be the perfect arrangement. You were straight and someone I'd never be interested in. You were messy and too masculine for my tastes."

My brows furrow at that. "Okay..."

"But then you just...grew on me. And I couldn't look away."

He stops and sucks his lips into his mouth. The pause is so long that I wonder if he's said all he wants, but he inhales and continues.

"I have issues. My family is one of them. There are other things as well."

"Like?" I press, and he meets my gaze.

"I had a...cold, unconventional upbringing. I spent most of my life struggling with things like my sexuality and the fact that my parents...they didn't love me. They still don't."

My heart stutters in my chest, and I rub at it, wanting to reach out for him but giving him his space.

"I don't know what I'm doing, Caleb. I don't know what we're doing. I don't know how to be your person. I've never been anyone's person."

"Whit..." I say, but he shakes his head.

"I didn't want this to get too dark too soon because I

know this isn't serious for you, and this is only the beginning of...whatever this is, but you should know what you're getting into with me. I'm...hard to get along with, not easy to be around. I know this. I fail to communicate, keep things in too long, and rarely open up. I'm a mess. I look like I have it all together, but inside it's...chaos."

"Whit..." I say again, and I reach out this time, tugging him closer. His knees hit the edge of the couch, and my hands link with his. He stares at them intently.

"I'm willing to give it a go. I already handed in my straight card for you. What's a little chaos? I happen to like it. Have you met my family?"

Whit's eyes flash up and meet mine.

"I want you to open up to me, though. Try to at least," I say and then tug him closer, so he's straddling me.

"How am I supposed to do that?" he whispers as I bring his hand to my mouth and kiss it.

"How about once a day, you tell me something? Something you're thinking or something you want me to know about you?"

Whit contemplates that for a moment and then nods. "We can try that."

"Good."

And then I lean my forehead against his and run my hand through his hair.

"Thank you for telling me that."

He nods, looking uneasy. "I've never done that before."

"That so? Must make me pretty special," I tease, and he shuts me up by kissing me deeply.

We lose ourselves in it, our tongues tangling as hands begin to explore. Because duh, how could I not when he's *right here*. He tugs my shirt over my head and then runs his hands down my chest and, with a trembling voice, says, "I saw you, for the first time, with no shirt and jacked off in the bathroom immediately after."

"Whit," half groan, half smile.

"I've never seen anyone like you. You're so...big. I've never been with anyone so big."

I flex my abs slightly, and they become more defined. Whit's fingers bump along them, and his eyes follow their path.

"God, you're sexy," he mutters, his eyes glazed, his lips swollen.

I reach over and tug his hips into mine, grinding up against him.

"Tell me more," I breathe.

He kisses me again, and when we come up for breath again, he adds, "Jacking you off is...."

"Tell me," I plead as he tugs the waist of my jeans down, freeing my erection.

"It's heaven, Caleb. Watching you..." he exhales shakily. "The things you do to me."

He runs a hand down my length, and I groan loudly.

"I dream of fucking you," he whispers, and my entire body trembles at that admission. "I'd make it so good for you."

His fist moves slowly over me, and I reach for the waist of his jeans.

"Please," I say, unbuttoning them and then dragging the zipper down. "I want to...."

Whit hangs his head while, with unsteady hands, I pull his boxer briefs down just enough to free his cock. I stare at it. It's thinner than mine but just as long, and I reach out and smooth my thumb over the bulbous tip. Whit inhales sharply as I drag my finger down the long thick vein underneath it.

"Tell me what to do," I say, my voice husky. I've never touched another man's dick before. I don't have any clue what he likes.

"Whatever you do will be...God," his voice trails off on a moan when I begin stroking him. He arches his hips into my fist, saying, "Harder."

Oh shit.

I tighten my grip and begin working him up and down, and he does the same to me. I watch it all unfold, our hands grasping the other's dicks as we bring ourselves higher and higher until we're both gasping for air. We kiss sloppily. Our tongues flick into each other's mouths as we pant and groan.

"Fuck, Whit. I can't last," I manage to say, and then I feel my cock jump as I release myself into his palm. Shortly after, he follows, his eyes downcast, watching my hand stroking him. I can't tear my eyes away. I hear him moaning, his breath shattering, and then his come is shooting from his perfect dick, and I let it splash against my skin.

I have no qualms about a bit of mess, especially when it's his.

Whit slumps against my shoulder.

"God."

"I know."

We sit like that for a while, giving our bodies a minute to calm down, and then Whit lifts his head, those dark eyes meeting mine.

"Can I ask you something?" he asks.

"Anything," I say, running my fingers through his release lining my stomach.

"How are you okay with this? How are you not freaking out?"

I shrug, "I don't know, man. I should be, right? But with you, it just…feels right."

Whit huffs a laugh. "I can't believe this whole roommate thing was just a farce."

This is news to me. "Huh?"

Whit blushes faintly and then looks away. "I did it to piss my parents off. I posted an ad for a roommate because they expressly forbid it."

"You little rebel."

"And then you showed up…."

He looks at me, and I lean up, pressing my lips to his.

"And I couldn't say no."

"And just like that, you won the fucking lottery, eh?"

He pushes himself off me and tucks himself away. "It feels like it. Now let's clean up."

"Nah," I say and stay put. "I think I'll just stay here. Let your come dry on me, carry you around with me all day."

Whit narrows his eyes at me, and I chuckle. "Just kidding."

CHAPTER NINE

Things continue just like that for the next few weeks. Whit and I fall into a predictable pattern. In the morning, we part ways and go to class. After class, I go to work, head to the gym, and we meet up each night in the apartment. Usually, I end up on top of him, watching a TV show while he runs those fingers I'm obsessed with across my back and through my hair. He usually reads until I distract him with something more fun. And then we end up both kissing and humping, and finally making each other come with our hands. He never pressures me for more, and I don't ask.

He still never fully undresses, just pulls his cock out of his pants when we're messing around, while I'm in a near-constant state of undress when we are alone. I don't push him to show me more, although the longer I'm with him, the more curious I become.

What's he hiding?

Despite that little quirk, he's opening up more and more. Each day he tells me something he's thinking or something he wants me to know about him. Usually, it's the former rather than the latter. Still, knowing that he's trying with me makes my heart constrict uncomfortably. I know how hard it is for him to make himself vulnerable to people.

But for some reason, with me, he's making an effort.

I'm worth it.

That thought carries me through the next few weeks and pushes me through the times when he shuts me out. When he's cold and quiet. When he's tapping angrily on his phone and then disappears for a few hours to cool down.

I hate those moments. But he always comes back, pulling me into him and running those fingers all over me, pressing his lips to mine. It helps me forget, for a moment, how little I do know him.

"I have a debate this weekend," he says, setting his Kindle down on the chair and looking at me. I've just returned home from the gym and need a shower, but he's bombarded me with this little nugget.

"It's out of town, so I'll be gone until Sunday."

My heart sinks. I've grown used to falling asleep next to him. And hate the fact that he's not inviting me to come along. Not that we're out. Not really. Everything we do is done in private, except for that one time at the aquarium.

"There's nothing to be done about it, Caleb," he says, reading my face, and I grab a beer from the fridge.

"Stop reading my face."

"Stop being so easy to read then."

I roll my eyes, popping the cap off the beer, and catch it before it clinks onto the ground. I toss it into the garbage and then take a seat on the couch.

"What am I supposed to do all weekend if you're gone?"

Damn you. Invite me to come with you.

"Visit your family? Spend time with Mal?"

He grabs his Kindle and continues to read, brushing me off, and I narrow my eyes at him. He's usually more attentive than this.

"Something's up. What is it?" I ask, watching as he peers at me over his Kindle.

"Why do you ask?"

"You're acting shady."

He scoffs. "I don't act shady."

"Yeah, man. You do. You are right now. What don't I know?"

He clears his throat, and he runs a hand through his hair. "Nothing important."

"Whit..." I warn, and he looks back at the book in his hand.

"I'm staying with Magnus. We're sharing a room."

"That so?" I ask, my stomach clenching uncomfortably at that bit of info. Could have lived my entire life without knowing that, really.

Not that I don't trust Whit, but despite everything that's happened between us, we still haven't defined what we are. Not sure we're really a thing. We're just messing around, I guess.

"Yes, but there's nothing to worry about...not that I expect you to worry. I know this is just casual between us."

I raise an eyebrow at him. "I would prefer it if you didn't fuck him, Whit. Despite how *casual* this is."

His cheeks flush, and he shakes his head. "I don't plan on it."

"Good."

He clears his throat again and then continues to read. "That all?" I ask, not sure this conversation is really over.

"My ex will be there as well."

I shift on the couch and grip my beer a little tighter.

"And that's an issue because?"

"We've made plans to grab dinner together one night."

"That so?" I say, and Whit sets his Kindle down roughly.

"Stop saying that. It's aggravating. If you must know, we'd made plans to meet up before this…thing with us happened. I didn't want to cancel."

"Didn't ask you to," I say, taking a swig of my beer. "Like you said. It's casual between us."

I hate that fucking word. Makes me growly and irrationally angry.

Whit stares at me, trying to read me, but I just ignore his gaze and guzzle my beer. I glance down at my shirt, stained and wrinkled.

Real prize here. Bet his ex looks a lot like Magnus. Cute, pampered, petite.

"I'm going to the gym," I say, and Whit sighs.

"You were just there."

"So what?" I say.

I need to go rage row or something to get my mind off of whatever's happening between Whit and me. Apparently, it's casual enough for him to go on a date with his ex.

When I return from the gym an hour later, I see Whit's right where I left him. Unbothered by my little tantrum.

Fuck him.

His eyes meet mine, and he asks, "Feel better?"

"Peachy," I reply. "Going to go shower."

I disappear through the door and strip out of my clothes. When I step underneath the hot stream of water, I run my hands over my face and through my hair, resting my forehead on the cool tile. I'll get over it soon. I'm just feeling a little insecure. This whole year has been a whirlwind, and I've been knocked sideways so often that I'm confused about which way is up.

Washing quickly, I throw on a pair of sweats and lie face up on my bed, my earphones in my ears.

My eyes are closed when I feel Whit move against me. His scent envelops the space around me, and I squash the urge to pull him into me. I'm still pissed.

His fingers gingerly pull my earphones out, and he places them on the end table. Then his thumbs brush against my cheeks, his face hovering over mine. I can smell the mint on his breath.

Then his mouth is on mine, licking into me, his hands moving into my damp hair.

I try not to kiss back, but I'm helpless to stay away from him. I open my mouth and let him in, but I don't touch him. I'm feeling too clingy already.

"You're upset," he says when he breaks away from me.

When I don't answer, he kisses me again, his body pressed against mine. And despite everything warring within me, I still thicken just from having him nearby. It's pathetic, really. This casual thing we're doing. I'm all in, and he's....

"Are you using me, man?" I ask.

He freezes on top of me. "What are you talking about?"

"Are you using me? Is this an experiment to you? Fuck around with a guy who's not your type. See how long you can keep it up? Make a straight guy gay or some shit? Am I a game to you?"

"No, why would you...Caleb. I told you. I like you. I like doing things with you."

"Then why not make it more?"

"More?"

"More than just casual."

He looks pained. "I...I can't."

"But you did with your ex."

"That was a long time ago. Things are different now."

I sigh, and he presses a kiss to my neck. "I'll cancel with him if it makes you feel better. I'll do whatever you want if you stop being angry with me."

"Don't cancel. I...just...I don't want you with anyone else when you're with me, casual as it is."

Whit presses his entire body down on top of mine. For the first time since being together, I'm the one holding him. I like it more than I should.

"Stop saying casual like it's a dirty word. It's not. I haven't been with anyone else since we started this. And I don't plan on being with anyone as long as this lasts."

He wiggles a little on top of my still hard cock, and he adds, "Seems you still do want me despite being angry."

I scoff. "Don't be a smug asshole. You already know I'm constantly hard around you and willing to do just about anything. No need to rub it in. I already feel pathetic."

Whit sighs. "Don't. I love it. How needy you are for it."

My cock jumps at those words, and I run my hand under his shirt, caressing his soft skin and then clutch the nape of his neck.

"Do you?"

"Yeah," he says. "Want to try something new?"

My Adam's apple bobs. "Hell yeah."

Whit hums, pushes himself up, straddles my legs, and then he's tugging my boxers down until I'm fully exposed to him.

"I'm going to blow you."

My breathing accelerates at that little tidbit, and I clutch the sheets.

"This will be over embarrassingly fast," I mutter, and Whit smiles deviously.

"I am very good with my mouth. Just do me a favor, Caleb. Don't grab my head."

I nod, and then his mouth engulfs me. It's wet and warm, and his tongue is doing something that is making me whine as he continues to lower his mouth onto me. Holy fuck, he's still going. He's got to be like a fucking pro at this because I'm down his throat now, and he's not even gagging. He's a miracle worker.

Sweet Jesus, I see heaven.

His tongue does something that should be illegal, and I'm gasping, clutching on the headboard with one hand and fisting the sheets in the other just to keep my hands away from his fucking head. He pulls off slowly and then sucks on the tip of my already drooling cock before he swallows me down again.

"Oh mother fuck," I swear as he repeats the process, swallowing around me until I'm nearly weeping from the sensation.

I have never, *never*, had a blowjob like this before. And I thought hand jobs from Whit were life-changing. Blow jobs are ten times better.

Oh shit.

I'm going to be even more insatiable after this. I'm going to be unbearable. He's never getting rid of me.

He picks up the pace, and then his hand cradles my balls, tugging on them for a few seconds before one finger moves down a little farther and circles my tight hole.

And when he strokes it while deep throating me, I give up a strangled cry and come ridiculously hard. So hard that I see literal stars.

When I come to, Whit's wiping his mouth with the back of his hand and smiling down at me.

"I take it you enjoyed that."

"Oh, fuck off, you smug bastard," I manage to say and then pull him down for a blistering kiss. I can taste myself on him, and it only excites me more. This guy, I swear.

When we come up for air, I say, "How am I ever going to come back from this?"

Whit looks sad for a moment before the emotion is erased completely.

To lighten the mood, I add, "You do realize that I'm going to be begging you for those more often, right?"

"I don't mind. I enjoyed it. A little too much."

He pushes himself up and then slides off of me. "Give me a minute."

"Wait, did you just...."

He grabs a change of pants and disappears into the bathroom.

Okay, that's hot. I throw an arm across my face and lie there, my flaccid cock still out. Instead of putting it away, I just kick off my boxers and lie there naked.

When Whit returns, he crawls on top of me and tucks himself into my side.

Sighing, I pull him into me and nuzzle the top of his head with my face.

"You'll have to teach me how to do that so I can reciprocate. Not that you needed it tonight."

His hand strokes my chest. "You never need to reciprocate unless you want to, but it will be perfect if you do. I'm sure of it."

And I melt a little.

Okay, yeah. This may be casual for him, but it's not casual for me.

Not anymore.

WHIT

"We leave in thirty minutes," Magnus says, adjusting his bow tie in the mirror.

I watch him for a minute and then disappear into the bathroom. Oh, how my tastes have changed in the last month.

I glance in the mirror and grip the countertop as visions of Caleb writhing beneath me surface. Of him panting, begging, his lips on mine, his tongue plundering my mouth, those muscles flexing beneath my hands. So many muscles.

And that smile.

Hanging my head, I breathe deeply through my nose. This is getting a little ridiculous. I've never been so enamored with another person in my entire life. When I first met Caleb, I'd assumed he'd be a typical bigoted asshole, but he's proved me wrong so many times. He's so different than I expected him to be. The way he lets me hold him, how he nuzzles my neck, how he begs for it.

I'm obsessed.

Usually, sex for me is a transaction, something I do to relieve some of the tension building in me. It's nothing personal, and I derive a fleeting pleasure from it.

But with Caleb, I'm consumed by it. I give in to him much more than I should, and if I allow myself to take…well, I'm pretty sure I'd be ravenous.

He's becoming addictive, and we haven't even fucked yet.

I pull my cock out of my pants and tug at it. It's already painfully hard, and I find it easy to get off quickly, envisioning Caleb. Those thick, long legs stretched out in front of him, his cock hardening against his jeans, that backward hat he wears, that nipple ring, the way his scruff brushes against my cheeks when he kisses me.

His taste.

His moans.

His smell.

I gasp as I find my release, and as I try to gain control over my heartbeat, I quickly wash my hands and then look up and see my flushed cheeks in the mirror.

I need a minute or two before I reemerge into the bedroom I'm sharing with Magnus. He's been watching me closely lately, asking me questions about Caleb.

I'm not quite sure what to say. Magnus was a good lay, eager, and took my cock really well, but that was it for me. A transaction, like I said. Nothing more. I feel nothing for the poor guy.

Nothing like what I feel for Caleb.

Brushing my hair behind my ears, I think about how he wrapped his arms around me at the aquarium and surprised me by holding my hand in public. That day, I'd agonized over whether I should push him to out himself for me and decided that it would be best to keep my distance. I remember how hard it was for me to openly show any kind of preference for men out in public. The stares I got, the way people sneered. I didn't want that for Caleb, so I stuffed my hands in my pockets so as not to give off any vibes that he needed to do anything he wasn't conformable with.

But he did it anyway.

I remember how I'd struggled with my sexuality for years,

how I hid it, repressed it. But Caleb seems to have concluded that he's into men and then decided to go with it without agonizing over what it meant. For a man who was presumably straight a few months ago, he transitioned to being out relatively easily.

He seems completely unconcerned that he's with me now. With *me*.

I rub my chest, my heart thumping in it erratically.

I know he can't be with me, not really. There is too much he doesn't know.

I'm going to break him, yet I still can't stay away. I'm too damn selfish.

Inhaling deeply, I push out of the bathroom and nod to Magnus.

"Ready?" I ask, and he nods, following me silently to where we meet our teammates, Bev and Kate.

The debate goes well, and I'm proud of our accomplishments. And then it's time for me to meet up with my ex.

Donovan Gray.

I see him on stage, and he looks good, with immaculately combed hair, perfectly pressed trousers, and a button-up shirt. I remember a time when I preferred men like this. Men well dressed, well-mannered, and smaller than me.

Now my tastes run in a different direction entirely.

"Whit," Donovan calls out, nodding at me. "So nice to see you. Well done up there."

He holds out his hand, but I just nod at him, my hands clutched by my sides. I don't want to touch him, even if it's a harmless gesture.

"You as well."

His hand moves back, and he tucks it casually into his

pocket. "Would you like to head out now? I have reservations at a place we can walk to."

Being with him feels wrong, but I nod anyway, grabbing my coat and shrugging it over my shoulders. The two of us walk quietly out of the building, and when we exit into the cool fall air, Donovan glances over at me.

"You look good, Whit. Happy even."

"Thank you. I am," I say, and he faces forward. "How have you been? I was surprised when you reached out."

Donovan chuckles a little. "Ah, yes, I was worried you'd turn me down. I've been keeping tabs on you, if you will, for a while now. When I saw that we'd be competing tonight, I knew it was my chance to catch up."

"Keeping tabs?" I ask with a raised eyebrow.

"Yes, to say that I regret how we left things would be an understatement."

I shove my hands into my coat pockets. "Best to leave the past in the past. It's been years, and we've both moved on. It was for the best."

Donovan doesn't say anything, just side-eyes me. He always had such pretty eyes. I'd mulled over them for hours in high school. Now all I want to see are those blue eyes I've come to adore staring back at me.

"Are you seeing anyone?" he asks after a moment of silence.

"Yes."

"Is it serious?"

"It's..." my words cut off when my phone rings in my pocket. "I apologize. I have to get this."

Aunt Del's name flashes across the screen, and I debate taking the call. I'm out with Donovan, and I know he's been looking forward to catching up with me, but then I decide that I'd better answer.

She'd called to wish me luck at the tournament earlier and now probably just wants to follow up on how we did. The fact that since meeting me, she's kept in touch has changed something inside of me. She's offered me more parental love and affection in the past month than my parents have my entire life.

I hold on to it.

Clutch it with rigid fingers.

I'm not letting it go.

I swipe at her name. "Hi, Aunt Del."

"Whit," she says, her voice soft, concerned. "How was your tournament. Did you do well?"

"Yeah, we did."

"Well done, sweet pea." She pauses and says, "I just wanted to let you know that Caleb is in the hospital."

My entire body freezes, and I stop walking. I can't hear her words over the rush in my ears.

"Why?" I breathe out.

"There was an accident...."

"Is he okay?" I cut her off. I can't breathe. Fuck. I lean against a nearby wall feeling lightheaded. Donovan is in my line of sight, his eyes concerned.

I allow him to touch me, to keep me grounded as Aunt Del says, "It's nothing too serious. A concussion, a broken hand, and a lot of scrapes and bruises. I just wanted to let you know...."

"I'm coming," I say. "Send me the address."

"Oh no, Whit, I didn't mean for you to drop everything and head out here. Caleb mentioned how important this night was for you. That you're meeting up with some old friends. I just wanted to let you know...."

"I'm coming," I say and then add, "Address now, please."

Then I hang up, my hands shaking so brutally I almost drop my phone.

"You okay?" Donovan asks, his hands rubbing my arms. It feels wrong, him touching me, so I shrug him off.

"I need to go. My...Caleb. He's in the hospital."

Donovan's mouth opens and then closes. "Okay, let's get you back then."

I swallow roughly and let him lead me back to the hotel. I don't even say goodbye to him. I just jog to the elevators and disappear. I'm shaking so badly that when I enter the hotel room, Magnus jumps up from his bed and asks, "What's happened?"

He's wearing floral pajamas and a tight-fitting tank top. His hair is slightly mussed as if he's run his hands through it.

"I need to go. Something's come up. Can you find a ride home?" I ask.

"Well, yeah, but...where are you going?" he asks, his eyes concerned, but he knows better than to touch me. I won't allow it.

I rub at my eyes and pinch the bridge of my nose. "Caleb's in the hospital. I need to leave."

"You're shaking. You shouldn't drive. I...I can drive you there."

I look over at him as I haphazardly throw my clothes into the suitcase and zip it up. If Caleb saw me now, he'd be thrilled.

"You'd do that?"

"Of course, just because...just because it's over between us doesn't mean we aren't friends," he says, quickly grabbing his clothes and shoving them into his duffle bag. "I like the big guy. Plus, I get to drive your car. We know how you never let anyone drive it. So, it's really a win-win for both of us."

I huff out a broken laugh and then give him the keys.

"You're a good friend, Mag," I tell him, and he flushes.

"I know."

We arrive at the hospital in record time. Magnus is a fierce driver, speeding past cars and swerving around trucks. I wonder if I would have been safer if I'd driven myself.

He screeches into a parking spot, and I jump out, walking quickly through the hospital entrance. Magnus is jogging next to me, and when we enter, I immediately see Sem and Luke leaning against the wall, cups of coffee in their hands.

They're chatting like this is no big deal. Then my mind flashes to Caleb, who told me that this is normal for them.

Heathens, the lot of them.

"Where is he?" I ask, my eyes wild. I shove my shaking hands into my pockets.

God, I hate hospitals. So many bad memories in places like this.

"He's back there with Aunt Del. Hopped up on pain meds."

"What happened?" I ask curtly, and Sem and Luke both look at Magnus, standing awkwardly next to me.

"Who's the little dude?" Sem asks, his eyes sweeping over Mag's odd choice of pajamas. They've probably never seen a man who'd choose to wear feminine clothes. If this was any other situation, it would be laughable.

"He drove me here. We're on the debate team together. Why does this matter? What happened to Caleb?"

Sem eyes Magnus as Luke says, "We were riding the ATVs today, and his rolled."

"I knew those things were dangerous," I mutter. "And the way you all drive them. Like you're invincible."

"It could have been worse. All things considered," Luke responds.

I narrow my eyes at him, and he holds up his hands. "Look, my man, you shouldn't have come anyway. You're too late to visit. Only family back there now."

Frustration wells up in me. I hate hospitals. Despise them. I spent too many days in them growing up, but I drove all the way here and want to see him. To touch him, to make sure he's okay. It's a desperate, ugly feeling.

Casual. Yeah, right.

"I'm his fiancé. Will that work?"

Luke shrugs. "Maybe."

My eyes turn to Magnus, who's watching Luke and Sem warily, his face flushed. Probably because Sem is leering at him.

"You can take my car home," I tell him, but before he can answer, Sem steps forward.

"No need. I can give him a ride back."

I arch an eyebrow at him. "That's nice of you, Sem."

"I'm a nice guy."

Magnus shifts his eyes to me, and I ask, "Does that work? If not, you can take my car. I don't mind."

He swallows and then whispers, "Is he sane?"

I swallow back a manic laugh. "Most of the time, I believe."

"Fine. Then it works. This...man can take me home."

With Magnus securing a ride home, I walk up to the receptionist and explain the situation. The word *fiancé* slips from my mouth, and it feels so *right* for some reason. The woman behind the counter doesn't even bat an eyelash. She just scans my ID and then tells me the room number. Without even looking back, I make my way to him.

I need to touch him to make sure he's okay.

I need to hold him.

My body shakes the entire way there.

When I finally arrive, I push the door open with trembling hands and immediately see Aunt Del snoozing on a chair, a blanket pulled up over her. Then my eyes shift to Caleb, who's dozing on a bed, wires connected to his body, his face scraped, and a cast on his left hand.

I take unsteady steps toward him, and as if he can feel my presence, his eyes flutter open.

"Whit?" he asks, and my throat is so thick with emotion that I can't say anything, just nod as I gently run my hands across his face and neck.

He sighs as if he's missed me. "I'm okay, man."

But I need to see for myself, so I push the blankets down slightly and lift his gown up, my eyes widening when I see the bruises littering his skin. Touching them gingerly, I blink rapidly.

"Shit, stop doing that," he mutters.

I see his dick thickening, and my eyes shoot up to meet his.

"You know how it is," he says, his cheeks turning red, and I quickly place his gown back down and tuck him in.

"I was worried," I finally say, and Caleb snorts and then winces.

"I'm fine. Nothing too bad, nothing that hasn't happened before. It could have been worse. Could have been explosives."

I close my eyes, and he must sense that I'm close to losing it because he reaches out and grasps my hand, threading those strong fingers around mine.

"Come here, baby. Missed you," he says and tugs me until I can't come any closer.

"Not there, asshole. In bed. With me," he mutters and shifts over with a groan.

I shake my head, swallowing the lump that's formed in my throat. "I don't want to hurt you."

"It'll hurt more with you too far away. Come here. Missed you. Missed you so bad."

He pats the bed next to him, and I reluctantly crawl in next to him. Gently, I place my head on his shoulder, and he sighs in relief.

"Better," he mutters.

His arm cradles me to him, and I rest my hand on his chest. The thumping of his heart brings me a certain peace, and I relax a fraction more.

"How did you get in here?"

"You're my fiancé now," I tell him, and he grips the nape of my neck.

"That so?"

I nod, and he chuckles. "You'll have me married to you without me knowing it. Is that your plan, huh?"

"Would that be so bad?" I ask, and he presses a kiss to the top of my head.

"Nah. I could manage with you, I guess." He yawns and then says, "I'm so sleepy. Stay with me, yeah? Don't go back to your ex. I'm the better choice."

"I won't," I say, my heart clenching in my chest, and then feel him doze off.

I lie next to him, listening to his heartbeat against my ear, feeling his chest rise and fall with each breath.

"Sweet pea?" Del says, touching me gently, and I startle from my trance.

I didn't even hear her walk up to me.

"How did you get in here?" she asks, her eyes full of sleep.

"He's my fiancé," I say, and she blinks once, twice, and then her lips turn up into a smile.

"Well, that sure was quick, but I don't blame you. He's quite a catch."

I glance down at Caleb sleeping and can't help but agree. He will kill me when the pain meds wear off and finds himself saddled with me.

It seems Aunt Del didn't quite catch the sarcasm in my voice when I told her we were engaged.

"Come on, let's grab something to eat. You must be starved."

My stomach grumbles at the mention of food. How did she know?

I clutch at his hospital gown and whisper, "I shouldn't leave him."

"He'll be out of it for a bit. He's always loopy and sleepy when he's on pain meds."

"Don't tell me this has happened before."

Aunt Del rolls her eyes. "I have a to-go bag in my car for occasions such as this." She gestures to her blanket, pillow, and tablet by her chair. "With reckless boys like this, you have to."

I nod and then reluctantly slip out of bed and follow her down to the cafeteria. My body is abuzz with nerves, mainly from being in a hospital again but also because I left him when he asked me to stay.

I grab a sandwich and water, and then when she asks if I'd like to sit, I shake my head. "Need to get back to him."

Aunt Del nods her understanding, her eyes soft as she watches me.

"You're good for him, you know."

I swallow thickly and then glance down at her. "He's good for me."

She smiles. "I always hoped he'd find someone who'd love him, never thought it would be another man, but," she waves her hand in the air, "that doesn't matter, does it? He's happier with you than he's ever been with anyone else. The way he speaks about you."

I take a bite of my sandwich and swallow it as quickly as possible. My mouth is dry, and when I swallow, it sits in my stomach like lead.

"Will he be released soon?" I ask, trying to change the subject because I don't want to start blubbering.

"Tomorrow. Will you be taking him home? Or should I plan on him staying with me?"

"With me," I blurt and then take another bite of my sandwich.

"Good man."

She pants my shoulder, and then before we enter back into Caleb's room, she stops me.

"I don't mean to pry, but has Caleb told you about his mother?"

I shake my head. "I know she passed, but I don't know the details."

Aunt Del looks sad for a moment, shadows passing through her eyes.

"It was cancer. Came on suddenly and took her quickly.

The anniversary of her death is coming up. November twenty-third."

"God," I mutter, and she nods.

"She wanted to make it to the holidays but couldn't hold on. If…I just want to make sure that if you can't be there for him at that time, please convince him to come home. I know it's hard for him. It *will* be hard for him. I don't know how he'll cope with it."

"I'll be there for him," I say. "And we'll be there for Thanksgiving."

Aunt Del seems satisfied with my response because she hugs me tightly, and then we walk into the room. Caleb is still sleeping, and Aunt Del says, "I'll leave you my things just in case you need them, and I'll get a ride home with Luke. As his fiancé, you should be the one he wakes up to."

"Okay," I say and watch as she grabs her purse and tablet and then disappears outside.

"Whit?" Caleb mutters, his hand grasping the sheets, and I leave my sandwich on the table and climb into bed with him.

He immediately settles, pulling me into him with a grunt. I rest my head against his chest and rub my fingers across his neck, feeling that pulse strong beneath my fingers.

What am I doing?

This will not end well.

CHAPTER TEN

I wake up with Whit in my arms. What heaven is this, I think as I blink rapidly.

Shit, my hand hurts. My entire body hurts.

Groaning, I rub at my head.

"Careful," Whit says, grabbing my hand and placing it on my chest. "You have stitches up there."

Oh yeah. The hospital. The accident.

"Ugh," I say. "I need some water."

Whit hands me a Styrofoam cup, and I take a greedy sip. I eye Whit, who looks slightly disheveled.

"You look damn cute," I tell him gruffly. "Like you all rumpled."

Whit flushes prettily and then takes my cup of water and sets it back down.

"When can I go home?"

"The doctor will be back soon. So hopefully today."

"Where's Aunt Del?" he asks.

"She left when I got here."

I nod and then say, "I need to pee."

Whit slips off the bed and helps me into the bathroom, never leaving my side, just turning his back while I do my business.

When I walk back to the bed, my gown slips open, and I see Whit checking my ass out.

"I do a lot of squats to get this, babe," I say, and Whit arches an eyebrow at me as he helps me slip into bed.

"Stop looking at me like that, all stern and shit," I groan. "You're making me hard."

Whit opens his mouth to say something, but a knock on the door silences him.

A female doctor appears, and she smiles at us. "Hi, I'm Doctor Phillips. How are you feeling? Your fiancé was saying that you slept well last night."

My eyebrows rise, and I glance at Whit, who is tapping his fingers on his thighs. And then fuzzy memories of last night reappear.

"Yeah, love of my life, right here. He's the best," I say, and Whit shoots me a sour look.

The doctor chats with me and says that everything looks normal. I can leave as soon as the nurse comes to go over my aftercare instructions for the concussion.

When she leaves, I say, "Care to help me get dressed, fiancé."

Whit side-eyes me and grabs the plastic bag with all my stuff in it.

"It was the only way they'd let me in last night."

"I like it. I want a ring, though. How does that work with two guys? Do we both get a ring, or do you give me one? Or should I buy *you* one?"

"Shut up, Caleb," he says, and I undo my gown, and it falls to the floor, exposing my naked body to him.

He fumbles with the bag, drops it, and when he finally gets himself under control, he holds out my boxers for me to step into. It's a struggle because I'm half-hard as it is.

"Can't you control yourself?" he asks, sounding exacerbated yet pleased at the same time.

"You love it," I say as he helps me into my torn jeans and then my t-shirt. When I'm finally dressed, the nurse comes in and explains my aftercare instructions, and I can't help it. This is vital.

"How long until we can have sex?"

Whit's face is overwhelmingly crimson, and I smirk at him.

"As long as there are no symptoms like dizziness or headaches, you should be fine."

"Hear that, Whit," I tease. "I should be ready to go soon. This guy's insatiable. Can't go a few hours without me."

The nurse laughs at that, and so do I, but Whit is looking ready to murder me, so I drop the topic.

"I will make you pay for that," Whit mutters as he helps me into a wheelchair.

"Can't wait, babe. I can only hope for another spanking," I say.

We make it home an hour later, and Whit calls my aunt to tell her how I'm doing. Which is fine, all things considered. I have a slight headache, and my hand throbs. But other than that, the most uncomfortable part of me is my cock, which has missed Whit more than it should.

"I left you some meals in the fridge," Aunt Del tells us through the phone. "And once you're better, hon, come out and see us. We'd like to celebrate your engagement."

When we hang up, I arch an eyebrow at Whit, who is wiping down the already clean counters.

"When are we getting married, huh?" I ask, watching as he moves on to scrubbing the sink. "I'm thinking of a summer wedding."

Whit huffs and looks over at me.

I lean against the counter, then move toward him, wrapping my hands around his waist and tucking my face into his neck.

It's only then that I realize he's shaking and not in a humorous way.

"Hey," I say softly. "Hey, baby. Come here."

He drops the sponge, and with soapy hands, he turns into me and buries his head into my shoulder. "I'm sorry."

"No, no need to apologize," I say, running my hand up and down his back. It's tense under my fingers.

"I...I'm a mess. I hate...I...." He clutches at my shirt, and I press a kiss to his temple.

"Whit. Is it me teasing you about being engaged? I know this is casual...I was just being an asshole."

"No, it's...I hate hospitals. I just hated seeing you in there. You have to be more careful next time. I can't see you like that again."

I'm silent for a moment, and then I nod. "Okay, I'll do my best to stay out of trouble."

He exhales shakily and then explains, "I...I spent a lot of time in hospitals growing up."

"Why?" I ask, keeping him tucked into me. His fingers are tight against my shirt.

"I wasn't well...mentally."

I inhale deeply but don't say a word, just let the silence settle around us.

"I hated my life. Hated my parents. I...I tried to kill myself more than once. It didn't work. It never worked...."

"Shit," I mutter, and then despite my injuries and the way my body aches and trembles, I pick him up. He's heavier than I expect, but I'm still stronger. His legs wrap around me without protest, his face still tucked into my neck. I settle us on the couch, him straddling my lap, and me holding him tightly.

"I'm glad it didn't work, Whit," I say after a moment of silence.

"Do you think differently of me now?" he asks, his face still not meeting mine.

"No. I like you just the same. More probably. Because I get to know you."

He shudders beneath me, and I just hold him, my mind running rampant with this new information he's just given me. His home life must have been awful for him to have attempted suicide so many times. If I ever meet his parents, I'm going to kill them.

"Are you okay now?" I ask, needing to know what I'm dealing with.

"Yeah, moving away from my parents helped a lot. I haven't had an issue since freshman year."

"Good, you need to stay away then. Promise me you'll stay away."

Whit is silent, not acknowledging my request, not acknowledging me one way or another, but he doesn't move from my lap. Just stays there, tucked against me for what feels like hours.

When he finally moves away, he looks at me with red-rimmed eyes.

"I missed you," I say, brushing his hair behind his ears, and he presses his lips into the palm of my hand.

"Can I...can I show you something?" he asks, his voice wobbling slightly, his eyes shiny.

"Of course," I reply gently, and he swallows roughly.

And then he's pushing off me, and his hand moves to the back of his shirt. He tugs it off quickly in one swift movement, tossing it to the ground.

And I see it, his arms riddled with marks, lines slashing across his skin. The entire fucking thing.

My eyes flick up from the scars to his eyes, and he meets my gaze as he unbuttons his pants and shoves them down his legs.

Marks are there, too, on his thighs and hips, white lines in the fabric of his pale skin.

"It makes so much more sense now," I mutter, reaching out to trace the scars on his thighs and then moving up to the ones on his hips and then finally his arms.

And he lets me, his body trembling as I run my fingers across the history etched into him.

"You don't show this to anyone, do you?" I ask softly, tracing my hands back down his soft skin.

"No."

I meet his gaze and then take his arm in my hand and press a kiss to a long, jagged line on his forearm.

He trembles at the touch, and I do the same to the other side.

"I don't disgust you now?" he asks, his voice shaking.

"No. You're perfect."

"Are you sure?" he whispers.

I huff, "Apparently, I have no shame. Just look between my legs."

Whit glances down and sees my tented pants and lets out a choked laugh.

"Caleb," he says, trying to sound stern, but I'm too busy pressing a kiss to his hips. To those bright white scars.

"I'm seeing you naked for the first time. Sue me," I mutter, nuzzling his growing cock through his boxer briefs.

God, he smells good.

"Caleb," Whit says as I run my good hand over his thigh and clutch his ass. "You can't have sex."

"I'll be fine. Don't make me stop. Don't wanna."

Whit shakes his head quickly, and then he's stepping back, his chest heaving, his eyes glassy with need.

"Where you going?" I ask gruffly.

"The doctor said you need to wait. I won't be responsible for you relapsing."

"You make it sound like I'm a drug addict."

"I don't want to hurt you."

I press the heel of my hand into my erection and arch an eyebrow at him.

"This is torture. You are *torturing* me, Whit."

"You need to rest," he says, grabbing his jeans, tugging them on, and then pulling on his shirt.

I sink back into the couch with a groan and stare at the ceiling.

He moves back to the kitchen, and I hear scrubbing.

"Whit, what the hell are you doing?" I ask grumpily.

"I need to distract myself."

"By cleaning?"

"I need to...I need space to breathe, or else I'm going to

fuck you into a coma. Your aunt would kill me. Your cousins would bury me alive."

"You're killing me. Literally."

"Think of it as a safety precaution.

"Fine," I grumble. "You win, but when I'm better, I'm stripping you down, and we aren't leaving this apartment until I'm done exploring."

Something crashes to the ground in the kitchen, and I smile to myself.

Yeah, Whit, just you wait. Asshole.

Whit is attentive yet aloof for the next four days. He's careful not to touch me too much for fear that the monster between my legs will awake, I'm sure. But he never leaves me alone. He's always there looking fucking delicious and unavailable.

And when he needs to leave to go to class, he asks Mal to come hang out with me. And when Mal can't, Magnus is there, kicking my ass in video games.

"I met your cousin," Magnus says, sitting next to me on the couch. He's wearing a red crop top and black ankle-length skinny jeans. I've never seen a dude dress like him. In my entire life.

What must my cousins think?

The thought makes me chuckle.

"Which one?"

I look over at Magnus again and see his little brow furrowed, his tongue peeking out of the corner of his mouth.

"Sem. He drove me home from the hospital."

He bites down on his lips as his fingers press aggressively at the controller.

This is news to me, and now my focus is split between the screen and the little dude next to me.

"And how was that?"

He flushes and shrugs. "Fine. Didn't talk much. Just stared at me whenever he could."

I chuckle at that, and images of a confused Sem pop into my brain. "He's probably never seen a little dude like you before. What were you wearing?"

"Nothing too crazy," he says, and I snort, but it's cut short when he hops up from the couch and pumps his fist into the air.

"Killed you, motherfucker."

My eyes widen at that, and then I laugh, "You're fucking weird, tiny."

"I know, but best to just go with it, yeah?"

"Yeah. Guess so."

Mag leans back against the couch. "Sem asked for my number."

"Did he now?"

Mag flushes and shrugs. "Yeah, I gave it to him. Why do you think he did that?"

"Your guess is as good as mine. He's probably intrigued. Don't be surprised if you find him stalking you."

"Stalking?" he asks, looking at me nervously.

"He can get a little obsessed, and he has a way of finding things out...."

"Is he like, a hacker?"

"Nah," I say, leaning back and scratching my stomach. "Maybe."

Magnus groans and flops back on the couch dramatically, throwing a hand over his face.

"This is my life now. I should have never talked to you at

that coffee shop. Now I'm surrounded by big dudes who are slightly sociopathic."

"Thought you liked them big?" I ask, and he rolls his eyes.

"Yes, but not murderous."

I chuckle at that, and then Magnus joins me, his eyes watering from how crazy it all is.

Welcome to my life, little dude.

"Why are you all so big?" he asks me, poking at my arms. "Is there something in the water out there?"

"Hey, stop poking me," I mutter, and he does it again, the little shit.

"I thought you were big, but Sem's even larger."

He pokes my side, and I slap his hand away.

"You poke me again, you're asking for it."

Magnus gets a gleam in his eye, and then he *slowly* draws his finger to me until it gently pokes the skin of my arm.

And I'm on him, flipping him onto his back and straddling him, keeping him in place with my thighs.

He breathes heavily, a bubbling laugh escaping as I dig my fingers into his sides.

"Oh fuck," he giggles and writhes underneath me, his already short shirt riding up as I tickle him.

"Gonna make you pay," I grumble, and Magnus squeals as I tickle him even more.

"What is going on here?" a stern voice behind me says, and I freeze. Swiveling my neck, I see Whit standing in the doorway, looking murderous.

I push myself up and help Magnus stand. He pushes his midriff down and looks slightly ashamed.

"Sorry, Whit. We...I was provoking him."

Whit arches an eyebrow and then holds the door open. "Thank you for helping today, Magnus."

Mag quickly grabs his bag and offers me a shy smile before disappearing into the hall.

When the door closes, Whit folds his arms across his chest and watches me.

I shuffle on my feet and then sigh. "Come on, man. I'm not into him. He was just being a little shit."

Whit doesn't say anything, just eyes me.

"Aw. You jealous, baby?" I ask with a small smile, and he huffs in annoyance. "Nothing to be jealous of. I got a thing for you."

I step toward him and pull him into me and nuzzle his neck.

"Other guys don't do it for me. I think I'm gay just for you."

He relaxes under my touch, and then I press a kiss to his neck and nibble on his ear. "I'm horny as hell for you, though."

I arch my hips into him to prove my point, and he shudders against me.

"I want you now."

"Are you sure you're better?" he asks, and I nod, nipping lightly at the skin on his neck. Inhaling him.

"I'm ready. Have been for days, but you've made me wait. I want it, and I want it *now*."

Whit pulls away from me and eyes me, gauging how serious I am. Whether or not I'm lying to get my way. So, I let him look his fill while running my hand up and down his growing cock.

"Seems you're ready too," I tease, and Whit exhales shakily. "I want you naked, Whit. Both of us naked. And when we're done, I'm washing you in the shower.

Whit's lips tremble. "Thought about this a lot, have you?"

"You have no idea. The past few days have been torture," I say and then slide my fingers into his hair and pull him into a bruising kiss.

I moan into it, licking inside his mouth. He tastes so fucking good. God, I can't wait to strip him down and press my tongue everywhere. Pawing at the bottom of his shirt, I tug it up and over his head, dropping it to the floor. I take a moment to look at him and then groan loudly at how fucking perfect he is.

"Stop looking at me like that," Whit breathes, and I roll my eyes, fumbling with the button of his jeans.

"I can't help it. You're so sexy."

"You can't be serious."

"I'm deadly serious."

I hook my thumbs into his jeans and tug them down. They don't come off easily, so I crouch down and help him step out of them. And that leaves him in just his boxer briefs, his hard length straining against them. So, I nuzzle his cock, run my good hand up to his thigh, and tug his underwear off.

His cock bobs in front of my face, long and hard. Whit is visibly trembling, his hands threading through my hair, his thumbs brushing my stubbly cheeks.

"Caleb," he mutters, and I press a kiss to his swollen tip.

God, I've never sucked a cock before, but I don't even care because it's *him*.

"Tell me what you like," I breathe, and Whit shudders when I suck on him again.

"Whatever you do, it'll be perfect."

I highly doubt that, but I'm nothing if not enthusiastic.

So, I lick my tongue down to the base and then sloppily kiss my way back to the tip.

He's trembling. I can feel it in his thighs. He's trying to hold back.

"Such a control freak," I say and then slip him into my mouth.

He's warm and smooth and tastes musky. I'm already addicted.

Sliding him into my mouth as far as I can, I gag, and Whit groans. I love that sound, love making him go crazy, so I pull off of him and try again.

I gag again, and Whit's hands tighten in my hair.

I pull off him and press a kiss to the tip of him.

"Fuck my mouth, yeah? I know you want to."

"Caleb," he moans, rubbing the tip of his cock over my lips, smearing them with precum. Such a kinky fucker.

"Do it. I want it."

Whit watches me, and when I open my mouth, he exhales shakily and slides himself back inside. He starts off slowly, pumping carefully into me, making sure not to go too deep. I suck as best I can, but it's fucking messy. I'm drooling, spit dripping down my chin, and my eyes leaking as he begins to move faster.

"You're doing...so good," he moans, moving his cock farther into me.

I gag and clutch onto his thighs, but I'm so turned on I don't even care. I just like being owned, apparently.

"I'm so close," he says, and then his hips pick up the pace, his fingers tight in my hair. "Look at me."

I do, and his dark eyes, those fucking eyes, make me nearly come undone. So, I reach up and cradle his balls, and he nearly shouts at the sensation. And then he's trying to pull away, but fuck that. I'm all in. I grab onto him and yank him so far back into me, I have to breathe through my nose, and he's frantically trying to pull away, but then I swallow around him.

And he groans my name. Come hits the back of my throat, and I gulp it down. Greedy for it. Needing it. He tastes so damn good.

And then he sags, his cock softening in my mouth as he strokes my cheeks.

"Caleb," he mutters, and I finally let him slip from my mouth.

I look up at him, my face a mess. Tears stream down my cheeks, and my mouth is red and wet from how rough he was, but the way he looks at me. I know he likes what he sees.

"Come here," he says and pulls me up, pressing his mouth to mine and kissing me roughly. "I'm going to wreck you," he says, and I groan my acceptance.

He can have me.

Pulling away, he undresses me, and then he's on his knees, swallowing me whole. And holy mother, he's so much better at this than I am. Deep throating me like it's his job. I place my hand on his shoulder, and with my good hand, I gently cup the front of his neck, feeling myself inside it.

"Whit, Whit," I moan as he bobs his head. He reaches behind me, and as those fingers massage my ass, he pulls me again and again into that warm, wet mouth. And then one finger slides down my ass crack, stopping at my hole, playing with it, hinting at the things he wants to do to it.

And I shudder and spray down his throat. Shaking like a leaf, moaning his name. It should be embarrassing, but it's been days since I've found release. I wanted to do this only with him. No one else.

Whit rests his head against my thigh, his finger still massaging my hole, and I stroke his hair.

"I'm going to fuck you," he says, his eyes closed, still kneeling on the floor.

"I know," I say.

"Not today, but soon."

"I can't wait."

And then he opens those dark eyes and stands, leading me into the bedroom.

"On the bed. Facedown," he says sternly. And I obey, just cradle his pillow beneath me and inhale his scent that lingers there.

I hear a drawer open and shut, and then he's spreading my ass cheeks, looking at me. And I should be ashamed, but I'm not. Nothing with Whit has ever been uncomfortable. It's been remarkably easy.

"Look at you," he says, running a finger down my crack again and stopping at my hole.

I grunt and arch my hips up a little, and he pauses.

"Greedy, Caleb?'

"You know it," I mutter and breathe deeply and turn my face into the pillow.

A cap flips open, and I feel cool liquid slide down, and then his fingers are there again, rubbing it up against me.

"Ready?" he asks, and I nod.

And then one finger slips into me, and I groan at the weird sensation of being invaded down there.

"Relax," he says, and I do my best as he massages his way in. More lube dribbles down my crack, and he works it inside of me. And when he's knuckle deep, I gasp.

"So good," I mutter as he moves in and out of me, his finger crooking, searching.

"Oh fuck," I nearly shout, and Whit chuckles.

"There it is," he says and does it again. I nearly come off the bed, my cock already hard again.

"What the fuck...." I moan as he does it again and again. I'm panting now, unable to catch my breath. My heartbeat thunders in my ears, and before I know it, he's added a second finger, scissoring them, opening me wider, each time hitting that spot inside of me that's driving me wild.

"Whit," I moan. "Please. More."

I'm on all fours now, my ass in the air, my elbows bent, my forehead on the bed beneath me. I'm arching back into him, fucking myself on his fingers. So desperate.

"Such a slut for it, hm?" Whit says roughly, and I whimper.

"Yes. For you. Yes. More. More. More."

Whit suddenly shifts on the bed, his thighs bumping mine. He reaches around me and clutches my cock in his hand. And then he's working me from both sides, and my eyes cross. He thrusts in with his fingers as his hand moves down my cock. It's too much. Too much. I'm writhing, whimpering, grasping for something to hold onto. He's hitting that spot just right, and I'm nearly sobbing with the need to explode. To find relief.

A third finger enters me, and I'm so full. So fucking full. How have I never done this before? How have I gone my whole life without this?

When he bites down on my ass cheek, thrusting in and down simultaneously, I cry out, coming over and over onto his silky sheets. My entire body tingles, ass clenching around his fingers, my cock jerking in his hand.

And when it's over. I can't move. So, I drop down into my own mess, not even caring that I'm sticky.

Whit's fingers are still in my ass, and I don't even ask him to leave. Just want to keep him inside of me.

"Stay," I mutter, and Whit presses a kiss to my back before slowly slipping his fingers from me.

He massages my cheeks and then spreads them, watching my pulsing hole. I should be blushing at how intimate this is, but I'm too fucking satiated to do anything but smile.

"You did good," he says, pressing his thumb to my hole, and my ass sucks it right in. I'm apparently a cock slut. Who knew?

"You sore?" he asks, and I shake my head.

"Did you like it?"

"What do you think?" I ask, and he presses another kiss to my back.

"I think you were made for it."

I glance over at him, and he's smiling softly, his cheeks flushed.

"Give me a sec, and I'll get you off, k?"

He shakes his head. "No need. Already did."

My eyebrows rise, and I smile back at him.

"Fine, then give me twenty minutes, and we can do that again."

CHAPTER ELEVEN

Whit scowls at me until I push myself up, and we go to the shower. I turn it on, and I hear him strip his sheets.

"You do know that you should probably buy more sheets. Several more, in fact. I plan to do that multiple times a day," I tease when Whit appears in the bathroom, his hair tousled, his hands on his hips.

He's naked in front of me, and I love it. Those white stripes across his skin only making him sexier.

Fuck. I must love scars or some shit because this is really doing it for me.

"Wrap your arm," he says, holding out a plastic bag.

"Yes, dad," I say, and he helps me secure it, and then he points. "In the shower, Caleb. And don't get your stitches wet."

I roll my eyes but step inside, and then he's right there behind me, pulling me into him, his hands splayed on my chest.

"Going to wash me too? Make sure I'm all nice and clean?" I ask with a small laugh, and Whit reaches around me for the soap and begins to lather me up, which is seriously the sweetest kind of torture.

"Do I get to wash you too?" I ask and reach behind me and grab onto his ass.

His cock is nuzzled nicely between my cheeks, and I have the strongest urge to lean forward and invite him to just fuck me. Hell, I'm already prepped, but I don't get the chance because he turns me around and begins washing my front, his face set in severe concentration.

"You take this very seriously," I tell him, and his dark eyes meet mine.

"There's nothing wrong with being clean."

"Nothing at all, especially when you're the one cleaning me," I say as he washes my cock with methodical precision.

"Come on now," I grumble when he squats down and washes my legs.

"Now rinse," he says, and I puff out a breath but turn obediently, rinsing the suds from my skin.

"Now my turn," I tell him, and I hold out my hand for the soap.

"I am halfway done already," he grumbles with narrowed eyes. He's right. He is. Half of his body is already covered with suds.

I tilt my head and wiggle my fingers. "Now, Whit. Don't rob me of this. I've wanted you naked for a decade. You wet and naked is in the top five hottest things I've ever seen. Let me touch you."

He sighs and slaps the soap into my palm, and I take my time rubbing it over his smooth skin, making sure to spend time between his legs. A lot of extra time.

"God, you're so fucking hot, dude," I say, and then, despite huffing and tapping those fingers on his thighs nervously, his cock hardens, and I lick my lips.

"Took you long enough," I say, and then I'm on my knees.

"I'd prefer you naked," I tell Whit, and he huffs in mock annoyance, pulling on a long-sleeved shirt instead and some track pants. I'm only clad in sweatpants. Didn't even bother with underwear. Easier access for Whit if he gets any genius ideas.

"I would rather not."

I want to pout but just follow him out to the couch and crawl on top of him, tugging his shirt up until his entire torso is exposed. I rest my face on his bare skin and sigh.

"Better."

"You're ridiculous," Whit says but slips his hands through my hair anyways and turns on the TV. It plays in the background, and I only pay attention to it halfway. Whit's not even looking at it. He's reading his Kindle, his fingers lightly massaging my neck.

"What we doing this weekend?" I mutter against his skin. Then I scoot my head over a little to the right and bite down on his nipple.

He hisses and pinches me.

"Behave."

I do it again, and he tugs on my hair. "You are seriously like a child."

I reach up and press a kiss to his lips.

"Just needing a little attention. So, what we doing this weekend?"

"I was planning on staying home and reading."

"Don't be an asshole," I say, pressing my lips to his again.

He cradles my head and gives me a slow, filthy kiss. His tongue licks inside my mouth, and I can't help but get lost in his taste. When we pull away minutes later, both of us panting, I snuggle up against him again and sigh. I love the feel of his skin against mine. He should be naked all the time.

"Mal's having a bonfire on the beach. We should go."

"I'd rather not."

"Bummer. I'll just have to go with Magnus then."

Whit tenses underneath me and then grumbles, "Fine. I'll go."

I smile into his skin and turn my face back to the TV. Welp, that was easy. Seems Whit's a jealous fucker. Not that he has any reason to be. I'm into him. Big time.

Being with Whit has been wild. I've never been so infatuated with another person. Since that first meeting, seeing him looking so serious and put together, he's consumed almost all of my attention. It's as if he's all I can focus on. The fact that he's a guy no longer factors into it. I'm just into him.

Saturday arrives before we know it, and Whit and I are heading down to the beach. I'm in my flannel shirt, jeans, and a backward baseball cap, driving Whit crazy. I can see him watching me, subtly adjusting himself in those tight pants of his.

Serves him right. He teases me by just existing.

This morning he dared to walk out of the shower completely naked, bent over to grab his clothes, giving me a nice view of his ass, and then left for class. He knew what he was doing to me too. He fucking *smirked* when he left. I feel some sort of vindication that he's just as horny as me.

"You assholes made it," Mal smiles, lifting up two

unopened beers and handing them to me. People mull around us, some drinking, others dancing. Mal's bonfire is always a hit this time of year. Anything Mal does is, actually. People just flock to him.

"Had to drag this one," I say, shooting my thumb over my shoulder.

Whit slides up next to me, and Mal fist bumps him. Then Whit opens my beer for me and hands it to me.

"Thanks, babe," I say and pull him into my side, pressing a kiss to his temple.

"You guys are too cute. Makes me want to barf," Mal says.

"Getting you back for smooching on Bree. I can't get those images out of my mind," I say.

Mal looks pleased and then tells me, "Sem and Luke are here. Been half-heartedly looking for you."

"Meh, they'll find me. I'm sure they've found someone to harass."

Whit and I mingle for a few more minutes and then find a seat on the beach. Whit sprawls a towel out and lowers himself onto it, spreading his legs, and I crawl between them. This dude actually wanted to bring *two towels*, one for each of us. I'd told him in no uncertain terms that no, we'd be sharing. Thank you very much.

I rest my head against his shoulder, my legs stretched out in front of me.

"We should've brought two towels. You're half in the sand," he scoffs.

"Aw, looking at my legs, Whit? I know they're impressive."

He huffs in my ear and then slips his frozen hand under my shirt.

A hiss escapes me, and he chuckles lowly. I glance up at

him, and his eyes are sparkling. Gah, this guy. Drives me insane.

"Feel free to feel me up," I say. "You know I'd never say no to you."

Whit tugs on my nipple ring, and I bite back a moan.

"Hey, you two!" a feminine voice says to our left, and I bite down on my bottom lip as Bev stalks toward us.

"Oh, you're so damn cute together," Bev says, moving to stand in front of us. In her arms is a stack of flyers.

"Thanks," I say, beaming up at her.

Whit says nothing.

She quickly grabs a sheet of paper and holds it out to me.

"What's this?" I ask, looking at the colorful print lining the front of it.

"It's a flyer for our LGBTQIA club. Anyone's welcome, but I thought you may want to join since you're out now. Each month, we have socials and a support group for those who need it."

"This looks cool," I say, folding the paper and placing it in my pocket.

Bev bounces on her feet. "Awesome! We've been trying to get Whit to come for ages, but he won't."

"I'm busy," Whit grumbles.

Bev rolls her eyes and then places a hand on her hips. "How do you stand him?"

"He grows on you, and it helps that he gives amazing head."

Whit coughs behind me, and I snort a laugh.

"Too gross. So, you'll come to a meeting then?" Bev asks, and I shrug.

"Not sure how I identify. Just know that I like this guy's cock."

Whit sighs heavily behind me, and I beam up at Bev, who's trying to hold back a laugh. "No problem. No labels are needed. Just come and bring your...."

"Boyfriend," I say without hesitation.

"Cool," she says and then waves goodbye, handing a flyer to another person as she leaves.

"Seriously?" Whit asks, annoyance lacing his tone.

"You can't get enough of me. Stop being such a party pooper."

"No one needs to know how much you love my dick."

"Ugh, stop saying that word. Makes me hard just thinking about it."

"You're ridiculous."

I lean my head back, and he presses his lips to mine, and I smile into it. He places a cold hand on my cheek and turns me farther into him until we're making out like teenagers. I would have continued to tongue fuck him if a tiny shadow didn't loom over us, interrupting.

"Um, hi guys," a voice says, making me slowly rip my mouth from Whit's. I stare up at Magnus who's wearing tight, ankle-length jeans, suspenders, and another midriff-baring shirt. This guy has style, I've got to admit. Dresses better than me, that's for sure.

"Hi, Mag. What's up?" I ask, trying to be friendly when I just want to get back to smooching Whit. I've got a major case of blue balls at the moment.

"Um...Sem, your cousin," he looks around, and I see Sem on the other side of the fire staring at us. He looks like a serial killer. "He's, well, I think he's following me around, and I'm not quite sure what to do about it."

"Warned ya," I say with a shrug.

Mag huffs a nervous laugh. "You did, but I didn't think you were serious. He's like lowkey stalking me."

"He probably has a crush on you. I mean, look at you. You look...very pretty."

Whit pokes me in the side, and I grunt.

Peering back at him, I say, "Nah, boo, you know only you do it for me, right? I mean, why else would I have accepted your proposal of marriage?"

"Shut up, Caleb," he says softly, but it's too late. Magnus already heard.

"You're *engaged*?" Magnus chokes out, his eyes wide.

"That's what they say," I reply and watch Magnus' eyes move over Whit and me. Like he's just now noticed that Whit's hand is under my shirt, and my lips are swollen from his kisses.

Magnus rips his eyes away from us and looks over his shoulder. Sem's no longer on the other side of the fire. No, he's now standing just close enough that he can reach out and finger the end of Magnus' shirt.

Magnus glowers at him and swats his hand away.

"Leave me alone," Magnus says and then turns back to us. "I'm sorry, I'm confused. Whit, I thought you were already...."

Whit cuts him off, his hands tightening against my abdomen. "*Enough*, Magnus. Please."

Magnus watches us with confusion before Sem starts tugging on Magnus' sleeve, and Magnus turns and arches an eyebrow.

"Excuse me, Goliath. Do you mind?"

I chuckle at Sem's frown.

"What are you wearing?" Sem asks, and Magnus rolls his eyes.

"Clothes. What are you wearing?"

"You look like a girl."

"And you look like an ogre. Go back to your swamp."

"Damn, what happened to the stuttering boy who approached me in the coffee shop?" I ask with a laugh.

"I'm no longer afraid. You're mostly harmless. Currently, though, I'm just annoyed with this...beast."

Sem takes a long swig of his beer and then snaps one of Magnus' suspenders.

Magnus places his hands on his hips and cocks them. "Seriously. I may be small, but I can still kick your ass."

Sem chuckles at that and then stands a little taller. He looms over Magnus and is at least twice as wide.

"Like to see you try, little girl."

"Oh, you're on. Just you wait," Magnus huffs and then stalks away.

Sem follows him.

"What was that?" Whit asks, and I shrug.

"Sem's intrigued, apparently. Never seen anyone like Magnus before in his life. Probably doesn't know what to do with him."

"I didn't think he was into men."

"He's not," I begin and then furrow my brow. "I don't think he is, at least."

"Well, sexuality is a spectrum, so there's a chance he could be more on one end than the other."

"I don't know, man. All I know is mine slid from one side to the other end when I met you."

"When we met?" he asks.

"Maybe not when we met exactly, but I was a goner for sure when you started holding me. Goodbye, heterosexuality."

He rests his chin on my shoulder and presses a kiss on my cheek.

We watch the fire for a bit. I drink my beers with Whit wrapped around me. His hands are both up my shirt now, one hand sliding through my happy trail, and the other flicking my nipple ring.

"You getting nervous?" I ask.

"Why would I be?"

"Because your fingers are driving me crazy."

He stills them and apologizes, but I just chuckle.

"Nah, I don't mind. I mean, I've got a raging boner but go right on ahead. Never apologize for putting your hands on me. I like you touching me."

"If you say so," he says and then adds. "I should've brought my Kindle."

"Can't live without it, huh? Even I can't entice you away from it for long."

"You entice me to do plenty," Whit says and presses a kiss to my neck. I arch my neck, and he sucks on it, bites at it.

"Leaving a mark, babe?" I ask when he moves his lips up to my ear.

"Perhaps."

I snort. "Perhaps, he says. This guy."

I can feel Whit smile against my temple, and I melt just a little more.

"Just so you know, you're free to mark me anywhere, anytime."

"I'm starting to realize that," Whit mutters, and then, "How about we make our rounds so we can head home. I think there are a few more places I'd like to mark you."

"Whit," I groan and shift between his legs. "We should be social, and you're making me want to just hide in our apartment all the time."

"*Should be*, being the correct term. There is no *need* to be social, Caleb."

"God, that big brain of yours turns me on. Why are you so convincing?"

"I am part of the debate club for a reason. Do you think I could perhaps, persuade you to leave now?"

I swallow roughly and then shake my head. "No, nope. Social for a little longer. Then we go home, yeah? We need to check up on Sem anyways. Make sure he's not being too much of a creeper."

I push up and stand, holding my hand out to Whit, who grumbles but reluctantly takes it. I pull him into me for a short kiss in apology, and then we mingle for a bit. We catch sight of Bree and Mal making out on a towel and then see Sem studying Magnus, who's swinging his hips to some music. Luke's chatting with a group of girls, one on his lap, and a bunch of other people I don't know are making out.

"I'm glad we're mingling," Whit says dryly, and I pinch his butt.

"We're outside, around other humans. It's important."

"I get enough socialization in class. I find the longer I'm alive, the less I want to be around…people."

I roll my eyes. "Then it's good you have me, babe. I'll keep you young and less cynical."

Something bumps into me, and I see two people who are so into making out that they aren't even looking where they're going. Hands are everywhere. Is that a boob?

"So, this bonfire is basically a mating ritual," Whit observes, and I squeeze his hand.

"It working?" I arch an eyebrow at him, and he huffs in annoyance. "This is making you want to mate with me, huh? Admit it."

Whit shifts on his feet and then says in all seriousness, "I'm afraid it is, Caleb."

My eyebrows rise this time, and I decide it's time to go home. I think Whit has a point. Better to stay in sometimes.

"Should head home then."

Whit nods with a small smile, and I quickly grab the towel we brought and speed walk to the car.

"Why did you decide on pre-law?" I ask Whit. I'm sprawled across his naked body, my entire body satiated from *multiple* orgasms. He really outdid himself this time.

He shrugs underneath me. "I'm good at it."

"That's all?" I ask, tracing my finger around his nipple. It puckers underneath my touch, and I pinch it slightly.

"If you must know, my parents decided on it."

"Your parents are shitheads. Shouldn't you be the one to decide your future?"

"Yes, but there are…extenuating circumstances that dictate what I can and can't do."

"Like what?"

The fingers of my good hand are tracing over the scars littering his arms, my thumb tracing the long jagged one that stems from wrist to elbow again. I'm a little obsessed with it, wondering what the story is with this one. He's yet to divulge any of it, though, which is fine. He can open up and talk to me about it later. There's no rush.

I lean over and press my lips to it, and he shudders beneath me, threading his fingers through my hair.

"Many things hinge on whether or not I get my trust fund at twenty-three."

"Like what?"

I wait for his answer, but he doesn't respond. A long silence stretches out between us, and I push myself up on my elbows to look down at him. And damn, he looks delicious. Hair rumpled and his eyes heavy-lidded.

I gave him such good head earlier. Still patting myself on the back for how his eyes literally rolled back in his head when I did that thing with my tongue.

"This another one of your secrets?" I tease.

He meets my gaze and sighs, "Pre-law or pre-med were the two majors I could pick from."

"Yeah, figured, but what else determines your trust fund is released to you? You made it seem like more than one thing was holding you back."

He clears his throat and runs his hands up and down my back, "Nothing else significant. Just some minor stipulations."

I don't believe him, but he seems to be getting agitated with this topic of conversation, so I let it go and rest my head back on his chest and listen to him breathe.

Whit's silent for a moment and then asks, "Is working with your uncle and your cousins really what you want?"

"Yeah, I'm a simple guy. It's job security, and I can make a steady income."

"You don't ever have any higher aspirations?"

"What? Being engaged to a dude who works with scrap isn't lofty enough for you?"

Whit squeezes my neck, "That's not what I meant."

"You kind of meant it. Admit it. Guys like you don't usually go for guys like me."

Whit admits nothing, just continues to run those long fingers of his across my naked skin.

When he says nothing else, I ask, "So where will you go to law school?"

Whit's hands pause and he says, "Harvard, most likely."

I lean up on my elbows and stare down at him. "Shit, that's across the country, Whit."

He swallows loudly. "Yeah."

"Have you been accepted yet?"

"No, I need to take the LSAT and then go from there, but that's the school of choice. My parents have insisted on it."

"What if you wanted to stay here? There has to be some good schools nearby?"

"There are but…I just don't know if it's possible."

"What if there's an incentive to stay?"

I move my fingers up his neck and cup the side of his face. He leans into it, and I kiss him softly.

"We barely know each other, Caleb."

"I know," I reply, kissing him again and then sucking on his tongue until he moans against me.

When I pull away, I press my forehead against his. "But I feel like I've known you forever. It just works with us. So…if you insist on Harvard, I'm sure I could find work out there."

Whit tenses beneath me, and I meet his dark stare. My heart stutters in my chest, and my stomach clenches a little at what his silence means.

He doesn't want me out there. *This is casual*. He told me what to expect when this started. It has an end date. I was stupid to assume. So damn stupid.

Can't forget this. Can't make this out to be something it's not.

I try and lighten the mood despite the painful tear in my heart. "Of course, that's only if you want me out there with you. I'd be crazy to follow you around. I'm not Sem."

He relaxes slightly at my words, and my heart fractures a bit more. "Can we table this conversation for another time, Caleb? I'd...I'd like to just have this evening with you without the future looming over us."

I nod and then press my head to his chest again. My eyes sting, and I blink away the sensation. Must be allergies.

Whit tries to start a different conversation, but I'm having a hard time following it because I'm just thinking that whatever I'm feeling, he's not. And with that comes shame. Shame of being so vulnerable, of not knowing how to stop wanting him.

I'm in over my head.

"I've ruined it, haven't I?" Whit finally says softly.

"Nah," I mutter and sink my face into his neck and breathe him in.

Who knows when this will be over? I gotta get my fill.

"You're acting...sad."

"I'm not sad, just coming to terms with some things."

"I'm so sorry, Caleb," he whispers, and my heart beats irregularly in my chest.

"Don't be. You were never anything but honest with me."

Silence engulfs us, and I should move to my own bed to have some fucking dignity, but I just can't. I don't want to be without him. So, I fall into a restless sleep, curled around him.

When I wake up, Whit's gone. The sheets are cold underneath me, and I turn over and press my face into the pillow, inhaling his scent. My neck still throbs slightly from the mark he left on me last night, and I rub at it absently.

I don't know if I'll ever get over Whit, of what this relationship has done to me. How it's changed me. My chest aches, knowing that there's a very good chance I will be waking up like this for years to come.

Silence permeates the air around me, and I wonder if this is the beginning of the end for us.

CHAPTER TWELVE

I decide to give Whit some space. He obviously needs it, so instead of lurking around the apartment like a ghost, I head to the gym and do whatever workouts I can with my broken hand. Then I chill with Mal and Bree until I can't stand to be around them for another minute. Watching them making eyes at each other only reminds me that Whit isn't around to gaze at like this.

Is this how I look with Whit?

Am I this pathetic?

Yes, yes. I think I am.

When I finally head home later that day and don't see Whit, I wonder if I should just pack a bag and get away for a little while. Clear my head. Tomorrow is my day off. No class, no work, so why not?

Yeah, that's a good idea.

I'm a fucking genius sometimes.

I'll get a motel or some shit and spend the day drinking and watching bad daytime TV. Better than overthinking this. Whatever this is. I'm already losing my mind with anxiety.

I'm in the middle of stuffing my plastic bag with shit I'll need when Whit's footsteps resound in the apartment.

"Caleb?" he calls out, and I freeze.

"In here," I say and turn to greet him when he comes through the doorway. God, he looks like a dream.

"Sorry I was late..." his eyes catch on my overstuffed plastic bag, and they narrow.

Maybe I should invest in a nice travel bag. I'm looking slightly pathetic at the moment.

"What's that?" He folds his arms across his chest, and I shrug and shove another undershirt into it. At this point, I don't even know what I've packed. It could be all socks, for all I know.

"Taking a mini-vacation."

"Why?" he asks, tapping his fingers on his arms.

"Need to get away. Think a bit."

"Think about what?"

I don't answer because what am I going to say? That I'm butthurt that he doesn't want me after this year? That my heart is breaking a little that he's going to move across the country? That I think I might, just maybe, wish he really was my boyfriend? Yeah, I've got nothing. Anything I utter at this moment will just make me look even more pitiful than I already do. This is just casual for him. I need to remember this. Nothing to see here.

So, I just move toward the bathroom, intent on at least grabbing my toothbrush, but am stopped when Whit grabs the bag from my hand and begins shuffling through it.

"You've packed three pairs of socks and an undershirt."

"You interrupted my packing process. It's normally very

precise," I say and head back into the room, dump the bag out, and start over.

I slowly begin packing again, and Whit sighs. He moves to my side and helps me, picking out one article of clothing, folding it nicely, and then placing it in the bag. He does this until all of my clothes are situated neatly inside the bag. Then he holds it out to me.

"Thanks," I say sheepishly, grabbing it from him. Our fingers brush, and tingles move up my arm. I've got it so bad.

Whit bites down on his bottom lip and nods. "You're welcome."

I move to the bathroom, and Whit watches as I pack my toothbrush and deodorant.

"Toothpaste," he says, and I shove it in my bag too. "Can I ask where you're going?"

"Dunno. Somewhere." I suddenly feel like an idiot. I kind of don't want to go anymore. The toothpaste falls out of my overstuffed bag, and I shuffle it around the floor with my foot like a tool.

Whit bends down and picks it up, placing it inside my bag once more. I simultaneously love that he's helping me pack and am devastated that he's not fighting for me to *stay*.

"How long will you be gone?"

"Tonight and tomorrow," I say, and Whit shifts on his feet, his hands in his pockets.

"That's all?"

"Yep."

"Can I...can I come with you?" he asks softly, and my heart thumps wildly in my chest. *Thank fuck*. The point of this whole excursion was for me to get some space from Whit, but I'm not sure I want to go anymore. I'll sleep like shit without him.

I'll miss him.

"Yeah, man. You can come with me. If you want to."

Whit doesn't even dally. He just jumps into action, grabbing his suitcase.

"We're only going to be gone for a night," I say, watching as he carefully folds a multitude of clothes and places them inside.

"I know, but it's always good to be prepared." He grabs the lube, and my cheeks flush because, yeah, I'm easy, and I'm sure I'll let him do whatever he wants to me tonight.

He moves to the kitchen and packs a bag full of water and some food. It's like he thinks we're going on a survival hike, but I don't say anything and just let him do his thing. There is a method to his madness, I suppose.

Ten minutes later, we're buckled in his hundred-thousand-dollar car, and Whit asks, "So where are we going?"

I shrug and feel my cheeks heating. "Dunno."

"You don't know?"

"I was just winging it, man. Had no plans. Just wanted to get away."

"Okay, well, can I make a suggestion then?" he asks, and I side-eye him.

"Yeah, Whit. Go ahead."

"I know a place, and I'd like to experience it with you. Does that work?"

My mouth twitches into a small smile. "Yeah, babe. I'd like that."

He types something into his phone, and then we're on the road.

Whit flips on some music and says, "It's about two hours away. Is that okay?"

"Yeah."

I lean back in my seat and rest my head against the window, watching cars pass but mainly just staring at Whit.

Fuck that man. He's so damn smooth. He wiggled his way into my solo trip. And I didn't even blink twice.

We make our way out of town, changing freeways. I watch as our scenery becomes more arid, but I barely notice because I'm thinking about Whit the entire time. I work myself into such a state of neediness that I barrel into him when we exit the car, pulling him into my arms and smothering him against me.

"You okay?" he asks, his hands smoothing across my back.

"Yeah, I just...just wanted to touch you."

Whit holds onto me. "You can touch me all you want."

I breathe him in, and we stand like that for a few minutes until I finally pull away. And for the first time since arriving, I take in our scenery. We're in the middle of the desert. Large Joshua trees litter the red horizon, and small round tents surround us.

"What is this place?" I ask, and Whit offers me a small smile.

"They're called yurts. Come on. Let me show you."

We check in with a woman who smells a little too ripe for my taste, and then Whit leads me to a yurt at the back of the campsite with a large blue door. We have to bend down to enter it, but when we straighten, we fit perfectly. My eyes take it all in. In the middle of the room is a queen bed with a thick comforter. I sit on it and then arch my neck up to see a skylight just above.

"It's for stargazing," Whit says, looking a little nervous. I stand and turn in a full circle, taking in the overstuffed chair on the other end of the space and a small "kitchen", which is basically a table with a coffee maker on it.

"Do you like it?" he asks, and I nod, swallowing roughly.

"Thought I'd be staying in a Motel 6 tonight, so this is an improvement."

Whit sets our bags down on the chair and moves toward me.

"We can just stay in bed the whole time," he says, and I arch an eyebrow at him.

"Presumptuous much?"

His red cheeks darken, and I pull him into me. "Just kidding. You know me. I'm down for being naked with you all the time. Where are the bathrooms?"

"Just outside. They're outhouses."

Now it's my turn to be surprised because I've never envisioned Whit wanting to camp. Without a washer and dryer and running water.

"I know," he says, reading my face. "It's not really my thing, but I knew you'd love it. When my family traveled to Morocco, I stayed in one, and I loved it. I've wanted to come out here for a while now, and I thought tonight was a great time."

"You made a good assumption. I do love it. Never stayed in a yurt before. Didn't even know what a yurt was until now."

He smiles softly at me, and I groan at that look. He looks sheepish.

This guy.

"So, what now?" I ask.

Whit gestures to the door, "How about we just sit outside for a bit? See the stars we can't see in the city?"

I follow him outside, and the sun is already setting. It's chilly in the desert in the fall, and I shiver as the temperature starts to drop.

"I don't think I anticipated the cold," I say, and Whit chuckles.

"I have a blanket in the car."

A moment later, he's back, pulling me onto his lap and against his chest, and wrapping the blanket around the two of us.

We sit like that, my head on his shoulder, and his hands wrapped around my torso. My very own cocoon.

"It's beautiful out here," I say, and Whit nods.

"You're beautiful," he whispers.

My body melts into him, and I turn around, kissing him roughly. Gods, this man is doing things to my insides. And here I was supposed to have been spending this night thinking about what the hell I'm doing in a casual relationship with a guy who is eventually going to leave. Yet here I am, sucking on his tongue and letting him rub his palm against my cock.

"You're pretty too, Whit," I say, and he tilts his head, taking more of my mouth in his, licking his way inside. My insides are on fire from the mere taste of him.

"Let's go inside. We can stargaze and make out at the same time," I say, my voice husky. Whit nods, holding my hand, bringing me inside, and shutting the door behind him.

I pull off my shirt and pants without a second thought and slide into bed. Whit moves to join me, but I shake my head.

"Nope, underwear can stay on, but no clothes in bed. I want to touch you."

Whit huffs but strips off his clothes, leaving him clad only in his boxer briefs.

Could he be any sexier?

No, no, he could not.

"Better," I say, and then Whit crawls next to me, and we

lie on our backs, facing the darkening sky through the skylight. Stars sparkle endlessly above us, and for a moment, I wonder if my mom can see how happy I am from her place in heaven.

"This is awesome. I love it," I tell him, linking our hands and bringing one up for a kiss.

"I'm glad you like it."

We're silent for a while, and then I roll over and press myself against him. His hands run up the length of my spine as I drape a thigh over his.

"Can't stay away," I mutter, running my hands along his lean torso and nuzzling my face in his neck.

"I don't want you to stay away," he replies, and then our hands are everywhere, touching, massaging, exploring. It's driving me crazy, this insane desire I have for this guy. He must feel the same way because he seems just as insatiable. His mouth rarely moves from mine, his mouth eats mine, and then his hands are underneath my boxers, kneading my bare ass.

"Whit," I say, panting against him.

"Yeah?" he huffs.

"I want you to...want you to fuck me," I mutter, and he freezes for a second before he pulls me closer to him.

"You sure?" he asks.

"Yeah. Fuck yeah. I want you to be my first."

Whit closes his eyes and kisses me so slowly that it should be illegal.

"Okay," he says when he finally pulls his mouth away from mine. Then he rolls from underneath me and stands up, grabbing the lube from his suitcase. But then freezes as he makes his way back to me.

"I...I didn't bring any condoms. I didn't expect...."

"Shit," I mutter as I press my hand against my aching cock.

Whit sits down on the edge of the bed and tugs my boxers off. He starts palming my cock, and my back arches off the bed. God, my brain is scrambled. I can't think, can't remember why we needed condoms in the first place. All I know is that I need him inside of me like yesterday.

"I'm negative, are you?" I pant, my eyes wild with lust.

Whit's hand stills on me, squeezing gently. "Yes. I'm negative. I've never had sex without one before."

"Oh, shit. Okay. That's good, right?"

Whit begins stroking me again, and I gasp. "Just do it, Whit. We don't need condoms. I can't wait any longer. Been waiting too long. Far too long."

I'm rambling, but I don't even care at this moment. Just need him *inside me.*

"You trust me?" Whit asks, seeming confused that I would do such a thing. This man has serious issues.

I turn over on my stomach and clutch the pillow in my arms, arching my ass in the air. "What do you think?"

Whit stares at me for what feels like an eternity and then runs his hand across my ass and spreads my cheeks like he likes to do. He's staring at me, at my hole. His breathing stutters, and he traces a finger down the crease. Back and forth. He torments me until I hear the pop of a cap and feel lube trickling down my crack.

"Gods," I mutter as he quickly works one finger inside me.

I've gotten good at this, of bearing down and letting my body relax so he can move inside of me. We've been practicing.

I *love* practicing with him.

Beg for it usually.

"Look at you," he whispers almost as if he's in awe, and then he adds a second finger. He starts to scissor them, stretching me and making me see stars as he occasionally massages my prostate. He knows just where it is. It's like he's memorized my entire body.

I've done the same with his.

"You're doing so good, Caleb," he says softly, and I melt at the reassurance. This is a big step, letting someone in like this. And yet, I'm not afraid.

When he adds a third finger, I'm whimpering. "Whit, please. I can't wait any longer. Need you. Need this. Please fuck me."

"Almost," he says, his voice strained. I'm practically fucking myself back on his fingers, needy as hell for more of him.

And then suddenly, his fingers are gone, and I feel so *empty*. I look back and see Whit staring at me with those dark eyes.

"Are you sure about this?" he asks as he covers his cock with lube.

I nod, swallowing roughly.

"Yeah. Need you." I turn my face forward and lean my forehead onto my arms.

I feel Whit moving behind me and pressing down on my back, making my ass arch up even more.

"You're perfect," he says so softly that I almost miss it, but then it's forgotten because I can feel his cock at my hole, pressing inside.

I take it like I knew I would. His head slips in easily, and I gasp. He's thicker than his fingers, but he moves slowly, letting me adjust to his size until he's sinking in more.

"Good boy," he mutters, his fingers digging into my hips.

The compliment makes my chest inflate, and I bear down, and he slips in a little farther until he's panting.

"So tight," he says on a shaky exhale. "So good."

I feel a bead of sweat fall down my temple, and I turn my face. On an inhale, I push back the rest of the way, impaling myself on him.

"Caleb," he stutters, and I breathe deeply through my nose because he's long. Longer than his fingers, and he's bigger too. He stretches me deliciously, and I can feel the pleasure begin to bloom through its sting.

"God, you're big," I grunt, just letting myself *feel* him inside of me.

"You okay?" he asks, pressing a kiss to my back, making sure not to move inside me.

"So good. So full," I manage to say and then nearly come when he reaches around me and begins stroking my cock. Up and down, twisting his wrist deliciously, bringing me so close to the edge that I'm writhing under him. So full, so fucking full of him.

"Shit, Whit. Move. Move. Jesus. Fuck me. Please."

Whit's hand disappears, and then I feel those fingers digging into my hips, and he's pulling his long length out and pressing back in, slowly.

Too fucking slow.

"More. Faster," I gasp, and he does it again, a little harder.

It's not enough. I need more. I need for him to *wreck* me.

I look over my shoulder and see him watching his cock pull all the way out of me before he pushes it back inside. The sight is so fucking obscene that I can't help it. I press back and impale myself on him. Hard.

"Caleb," he groans and meets my eyes. "Don't want to hurt you."

"Wreck me. Fuck me. Now. I want to feel you for days."

Whit seems to think on this for just a moment, but when I lurch forward and slam back down on his dick again, he comes to a decision because he starts to piston forward, slamming into me. Tunneling that long, slick cock right up my ass. The bed lurches forward, and I wonder for a moment if we're going to take the entire tent down, but then all I can think about is how damn good it feels because he's tilted his hips just right, and he's hitting the pleasure spot inside of me so good.

"Oh Jesus," I cry out, lowering myself even more so he can just use me.

"You're such a slut for me. Aren't you, Caleb," he huffs, his hips slapping against my ass, his balls hitting mine. The sounds our bodies are making are literally pornographic, and I feel myself growing close to coming just from the sound of it.

"So damn greedy," he says and then wraps his arms around me and pulls roughly. I'm lifted up and off my elbows, my back pressed against his chest. Now I'm totally skewered on him, and I can't breathe.

Whit grabs my hair and tugs roughly, turning my head and pulling my mouth to his.

"You're mine. *Mine*," he says roughly and then slams his mouth onto mine, eating me, sucking me, his hips thrusting up in short bursts that make my cock weep. My entire body is shaking, trembling with need. How is this so good? Why was I ever straight? Pussy has nothing on this.

And then he shifts ever so slightly, and I cry out as he thrusts against my prostate just right, and without even touching myself, I explode across the sheets. Thick, white strips of come landing everywhere.

Whit grabs my neck and squeezes. He pumps up inside of

me once, twice, three times, and then he groans loudly, biting down roughly on my neck as he chases his own release.

We stay like that for a few seconds, catching our breath, and then Whit moves his hand from my throat, and I collapse forward, Whit's cock still inside of me as I struggle to breathe.

Warm, soft hands rub gently up my back and down my sides. Reverently. Worshipful.

"You okay?" Whit asks, and I nod.

"Need water."

Whit kneads my ass cheeks and then pulls out slowly, trying not to hurt me. I can feel his release dribbling out of me when he's gone, and I secretly love it.

"Here you go," Whit says, holding a water bottle out to me. His hands tremble slightly, and I bite back a smile as I push up on my elbow, drink it down, and then I collapse back on the bed.

"You wore me out," I manage to say and then wince at how tender I feel. How empty. "I want to do that again. Tonight," I add, and Whit runs a hand tenderly down my chest, stopping at my happy trail as he threads his fingers through it.

"Maybe," he says, and I arch an eyebrow at him.

"Why maybe?"

"You'll be sore. We should give your body a rest."

"Fuck rest. I want it again. Give me a few hours."

Whit chuckles and then presses a tender kiss to my lips. He helps me clean up, and I let him, even though, secretly, I want to tell him to fuck off. I want to feel his come on me when I fall asleep, but I'm pretty sure he wouldn't go for it. He's too much of a neat freak. So, I arch my hips up as he wets a towel and cleans my cock, ass, and thighs.

Then he lies down next to me, and I move on top of him.

"That was…amazing," he tells me, and I preen.

"So, your first time without a condom was memorable?"

"Yeah, Caleb. It was. You were."

I scoot a little closer. "Good, I want you to remember me."

Whit's fingers dig into my skin a little harder than usual, and he whispers, "Always."

And we fall asleep with me in his arms.

I knew it. After a taste of it, I wanted more. Waking up on top of Whit, my ass deliciously sore, I try to convince him to do me again, but he just shakes his head and suggests hiking.

"Have you ever hiked a day in your life?" I snort, and he eyes me with irritation.

"I have. The Swiss Alps, if you must know."

"God, you're such a snob," I say, tweaking his nipple and making him hiss, but I kiss it better. Far longer than I probably should.

"I'm not fucking your ass again today. I don't want to hurt you."

I glower at him and then sigh, rolling off him and throwing an arm over my head.

"Fine. Hiking it is. But just know I'm going to try and change your mind."

"And just know that I have a will made of steel."

I snort even louder at that, and I belly laugh, unable to stop.

"Stop laughing at me," he grumbles, and I eye him through the tears in my eyes.

"Will of steel? Pompous much?"

"It's just how I talk."

I roll over, still chuckling, and nuzzle his jaw. "And I love how you talk. Gets me all hot and bothered. Care to stick your dick in me and help me out?"

Whit shoves at my shoulders and slides off the bed.

A minute later, he's tossing my clothes at me.

"Get dressed."

My ball cap hits me square in the chest, and I lift an eyebrow.

"I didn't pack this, Whit," I say and tug it on. I'm now lounging back on my elbows, wearing just the hat and nothing else.

Whit glances over at me and exhales shakily.

"You sneaky bastard," I say and then make sure to flex my muscles, giving him an excellent view of my V-cut abs.

The way he's looking at me has my cock perking up.

"You *so* can't resist me now."

Whit fumbles with his clothes, and I chuckle lowly.

"Come on, Whit. Fuck me. It's your dream come true. Me in my hat and nothing else."

He turns to look at me once more and then sighs dramatically, stalking toward me with purpose.

"Fine, but you're riding me this time. That way, you can control it. Go as slow as you want."

As soon as he's close enough, I grab him and throw him down. He lands with an *oomph*, and I crawl on top of him. His cock is already hard, and I pump it a few times until he's arching into my fist.

"Prep first," he grunts, and I lean over, grabbing the lube, making quick work of slathering it onto his cock, but I'm too eager to do any more. Fuck waiting. So I grab him and find my hole before sliding down. In one single thrust.

"Slow," he hisses and grips my hips, trying to still me. But fuck that.

"Fuck slow," I mutter and pull up before slamming back down on him.

He groans loudly as I start to ride him, my thighs bunching and pulling as I move on top of him. His hands grip me, but he lets me control the speed and roughness of it. And hell. It's fast and furious.

"Like seeing you under me," I moan. And damn, what a picture he makes, flushed cheeks, wet lips, hooded eyes.

He's porn. My porn. Mine.

Mine.

His hand slides up from my thigh and grabs onto my cock, pumping me in time with my thrusts.

"Can't get enough. Need to do this. All. The. Time," I gasp as he begins to arch his hips up, tunneling into me roughly.

So much for taking it slow.

And then I feel it, the subtle shift of his body, and he's hitting my prostate as his hand works my cock faster.

"Oh shit. Shit," I say, grabbing onto the headboard on the bed and pounding down onto him.

And then I'm coming. My ass clenches around his cock which pushes him over the edge. He groans, his eyes rolling into his head as he fills me with his come. It's so hot that I keep bouncing on his cock until he hisses.

"Stop. Stop," he begs, nearly breathless, and I whine but comply. I collapse on top of him and press my cheek to his chest.

"You did not go slow," he chastises, massaging my ass cheeks.

"Like you were going slow either," I mutter. "At the end, you were pounding into me like your life depended on it."

Whit huffs, and then he runs his fingers from my ass to my hair, tugging softly.

"Did I hurt you?"

"Nah. Felt good. Want to do it again. Give me a few hours."

Whit's fingers pause, and he grabs onto my chin, tilting my head up so I can see the seriousness in his eyes.

"No. No more. You need to heal."

"I have an amazing hole. It's been blessed. No need to heal."

His eyebrows bunch together, and he watches me for a moment before those serious lips arch into a smile.

"You, Caleb, are absolutely ridiculous."

"Nah. I'm perfect, remember. Plus, I have the hat. You're a sucker for it."

"It was a very nice touch."

"A nice touch, he says," I mutter, and then he presses a kiss to my lips and rolls us over, slipping out of me. My good hand is tucked beneath my head, and I watch as Whit just looks at me, his eyes sliding from my face to my flaccid cock. And then his hands grip my thighs and spreads them wide. When I am spread to his satisfaction, he cradles my balls in his hand and lifts. And then he's staring at his release dripping from me.

Oh, fuck. That's hot.

"Like what you see?" I choke out.

"Shameless," he says, his cheeks red.

"Just for you."

He meets my eyes and then gently lets me go. He stands up and goes about his cleaning ritual, making sure I'm nice and tidy before he hands me my clothes that ended up on the floor earlier.

"Still up for a hike?" he asks.

I clench my ass and feel soreness there, but it's nothing I can't deal with.

"Yeah."

We spend the next few hours exploring the vast expanse just outside the yurt. The entire time, our hands stay linked, and I insist on frequent breaks where I tug him into me and kiss him. Extensively. Need to be thorough.

When we make it back to the yurt, it's time to head back to civilization. But I don't want to go.

"We have to," Whit says, folding our clothes. "You have work tomorrow."

"Don't remind me. How am I supposed to get through an entire workday when I have your cock waiting for me at home?"

Whit shoots me a look and then grabs my stuffed plastic bag and his suitcase. "You had my cock before, and it wasn't an issue."

"Oh, it sure was. I was hard *all the time*. And now I know what it's like to have you naked *and* inside of me. I'm going to be miserable at work. Just counting down the hours until I can come home and sit on you."

"Get in the car, Caleb," Whit says, throwing our things in the trunk and sliding into the driver's seat.

I fold myself in next to him and lean my head back, turning my gaze to him.

"You're staring," he says as we make our way back down the dirt road toward the freeway.

"Can't help it."

He side-eyes me, and when he merges onto the freeway a few minutes later, he says, "I'm going to contact a lawyer."

My heart stutters in my chest. "Yeah?"

"Yeah. I want to see if I have any options...any other choices."

A smile sweeps across my face, and I lean forward and press a sloppy kiss against his cheek.

He flushes and wipes at the wetness lingering on his skin.

CHAPTER THIRTEEN

WHIT

1 MONTH LATER

The following month is a blur of late nights spent making out, sex, and *more sex*. Caleb is insatiable. He warned me he would be, but I didn't believe it. What straight guy goes from liking pussy to taking it up the ass?

No one.

I think I've found the exception to the rule.

Of course, it would be Caleb. He's broken every expectation I've had of him. There are some days when I don't think I can keep up with his sex drive. The first week, after staying in the yurt, my entire body ached from the physical exertion of driving into him and maneuvering his muscular body until we both found relief. He'd caught on to how exhausted I was, though. He always seems to be able to read me. So, the following week, he'd done all the work. Lifting himself onto me, riding me. I'm not sure what I like more, being in control or watching Caleb get off on using me.

After a debate meeting, I unlock the front door and walk into the apartment, immediately spotting the discarded clothes.

It should annoy me, the mess, but for some reason, it doesn't. I'm likely too enamored with him to let it get to me. I set my keys down and turn to see Caleb leaning back against the couch, completely naked. His muscular thighs are spread wide, his hand slowly stroking his cock, his eyes hooded as he watches me move toward him.

I pretend to be annoyed and arch an eyebrow. He merely strokes himself faster.

"You know the serious look you're giving me is only making me hotter," Caleb says.

My eyebrow lifts higher, and Caleb groans. "What if I'd brought a guest over, Caleb? Is this really the first impression you want to make?"

Caleb smiles at me, and I melt a little inside. He's the sexiest man I've ever seen.

He arches his hips, full-on fucking his fist now. "Come over here, Whit. I've been waiting for you. Need you."

I scoff but am already deciding which way I want him. This morning I'd taken him from behind. His back to my chest, slipping inside of him while he was still half asleep.

"You had me this morning."

"Not enough. Need more."

I roll my eyes in faux exasperation but still drop my messenger bag and tug off my shirt and pants as quickly as possible.

WHIT

Caleb is snoozing on the couch, his head in my lap as the TV plays quietly. My fingers thread through his hair which is longer than a month ago. He needs a haircut. Though I do like this as well. More to grab onto.

I like anything Caleb, apparently. He's making me rethink my entire future.

My phone buzzes in my bag, and I lean over to grab it. Seeing the familiar number on the screen, my heart speeds up. I feel sick. This is the call I've been waiting for, so I answer it without hesitation.

"Yes?" I say as quietly as I can.

Caleb clutches my thigh at the interruption and sighs softly, still asleep.

I continue to massage his scalp as the lawyer on the other end of the line confirms it is indeed me.

He then gives me the bad news. My stomach clenches, and I feel like I'm going to throw up.

There's nothing to be done. I'm stuck.

If I want my trust fund to be released to me when I turn twenty-three, I need to go through with it.

With everything.

My chest constricts, and I gulp down air. I can't breathe. The room is closing in on me.

"Whit?" Caleb says sleepily, his blue eyes blinking up at me.

I'm so sorry.

So sorry.

"You okay?" he asks, concern lacing his voice.

"I..." My lungs constrict, and I clutch at my chest. My

vision blurs, and I lean forward, placing my head between my legs, doing my best not to pass out.

The hope I'd had is gone. I hadn't even thought that things could be any different until I'd met Caleb. And for a month, one blissful, life-changing month, I'd let myself *hope*. But it's all lost now. Everything is ruined.

"Whit?" Caleb says, those strong, thick hands rubbing my back so softly. So gentle. Always so gentle with me.

I can't lose him. I can't.

"Fine. Just...need...a minute," I gasp.

He's so patient, waiting it out with me until my breathing comes easier and my vision isn't blurry. I still want to throw up, want to purge this feeling out of me.

"What was that?" he asks, cupping my face in his palms and pressing a kiss to my sweaty forehead.

"Just bad news," I say, and Caleb nods.

"You want to share?"

I shake my head. I can't do it. Not yet. The anniversary of his mom's death is coming up. Then Thanksgiving. Not yet. Not yet.

"Is it serious?"

I shake my head, even though it is. I feel like my heart is being ripped from my body.

The choice I have to make.

Is it even a choice?

"I...I overreacted. I'm...I'll be fine," I tell him, clutching at his hand and turning it to kiss that rough palm. Because I have to be fine with whatever I choose. And I don't know if I can choose this. Not after everything I've been through. Can I give it all up?

Caleb's thumbs rub over my cheeks. "Okay."

He doesn't sound convinced. Not that I expect him to. I'm a liar. He will *never* forgive me once this is over.

My eyes start to water, and Caleb's face crumples as he pulls me into his chest and holds onto me.

I should have never let him be my roommate. I should have let him go about his life, never knowing me. It would have been simpler, better. But I was too selfish. Wanted him too much.

CALEB

"Hey, um…you okay?" Magnus asks, sitting down next to me at the long table. I play with a bit of fall-colored confetti and shrug.

The LGBTQIA social is in full swing. Today everyone's gathered for the annual Friendsgiving before heading home to spend time with their families. And despite making a few good friends since joining, I want to just go back to the apartment to be with Whit. Ever since that phone call last week, he's been distant. Pulling away.

I can feel it growing wider each day. His moods are darker, and he's disappearing into his mind far too often. I can see the torment the most when we have sex. It's almost desperate, with him clinging to me, those dark eyes boring into mine as if he's committing each thrust, each brutal kiss, to memory.

It's hot, this new kind of intimacy, but at the same time, it's disconcerting. Am I losing him?

"Whit's just being weird," I tell Magnus and lean back in my chair, folding my arms across my chest.

"How so?" Mag asks, turning toward me and peering up

with those sweet hazel eyes. He's wearing his signature llama bowtie, a purple button-up shirt, and white pants.

What dude wears white pants?

"He's just being distant. Cold. It's confusing," I say, rubbing a hand over my face, the stubble tickling my palm.

"He's hard to read," Magnus says, nibbling on his lower lip, looking...I dunno...guilty. What does he have to feel guilty about?

"That he is," I say and then ask. "Was he like this with you when you two were...you know."

Magnus shakes his head. "It was never like that with us. It was more...transactional between us. It was convenient. With you...I've never seen him so happy."

I close my eyes and tilt my head back. Fuck, I'm getting a headache.

"Look, Caleb, I've known Whit for four years, and I still don't know him all that well. Everything I *do* know is usually something that I happened upon by accident."

I eye him fidgeting in his chair, and I turn toward him, knocking my knee into his. "You have something to say, Magnus? You know something?"

Magnus blinks rapidly and shakes his head, looking nervous.

This little shit knows *something*.

"Nope, got nothing."

I narrow my eyes at him and lean into his space, our foreheads nearly touching.

"Please tell me. He's shutting me out. I'm losing him," I say softly, and Magnus frowns.

"You looking sad is...well, it's depressing," he mutters and then presses a hand to my knee and squeezes. "He loves you, you know. The way he looks at you. He's never looked at anyone like that in the four years I've known him."

I swallow thickly and shake my head, "It's not love. It's casual. For him, at least it is."

Magnus looks despondent at that and squeezes my knee again.

"Trust me..." he begins and then freezes when a shadow moves across us.

"Oh, bother," Magnus says and removes his hand from my leg. "Hi, Whit," he says weakly.

Whit eyes Magnus, his eyes spitting fire, and Magnus shoots up from his seat, gesturing toward the food table. "Food's getting cold. Gonna go get something to eat. Bye!"

He disappears into the crowd, and I raise my eyebrows at Whit, who's frowning at me, his arms crossed over his chest.

"Hey," I say, leaning back and spreading my legs in front of me. "You're late."

Whit ignores my comment about his tardiness and says, "Why is it when I leave you alone with Magnus, I always end up finding you two touching."

"He's touchable," I say. "Like a bunny or a hamster. He's very tiny."

Whit scowls at me, and I smirk at him. "You were literally in his ass for over a year and you don't see me getting jealous when you spend time with him. Which is often, by the way, but heaven forbid he touches my knee."

Whit's eyes are so narrow now that I can barely even see the brown of his iris.

Enough of this shit. I reach forward and pull him onto my lap and then smash my lips to his. He tries to fight it, to push away, but ends up relenting a moment later. Opening up to me, surrendering in his own way.

I tilt my head to get a better angle and lick into his mouth, our tongues tangling obscenely for a few minutes until we hear jeering from the crowd.

"Ew, keep that PDA locked up!" someone shouts, and I pull my mouth away from Whit and glance over to a group of people shooting us looks, some amused and some annoyed.

"Don't be jealous that I have the hottest piece of ass here," I respond loudly, and Whit's ears burn.

I laugh and press a kiss to his temple and then whisper in his ear, "There's nothing to be jealous of. Can't get enough of you. They all know this."

And isn't that true? I'm a sex maniac when it comes to Whit. I love how he dominates during sex, how he takes control. Even when I'm the one on top, he still manages to dominate.

"By the way, my ass still hurts. Think I saw a handprint on my left cheek," I say, and Whit shifts on my lap and brushes his thumb over my bottom lip before pressing it into my mouth.

I suck on it a moment and then bite down softly. He sucks in a deep breath and then pops it out.

"Shouldn't have been such a smart ass then," Whit responds, and I roll my eyes.

He'd given me the spanking of a lifetime earlier today, and my ass is still red from it. Chaffed like a motherfucker when I pulled my pants on.

"Worth it. I'd do it again if it gets you to do that thing with your tongue again."

Whit huffs and then moves to stand, but I pull him into me, holding him tightly.

"Not yet."

He shifts on my lap and then relaxes into me.

"You've been distant," I say softly into his ear.

"I've been busy."

It's the same excuse he's used all week, and I don't buy it.

"Nah, there's something else. Will you tell me, Whit? Let me in?"

Whit stiffens and says, "There's nothing to tell, Caleb."

I roll my eyes and then press a kiss to his neck before relaxing my arms and letting him move off of me.

He holds out a hand to me, and I slip my fingers through his and stand. We move toward the food table, and Whit hands me a plate.

"Are you packed for our trip?" he asks, and I send him a look.

He should know me better than that.

Whit sighs heavily. "Fine, we'll pack when we get back. And you *will* be using that duffle bag I bought you. If I see that plastic bag one more time...."

"That bag served me for many years," I reply as I shovel food onto my plate.

"You got it at a Walmart. I threw it away, by the way."

I shrug. "I'll find another."

He glowers at me, and I smile widely at him. "Just kidding, babe. I love the bag you got me. I promise to use it from now on."

I lean over and press a kiss to his frowning mouth.

When I pull back, I watch him roll his lips between his teeth and look at me. Then he leans forward and says lowly, "When we get home, I'm going to spank that ass red again and then fuck you into the mattress. Maybe I'll even find another one of your deplorable plastic bags and tie you up with it, so you'll have no choice but to let me do whatever I want to you."

Oh shit.

I inhale sharply and then adjust myself subtly as I move through the food line, needing to get this show on the road. Being tied up by Whit is a major fantasy of mine and there is no time to waste.

He chuckles darkly behind me, and I send him a glare as we sit down.

"You know when you say things like that, how I get," I hiss. "You're literally torturing me. And at Friendsgiving, no less. It's shameful, man."

Whit reaches under the table and brushes his knuckles across my hard length, and I nearly choke on my mashed potatoes.

"I think we should just go now," I say, pushing my plate away, but Whit spreads his napkin on his lap and picks up his fork.

"I think I'll stay for a while."

I stare at him and watch as he smirks at his plate.

This guy.

Whit packs for me. Look, I was going to do it myself but gave up after he loomed over me, commenting about how negligent I was by just stuffing my clothes into the nice leather duffle bag he bought me. How that's careless is beyond me, but he sighed in satisfaction when I gestured toward the bag and my pile of unfolded clothes. Instead, I sat on the bed and watched him fold my clothes nicely, and then when our bags were packed and waiting by the front door, he did as he promised.

He tied me up and fucked me into the mattress.

Needless to say, I slept like the dead that night, too sore to move a muscle.

Whit is beneath me when I wake up, his hands kneading my tender ass. The fingers that tortured me so deliciously last night are offering some comfort, and I nuzzle further into him at the gesture.

"Don't stop," I mutter.

"We've got to head out," he says, and I groan.

"Not yet. Just a few more hours, then we can go."

Whit runs those hands up my back and massages my neck. "Your aunt wants us there soon. I have to help with the pies."

I reluctantly lean up and stare down at Whit, who's looking deliciously rumpled. Love seeing him like this.

"Pies?"

He flushes. "I happen to be great at making pie."

I smile widely and press a sloppy, morning breath kiss on his mouth. "You're full of surprises. I'd be hard again if I wasn't so wrung out."

"I bet, but there wouldn't be time for that anyway. It's time to get up," he says but continues to massage my back and neck. The incentive to move and get going is nonexistent. So, I just lie there and let myself be pampered by him.

After a few minutes of silence, I begin to doze again, and Whit says, "Your aunt told me the significance of this week."

I tense against him, but he soothes it away until I'm putty in his hands.

"I haven't really thought about it, to be honest."

"Will you promise to tell me how I can help, Caleb? Will you let me be there for you?"

I press a kiss to his skin again. I can't stop kissing him. All I want to do all day is run my lips across his body.

"Yeah."

We're silent for a moment, and then I say, "You can come with me to visit her. If you want. I'd like to introduce you."

Whit's fingers grip me tightly, and he shifts beneath me. "I'd love nothing more. I'm sure she was a wonderful woman."

I exhale a shaky breath. "She was the best."

We lay like that, my body cradled on top of his, before Whit finally says, "We really need to move and get going, Caleb."

"Give me an incentive," I mutter and press a kiss against his shoulder.

He thinks about it for a moment and then says, "I'll eat your ass in the shower."

I'm out of bed in seconds flat.

Whit follows me with a victorious smile.

Win-win if you ask me.

I lean back on the smooth leather seat of Whit's car and close my eyes.

"You do amazing things with your tongue," I say and listen as Whit starts the engine and begins to drive. "I'm going to be dreaming about it for years to come."

"Hopefully, more like *decades* with how much you screamed."

I open one eye and look at Whit, who looks smug, those long fingers firmly gripping the steering wheel.

"Shut up, man. Never had my asshole licked before. It was transcendent. Saw Jesus for a moment there."

He chuckles, and then I ask, "Can I do that to you? Would you let me?"

Whit glances over at me and then back at the road. "If you want."

I close my eyes and fold my arms across my chest. "Oh, babe. I so do. Tonight, yeah? I'm going to eat you so good."

Whit huffs, and I smirk.

I spend the next two hours in traffic thinking of how I want to make Whit come. When people say guys think about sex all the time, it's true. It's all I think about, really. By the time we arrive at my aunt and uncle's house, I stare despondently at my hard cock, and Whit rolls his eyes.

"You have deep-seated issues that need to be resolved," Whit says.

"My issue is you being so sexy," I pout, and he brushes a hand over my hard length, which isn't helping matters.

"Better get it under control," Whit says and presses a kiss to my cheek. "Here they come."

I look out the windshield and see my aunt walking quickly toward us, followed by Sem, Luke, Anne, and Liam.

"Motherfuck," I mutter and place my jacket over my crotch.

Whit smiles widely at me before sliding out of the car and is enveloped by my aunt's small frame. He leans down and presses his cheek to the top of her head, and my heart melts a little.

I know how much my aunt's acceptance of him means and how much he enjoys the weekly phone calls he gets from her. She's good at that, making sad boys feel loved. I know. I've been there.

Sem, Luke, and Liam line up to slap Whit on the back, and then Anne pulls Whit in for a crushing hug.

And for a moment, while I watch, I wonder if he was ever hugged as a boy. If those cold parents of his ever showed him an ounce of affection. Well, if they didn't, fuck them. I'll give him enough hugs to last him the rest of his life.

"Was traffic bad?" my aunt asks, and I nod, pulling her into me and lifting her off the ground.

"Put me down," she squeals, and when I do, I move toward Anne, pulling her into me in the same manner and she lets me twirl her around. She's tiny, kind of like Magnus. Her messy bun bops me in the face as I set her down.

"Glad you made it this time," I tell her, and she smiles widely at me.

"Glad I did too. Your fiancé is a hottie, by the way. I'd love to paint you both. As a wedding present."

I sling an arm over her shoulder. "Sounds like fun."

She winks at me, and I call over to Whit, "Hey, babe. Anne's going to paint us. Nude. For a wedding present."

Whit flushes crimson, and I beam at how he shifts uncomfortably in front of my aunt.

"Don't want to think of you two naked together. Seeing that once was enough," Luke chimes in as I wrap my arms around Whit and rest my chin on his shoulder.

"Alright, Whit. Let's get started on those pies, then you boys can head out for some wheelin'," my aunt says, and Whit glances back at me.

"I'm not letting you drive me around in that truck," he tells me. All stern and sexy.

I smack a kiss on his lips and shake my head. "Nah, babe. You're going to drive me."

He sputters, and I smack his ass. "Better get in and make those pies. We've got shit to do."

He glowers at me but follows my aunt inside, and I watch him go, my eyes always on him. I can't tear them away.

"Well, you two look happy," Anne says, poking me in the side.

"We better be. We're getting married," I say.

Yeah, I've rolled with it. I know it's all a misunderstanding. Whit and I haven't discussed this being more than casual, but for right now, he's my fiancé and we're getting married.

Not going to lie. I've dreamt of it too. Whit waiting for me at the end of an aisle, his dark eyes watching me as I approach. Him sliding a ring on my finger.

Sue me. I'm a sap when it comes to romance, apparently. Who knew?

Anne leans over and asks, "So you into all guys now, or is this just a Whit thing?"

I look at the door where Whit disappeared, and I shrug, "Think it's just a Whit thing. He's it for me, you know."

She nods. "Yeah, when you know, you know."

"Yeah," I agree, and then my future musings are interrupted by Liam, Sem, and Luke shouting for me.

CHAPTER FOURTEEN

"This is not working," Whit says, frustration evident in his voice as the gears grind loudly. He clutches the stick shift and tries to put it into gear, but it lurches forward and dies instead.

I laugh softly and then cover my hand with his.

"You got this, babe. Don't get discouraged. Betsy just needs a little coaxing."

Whit huffs and shoots me an annoyed look. "I hate Betsy."

I pat the dashboard and shake my head, "Betsy, don't listen to him. He's just a grump who hates not being perfect at something."

Whit grumbles something under his breath, pushes the clutch in, and starts the truck again. He shifts it into gear, and we lurch forward.

I hang onto the oh-shit bar as he moves into second gear, the engine whining as he does.

"You got this," I tell Whit as he maneuvers the truck over

the uneven ground of my aunt and uncle's property.

"I don't think I do," he says, but he keeps the truck from dying as we traverse the open land.

"Up this hill," I say, and Whit shakes his head.

"No way."

"Come on, Whit," I say. "Live a little."

"This truck has no doors. The seatbelts look flimsy. That hill looks too steep."

"It's not that steep."

"What if we tip over."

"Rolling isn't a big deal."

Whit stops the truck, and it dies. Then he turns to look at me, his eyes serious.

"Caleb, you're not to roll large machines. Ever. Again. I forbid it."

I smile softly at him. "You worried about me?"

"Of course, I am. You're...reckless."

"Nah, babe. I'm living." I say, and then I hop out of the truck and slide in next to him, using my strength to move him to the passenger side.

"You will not..." he says frantically. But I chuckle evilly, revving the engine loudly, and Whit scrambles to put his seatbelt on. It clicks, and Whit grabs onto the bar in front of him, his knuckles white. Then I'm revving forward, shifting from first to second gear as Whit mutters curses under his breath.

Wheels spin as we make our way up the rocky hill, and Whit's gone a lovely shade of white.

"You've got this, Betsy," I say, and Whit turns to glower at me and then scolds, "Caleb van Beek, put your seatbelt on right now."

I smirk at him as we skid and slide our way up to the top of the hill. At one point, we get stuck, and I have to stop the truck. We're tilting slightly, and Whit's promising to do all sorts of filthy things to me.

It's not motivating me to stop.

So, I just let us roll back a bit. The truck slides to the left, the tires slipping over the loose rocks beneath us, and then I put Betsy in gear, and we lurch forward, taking a slightly different path up the hill. When we finally make it to the top, Whit is breathing heavily, his eyes wild.

"You do that again, and you will be very, very sorry."

I eye him with a smile and then snap on my seatbelt.

He looks a little less worried now, though he's still fuming.

"Promise," I say, and Whit opens his mouth to reply when I let go of the clutch, and we crest the hill and begin our very slippery descent.

When we make it back to the house hours later, Whit marches straight into the house, muttering something about a shower. He's pissed. Though I saw him smiling a few times, he'd bite them back if he caught me looking.

"What did you do to him?" my aunt asks as she watches Whit disappear upstairs. "You better not have scared him away. I was looking forward to planning your wedding. And I want grandbabies."

"I want those things too," I say and then take the stairs two at a time, looking for my man.

I find him washing the dust away from our little adventure in the shower.

So, I join him, wrapping my arms around him and pulling his wet body into mine.

"Don't be mad," I say, and he ignores me, continuing to wash himself.

"I'll let you do whatever you want to me. As punishment."

He pauses for a moment and then says, "You'd do that anyway."

I run my hands down his chest and cup his soft cock in my hand.

"Maybe, I'll just *not* fuck you," Whit says, and I gasp, turning him in my arms and glowering at him. "That would be punishment enough."

His eyes sparkle with mischief, and I lean in to press a kiss to his lips, but he turns his face away, and my mouth hits his cheek.

"Seriously?" I whine. "You can't still be mad at me."

Whit arches an eyebrow at me and says, "Hands on the wall, Caleb. I'm going to wash you."

I watch him for a moment. He has this look in his eyes, and I'm worried for a moment. Whit's out for revenge, and I feel I'm going to be very, very sorry soon.

"On the wall, Caleb," he bites out, and when I do as I'm told, he ends up washing me like he said he would. And spends way too much time caressing my cock, bringing me so close to orgasm that I'm thrusting my hips forward, seeking release. But then he suddenly steps away and tells me to rinse.

I'm panting, my cheeks red, my heart thundering in my ears. Is it possible to expire from blue balls?

"You can't be serious," I mutter, and it's Whit's turn to chuckle darkly.

"I'm very serious, Caleb. I told you to stop being reckless, but you didn't listen. You didn't even wear your seatbelt."

I frown at him and then reach for my aching cock, but he grabs my hand, pushes it against the wall, and leans forward, his mouth on my ear.

"Touch yourself today, and I won't fuck you for a week."

"You can't be serious!"

"Try me."

I groan and sag in disappointment when he leaves the shower. Rinsing off, I glance at my sad, weeping cock and apologize for the punishment Whit has in store for both of us.

"Ready to go?" Whit asks, holding a bundle of flowers in his hands. I don't know where he got those, but my heart melts a little at the gesture. We're going to go visit my mom's grave before dinner. To be honest, I've been so distracted by Whit that the fact my mom died a year ago today almost slipped my mind. Almost. That kind of traumatic event is hard to forget.

"Yeah," I say, shrugging on my Carhart jacket, and tugging my hat low on my head. I notice how Whit stares at me, those eyes assessing and concerned.

His hand slips through mine, and he leads me to the car, where he opens the door for me, and I slip inside.

Then he drives me the twenty minutes into town, where my mom was laid to rest. When he parks the car and kills the ignition, I lean back against the seat and rub my face.

"Why is this so hard?"

Whit doesn't respond, and I look over at him.

"I don't know what to say, Caleb. I've never been faced with the loss of someone I loved. But I know that if we love someone deeply, we can never really lose them. They become a part of us even though they might not be here in body."

I stare at him, this wise man, and then swipe at my eyes. "Yeah. A part of me. I like that." My voice breaks slightly, and I look out the window.

"I'm so sorry for your loss, Caleb," Whit says, his voice gentle and sweet, and I blink rapidly.

"We should go."

As soon as we step from the car, I clutch Whit's hand in mine and pull him through the graveyard until we finally stop in front of a simple marble stone.

Arabella Lee van Beek

"She was just forty," I tell Whit, who crouches down and begins cleaning away the debris from the site. Even though he hates getting dirty, he obviously has no qualms about doing this for me. For my mom.

God, I'm so in love with this guy.

The thought shocks me so much that I can't breathe for a minute. My heart clenching painfully in my chest. I have no business loving this man. And yet, I do. I can't help it. He burrowed his way into my heart, and I'm not sure there's a way to remove him without cutting a piece from me.

When Whit glances up from where he's crouched, those eyes meeting mine, I bite back a sob.

Fuck.

If he notices my mini-meltdown, he doesn't say anything. He probably thinks I'm emotional from the loss of my mom. And I am, but I know that I'm going to lose him too, eventually. I'm not sure I can withstand the loss of both.

Whit reaches up for the flowers, sets them gingerly in front of my mom's name, and then says, "Nice to meet you, Ms. van Beek. I'm Whit."

I exhale shakily and rub my eyes.

"Your son is amazing. You'd be proud," he continues, pressing those fingers to her name.

Shit, this guy. I sniffle and bite down on my bottom lip to keep everything inside.

"Whit," I whisper, and he looks up at me again. Pain and sympathy filter through those eyes, and I pull him into my arms. I clutch him to me, my tears falling quickly now. I bury my head against his neck and let it go, the sadness and loneliness that I've felt since she's been gone. It's a gaping hole that hasn't really healed with time. I've just gotten used to the feeling of brokenness, the hopelessness.

Whit's helped me live through it. He breathed life back into me.

"She would have loved you," I manage to say, my voice broken and wobbly.

"I'm sure I would have loved her too. She made you, didn't she?" he says, and I clutch onto him tighter and almost utter those three life-changing words but swallow them down.

Not here. Not now.

"Thank you," I say instead. "For coming here. For the flowers."

"Of course," he replies and runs his hand across my neck and squeezes.

We stand like that for what feels like hours before we head back. The sun's setting in the distance as we drive back to my aunt and uncle's house, and I hold Whit's hand the entire way home.

It's enough, I tell myself. What we have right here, right now.

As long as he stays with me, I can be whatever he wants me to be.

Dinner is a quick affair consisting of pizza and beer, and then Whit and I head upstairs while everyone heads outside to drink by the fire.

I'm emotionally worn out from visiting my mom's grave, my eyes swollen and red-rimmed. I just want to be held, fucked, and then held some more.

For a moment, I worry Whit's going to keep punishing me for earlier, that he's going to withhold what I *need*. But when we get into our room, he locks the door and moves toward me, pushing my flannel onto the floor and then lifting my t-shirt up over my head.

"So, I take it you're no longer punishing me for earlier," I say softly, and Whit looks at me as he unbuttons my pants.

"I'll fuck you tonight because you need it, Caleb. But you're going to earn it."

I don't know what that means, but I don't care. As long as I can be close to him, I'll do whatever he wants.

He pushes me onto the bed and then stands there, watching me, those eyes traveling over me in excruciating detail. My entire body is trembling with need, and my cock hardens to full mast when he starts stripping. Slowly. Much too slowly.

"Come on, Whit," I plead, and he steps to the edge of the bed and trails a finger down my sternum.

"There will be no rushing tonight," he says.

I groan, and then he runs that finger over my nipple piercing, and he says, "You know I have excellent control. I can fuck for hours."

"You're full of shit," I breathe shakily. Because I can barely last ten minutes with him inside of me.

"You have very little control, Caleb."

"Not my fault," I bite out, and he trails that torturous finger to my happy trail and slides through it.

"You're too eager. You have no patience. Have you ever been edged?"

I shake my head, and Whit runs his finger across the head of my swollen cock as he leans down and says lowly, "I'm going to bring you to the edge so many times, you will cry, and I'm going to enjoy doing it."

I'm sweating, my cock aching painfully, and Whit's still inside of me. When he said he could fuck for hours, I thought he was joking.

He wasn't.

He was being serious.

The things he's done to me over the past two hours, I can't even think about it, or else I'll come.

I writhe underneath him, impaled on his long length as he slowly pulls out and then pushes back into me.

"Please," I mutter, my mouth dry and my body trembling. Every nerve ending in my body is lit up, and my skin is hypersensitive to touch.

"Begging won't help," he mutters as a bead of sweat rolls down his cheek, and he shakes his head. "You can go longer." And then he lifts one of my legs up and drives into me, hitting me in the prostate repeatedly until I'm gasping. I'm so ready to come, prepared to feel the headiness of release, but just when I think he'll take pity on me, he pulls out. My hole feels empty.

"Whit," I groan, and he swipes at his forehead.

He's a mess, the exertion of fucking me for so long taking

its toll on him. I can tell, but instead of stopping, of giving in, he keeps on going. The sight of him completely wrecked and on the verge of recklessness is an aphrodisiac all on its own.

"You too sore, Caleb?" he asks, reapplying lube into my sensitive hole, and I groan at being filled again. Need it. Want it. More.

"Never," I breathe and then arch up as he crooks his finger inside of me.

"Good boy."

His mouth swallows me whole, and I gasp as he sucks my cock for the third time tonight.

Oh god. This is awful. Amazing. Terrible. I need relief.

His head bobs, his throat swallowing around me, and I'm clutching at the sheets to keep my hands off of him. Then he's pulling away again, his lips red and swollen from taking me deep, and I whimper. Literally whimper.

Not the first time I've done that tonight.

"On your knees," he says, wiping at his mouth.

"Can't," I moan. My body is limp, and I don't know if I can move.

"On your knees, Caleb."

When he says my name like that....

I roll over with a grunt, the sheets against my cock making me bite back a groan. Everything is oversensitive, and I feel like just the slightest touch will set me off.

Holy fuck. Edging is no joke.

"Do not come on the sheets," he says and lifts my hips roughly before he enters me from behind, tunneling in and out of me until I'm breathless once again.

"Enough," I moan. "Enough. Please, Whit. I'm sorry. I'm sorry. Enough."

My eyes are leaking, and my entire body is on fire. My cock aches. It's almost painful.

Whit exhales shakily, and then he pulls out, flipping me onto my back once more and spreads me so wide it's X-rated.

"I'm going to watch you come," he says and then enters me again. Knowing that I can finally find release, I tremble so hard my teeth clatter.

He lifts both of my legs and places them over his shoulders, and then he's thrusting into me wildly, the headboard of the bed hitting the wall erratically.

I'm groaning so loudly that I'm sure my family can hear me from outside.

"Can't," I breathe. "Can't. Oh fuck...fuck. There. There. Fuuuuuuck. Yes!"

My cock jumps, my balls drawing up tightly, and my release happens so suddenly that I have to grasp onto the headboard to keep me grounded. I swear I grab on so tightly I hear it start to crack. My come shoots across my entire torso, hitting my neck and chin, and I don't stop coming until I blackout.

And when I come to, Whit's pounding into me so roughly that I'm moving up the bed, my head knocking against the wall. Then he's clutching me so tightly I know there will be bruises tomorrow. His moans and grunts echo above me, and I feel the warm heat of his release inside of me.

And then it's over.

I feel like I can't move.

I'm never moving from this spot again.

I'm dead.

"You broke me," I say, my eyes closed, my entire body trembling from the aftershocks.

"You learned your lesson?" he asks through heavy breaths.

"Nah," I manage to say. I can't even smile. My face doesn't work. "Give me twenty, and I'll be ready to go again."

Whit arches his hips inside of me again, and I gasp. Shit, I'm sore.

"I think you have," he whispers, licking at my chin. The thought of him cleaning up my release makes my dick twitch.

"You did well," he says, pressing his lips to mine.

"You're an animal," I mutter.

"Perhaps don't test me again."

I scoff and then pull him onto me. His skin slides against the wetness coating my abdomen, but he doesn't complain. Just lets me hold him.

We doze like this for a bit, and then Whit forces me into the shower and washes me. I'm too drained to move, so I slump against him, and when we crawl into bed, I fall asleep almost immediately.

When I wake up, I realize that the anniversary of my mom's death has passed with minimal emotional damage.

Because Whit distracted me.

In the most delicious way.

At that moment, I know I've fallen even more in love with him.

Fuck.

I'm in too deep, and there's no going back now. I'm setting myself up to get torn apart.

"You two awake yet?" Sem asks, pounding on the door, and I grumble, pulling myself closer to Whit.

"Go away," I shout, and Sem kicks the door lightly.

"Whit's requested in the kitchen."

"Ugh," I say, and Whit pushes at my shoulder. Once again, I've ended up on top of him, and instead of moving off him, I just nuzzle further into him.

"Come on, cuz! Ma is asking for him."

"I have to go," Whit says, shoving lightly at my shoulder, and I grunt and grumble but roll off of him. He pushes himself up, but before he heads to the bathroom, he leans over and presses a kiss to my cheek.

"You okay?" he asks.

"My ass is sore. You tore me up," I mutter, smiling softly up at him.

He glances down at my bare butt and trails his fingers gently over it.

"We should take it easy then."

I snort. "Nah. I'm good."

He arches an eyebrow at me and then asks, "You okay today, Caleb?"

My smile fades, and I swallow roughly. "Yeah, man. Thanks. For the distraction."

He nods and then presses another kiss to my temple before disappearing into the bathroom.

Sem kicks at the door again. Not wanting him to let himself in, I move to the door and open it, not caring that I'm completely naked. He's seen it all before.

Sem glances down at my cock and then looks me straight in the eyes.

"You moan like a whore."

"Jealous that your sad dick isn't getting wet?" I ask.

Sem stares at me thoughtfully, "Sex with a guy that good?"

"You have *no idea*," I groan, and he holds out his fist, and I bump it.

Sem smiles widely at me and says, "Now put that tiny dick away and come help me with the Jeep."

While Whit helps my aunt in the kitchen, Sem, Luke, Liam, and I spend the morning working in the garage.

"So, tell us Caleb, are you a top or a bottom?" Luke asks, his head tucked under the Jeep's hood, still tinkering with the engine. When I don't answer right away, they all pause and stare at me.

I clear my throat. "None of your business."

They continue to stare at me, and then Sem says, "He's a bottom. Have you seen how they cuddle?"

I slug him in the shoulder and then shrug, "So what if I am? Have any of you been fucked in the ass?"

They stare at me some more, and I laugh at their expressions of confusion.

"It's not for everyone. And not for the faint of heart." I smirk.

They blink at me, and then Luke says, "Shit, you do take it, don't you?"

"Yep. Don't be jealous."

"I'm not," Luke says with a shake of his head. "Although Sem might be. He's been eyeing that friend of yours. The tiny, pretty one."

Sem grumbles something and then suddenly puts Luke in a headlock. They scuffle around for a moment, the two of them grunting like barbarians.

"Have not," Sem huffs.

Luke chokes out, "Have too, asshole. Can't deny it. I've seen you."

"I'm not gay," Sem bites out and then shoves Luke.

Luke coughs and stumbles forward. When he rights himself, he runs a hand through his wild hair. "Let's just be honest here. You've been spying on him. You're low-key obsessed with that twink."

"That true, Sem?" I tease, and Sem blinks at me.

"He looks like a girl." As if that's reason enough to follow

Magnus around.

"He does not," I reply and then say, "He's just...small. Pocket-sized."

Sem doesn't seem to hear me and adds, "And he's too smooth for a guy. No hair anywhere, and he wears these little shirts," Sem adds, gesturing to his abdomen, and now it's our turn to stare at him.

"That's quite the observation, Sem," I drawl, and Sem glowers at me.

"Seems obvious. Sem has a crush," Liam teases, and I see Sem blush for the first time in my life.

"I do not have a crush."

"Think you'll be a top or a bottom," I say, waggling my eyebrows at him, and Sem's face scrunches.

"I won't take anything up the ass. Ever."

"Don't knock it until you try it," I say.

Sem pauses for a moment, almost considering it, and then he shakes his head. "Stop putting this shit in my head, man. I'm not gay."

"I didn't think I was either. Until Whit. Now I can't imagine it any other way."

Sem looks at me and then glances away. "Whatever. Let's stop talking about this."

"I don't know. I think the twink is a fun topic of conversation," Luke teases, and Sem tosses a rag at him.

"I'm leaving until you change the subject."

Liam and Luke laugh as Sem walks away, but I chase after him and grab onto his arm.

"Hey, man. Sorry for teasing you," I say, and Sem shakes me off.

"It's all good."

"Just know I'm here if you ever want to process it...."

"Process what?"

"Your feelings for Mag."

"I don't have feelings for him."

I tilt my head and really look at my cousin. That wild blonde hair pulled back in a ponytail, those clear blue eyes. The tattoos snaking up his neck.

"Just come to me, yeah? If you need anything."

Sem stares at me for a minute and then turns away. "Nothing to talk about."

I watch him disappear outside and wonder if that's true or if he's repressing some feelings of his own.

CHAPTER FIFTEEN

Thanksgiving happens without a hitch. My aunt outdid herself this time. When it's time for dessert, I try each of the pies that Whit made. When I exclaim how good they are and he grins softly, I feel like a million bucks. If he'd let me, I'd compliment him every day for the rest of his life. Watch him blossom like a damn rose.

Look at me all poetic.

"I can't move. You'll have to roll me outside," I say, patting my overstuffed stomach. I, of course, ate way too much per usual.

Whit grabs the plates on the table and carries them to the kitchen. I'd help, but I'm not sure I can do it. I wasn't kidding when I said I couldn't move.

"So dramatic," my aunt says with a large smile. "I bet I'll see you sneaking more food in half an hour."

I scoff, but Whit chimes in, "That sounds like Caleb. He's always insatiable. Never can wait too long before asking for more."

He smirks at me, and I roll my eyes. I know he's talking about other things. Makes my pants tent beneath the table. Asshole.

"Because I was deprived as a child," I reply.

My uncle lightly smacks me on the back of the head, and I rub at it.

"What was that for?" I ask with a small laugh. "You know how it was."

My uncle grumbles, still eating. "You had it good, son. Your mom did the best she could. We all did."

My eyes sting at the memory of her, and I nod. "Yeah. I know she did."

It's a somber moment, and I sit with it for a minute. I've never had a father. My mom had a one-night stand with a man she'd met at a bar, and nine months later, I popped out. Not able to afford to live in the city with a baby, she moved in with her brother and wife. I grew up out here, my uncle being the only father figure I'd had. He was more reserved and rarely showed affection, but I always knew he loved me.

I've had a good life, albeit a little unconventional compared to someone like Whit, who grew up prim and proper. And rich.

"Whit, come sit a minute. Have we told you the stories of all the trouble Caleb got into growing up?" my aunt says.

Whit lowers himself into a chair next to mine and shakes his head. His hand slips into mine, and I bring it up to my mouth, pressing my lips against his fingers.

"I've heard it mentioned, but nothing specific."

My uncle shakes his head. "Those boys were always in trouble. Still are. You should know what you're getting into before walking down the aisle to this guy."

"Don't pretend like you weren't in on it too, old man," I say, and my uncle chuckles.

"A few times," he admits and then leans forward to whisper, "Don't tell your aunt. She'll kill me."

"Oh, I already know," my aunt says and then adds, "It was very irresponsible, Daniel."

My uncle laughs loudly at that, and Whit eyes me as if to say, *now I know where you get it from*.

Sem, Luke, Liam, and Anne amble in, and they take a seat at the table as we reminisce about all the stupid shit we did growing up. Whit looks horrified at some of the stories, and I can't help but lean over and press my lips to that frown.

"It's amazing you made it out alive," Whit says as he makes his way to the kitchen.

"I know," I chuckle, and Whit frowns.

"You could have blown yourself up. Putting batteries into a fire. Jesus, Caleb."

I rub at the back of my neck and look at him a little sheepishly. "We were curious what would happen."

"You lit the backyard on fire with gasoline."

"Yeah, that was Sem. Not me."

"You were a part of it," he says and then pulls me into him, his hand clutching my shirt. "No more of that stupid, reckless stuff when you're with me. Okay?"

I lean into him and rub my face against his cheek. "Yeah, babe. I'll tone it down."

"All the way down, Caleb. I heard Luke and Sem saying something about a homemade potato gun. I don't want you to be part of whatever they're planning."

I chuckle at that and press a soft kiss to his lips. "And if I'm a good boy and stay out of trouble...."

Whit scoffs and shoves me gently away. "I need to go do the dishes."

"Nah, let's go out on the ATVs instead," I say. "Dishes are boring."

"We need to clean up," Whit protests, but I tug him toward me.

"Do the damn dishes later," I say. "Let's go have fun. We only have one more day here."

Whit throws me a look. "What did I just say about not being reckless. You shouldn't go out on the ATV. You just got your cast off. Do you want to break your hand again?"

I wiggle my fingers at him and say, "I'm fine. Feel like brand new."

Whit sets a dishtowel down and turns to face me completely.

"No. You're *not* to set foot on that thing. Especially since you always let your cousins convince you to do idiotic things. As history suggests, you don't make the smartest decisions when coupled with them."

I pull him into a slow, dirty kiss and then lean back, "All that fancy language makes me hot and bothered. You worried about me, babe?"

He narrows his eyes at me. "I just know how irresponsible you are out there with them."

I run a hand up his arm and then into his hair. "Why don't you join me then. Keep me in check."

He watches me for a moment, contemplating it, and then sighs. "There's no stopping you, is there?"

"Nah."

He sighs dramatically. "Fine, but *I'm driving*. Let me at least check in with Anne and make sure she's okay cleaning up by herself."

Anne, of course, waves him off, saying she'll finish the dishes, and then Whit follows me outside. I hand him the keys and watch as he warily mounts the ATV.

"You're turning me on big time, sitting there," I groan, flipping my hat backward and climbing on behind him.

"Keep it together, Caleb," he chastises as I help him start the machine and instruct him on how to drive it. He listens intently, then revs the engine, and we move forward.

Slowly.

Holy shit.

"Snails are moving faster than us," I tease as Whit carefully maneuvers us over a small hill. Luke, Sem, and Liam are so far in the distance I can't see them anymore. Can hear them hollering, though.

"I'm keeping you safe since you won't do it yourself."

"Aw," I say and press a kiss to his neck as my hands roam his torso. "You care about me. Admit it."

Sue me, I'm fishing for answers...for anything. Might as well do something productive because Whit's driving the speed of a grazing cow right now.

"Of course, I care," he says, purposefully avoiding a bump and steers us onto a bit of flat land.

My hands slide under his shirt, and I sigh into him. Touching him hasn't grown old in the least. I can barely keep my hands to myself. I never want to keep my hands to myself ever again.

"You're distracting me," Whit says as I play with his nipples. "It's not safe."

"You're driving so slow I think if something happened, we'd be able to avoid getting hurt."

I tug on his nipples roughly, and Whit stops the ATV

abruptly. He turns to look at me, his eyes flashing. "Do you mind?" he asks, cutely annoyed.

"I can't help myself," I say, moving my hands to the waistband of his pants and playing with the button of his jeans.

"We could find a tree, and I could blow you so good," I hint, and Whit huffs, starting the ATV again and turning it around, heading back to the house.

"You are not blowing me behind a tree," he mutters.

Sadly, he doesn't stop anywhere, much to my dismay. He just keeps plugging along. And before we even make it to the house, my cousins come racing past us, dust flying in the air as they whoop and whistle loudly at us.

"This is embarrassing," I say, laughing softly. "We look like total losers."

"We're being *safe*," Whit hisses, and I spend the rest of the slow ride home giving him a hickey.

He rubs at the fading mark on his skin as he slides into the car, and we begin the trip home. We had one more day at my aunt and uncle's house before needing to head back to campus. With the end of the semester looming, we both have projects to work on. Whit especially needs time to study. He's so fucking brilliant. That brain of his really gets me going.

"I can't believe you did this to me," Whit says grumpily.

"You let me do it. Secretly, you love it," I say as I fiddle with the radio. Soft music floats through the speakers as Whit glances at me.

"Your aunt saw it. She stared at it until your uncle told her to stop. It's enormous."

"It was a lot of work. Not my fault you taste so good," I

say, and Whit huffs.

I lean over and nibble on his ear. "Plus, hickeys aren't a big deal. Pretty sure everyone heard us fucking this weekend."

He grabs onto my hair and pulls me in for a quick, filthy kiss. Shit, now I'm going to spend the rest of the trip hard, thinking what that mouth can do to me when we get home.

"That's because you can't keep it down," Whit says.

"How can I when you fuck me so good," I reply and lean against the seat and palm my cock. "Don't be mad, baby. Love your cock."

Whit flushes, gripping tightly to the steering wheel and biting down on his lower lip. God, he looks good like this. Horny and hot for me. I love knowing how I affect him.

Suddenly, his phone buzzes, and he lifts it from the cupholder. The flushed look he wore a moment ago disappears, and he pales. Concerned, I glance at him and watch as he shifts his knee and starts driving the car with it as he texts back.

"Everything okay?" I ask as he sets it back down.

"Yes," he says, but it doesn't sound very convincing. That and his fingers are tapping nervously on the steering wheel.

His phone buzzes again, and he picks it up again, responding quickly before shoving it under his thigh.

"Want me to text back for you?" I ask, and he shakes his head.

"I've got it."

"Is it your parents?"

"No," he responds curtly, and I hold up my hands and let it go. After this amazing weekend, I don't want to start anything right now. I just want to ride the bliss into tomorrow. I sneak looks at him, though, and he looks both angry and upset. Anxious too.

Shit. This can't be good. Usually, he's upset when he hears from his parents, but it's nothing like this.

Then his phone rings, and he cringes, holding the phone up to his ear and talking abruptly in Romanian. His voice is terse and clipped, and he's gripping the phone so tightly that his knuckles are white. The conversation continues for longer than I expect, Whit's voice rising with each word.

And when he finally hangs up, he slams his phone into the cup holder and shouts, "Fuck!"

The swear word coupled with him yelling has me reaching over and running a hand down his thigh. He's trembling.

"What's wrong? What happened?"

He breathes deeply through his nose, his nostrils flaring, and says, "Nothing. I just need...fuck! FUCK! FUCK THIS!"

He hits the steering wheel twice and then breathes deeply again, trying to get control over his emotions.

"Hey, pull over, babe. Let me drive," I say, really worried now. He's never had an outburst like this before.

Whit inhales deeply through his nose again and shakes his head. "I'm fine. I'm fine. I just need to think. *Let me think.*"

He breathes deeply, calming himself, but I see the tremble in his limbs, how he's tapping a nervous rhythm against one thigh. And he's silent the entire ride home, not looking at me once. Not reaching for me. It's like I've ceased to exist.

When we finally get home, Whit shoots out of the car, grabs our bags, and takes the steps to the apartment two at a time.

He opens the door, tosses the suitcases inside, grabs his phone, and begins tapping on that damn screen again. What the fuck is going on?

"I have to go out. I'll be back," he says without looking at me.

"Why?" Now, I'm really starting to lose my shit. "Where you going?"

Whit *finally* looks at me, those dark eyes wild with some emotion I can't name.

"I'll be back."

And then he's gone, and I'm left in our empty apartment, confused and apprehensive about what this all means. I find myself unpacking our clothes and pacing the apartment, waiting for him to return. But he doesn't. One hour turns into two. Then three.

I end up dozing on the couch when a sound wakes me.

"Whit?" I ask, sitting up quickly, and I see Whit standing in front of me, a frown on his face.

"What is it? Where were you? Are you okay? I was worried."

He stares at me, a solemn look in his eyes, and then he grabs my hand and pulls me to the bedroom.

Undressing me.

Pushing me down.

Thrusting into me.

His eyes never leave mine, and when he kisses me, it's with such desperation that I cling to him.

Why does this seem ominous?

Why does it feel like the last time?

He clutches onto my hair, his thumbs brushing over my temples as he kisses me deeply, our tongues warring with each other as he pumps in and out of me.

"Whit," I murmur, needing him to reassure me that everything will be okay, but he's silent. Just continues to torment me with his mouth, hands, and cock until I'm coming.

He follows shortly after and then falls onto me, holding onto me, his whole body shaking.

"What is it?" I ask, unnerved.

"I'm sorry," he whispers.

"What for?" I ask my heart rate tripling. God, this is bad. Really bad.

He's silent for a moment, and then, "I tried to fix it, but I couldn't."

"Fix what?"

He shakes his head and digs his fingers deeper into the skin of my shoulders, marking me with bruises.

"I have secrets. And I can't keep them anymore."

I still beneath him. On a trembling exhale, I say, "Tell me."

Whit shakes his head, wetness seeping into my skin from where he's laid his head.

Shit.

"Whit, tell me. You're scaring me."

He sniffles softly and mutters, "I don't want to tell you. Can I have just one more night with you?"

I run my hand through his hair, wanting to let this whole thing go, to put it off. To have one more night with him. But with how he's been acting, I know I'll be worried sick when morning rolls around. No, I need to know now. *I need to know.*

"I can't do that, Whit. I need you to tell me what's going on. Whatever it is, we can work through it."

Whit sniffles again and then pulls out of me slowly. His release seeps down my ass and onto my thighs, but I don't even notice. My sole focus is on him. Always on him.

He stares at me, sprawled out beneath him, and then looks away. His jaw works, the muscles bunching and flexing as he grinds his teeth.

"I'm engaged."

"To me, you mean?" I ask, but I know that's not who he's referring to, even as I say it.

"No, to someone else."

The words settle over me like a wet rag. I'm suffocating.

"You're shitting me, right?" I ask, sitting up slightly and staring at the side of his face with confusion.

He's not even looking at me.

"I'm not."

It takes a minute for the words to register, and then I'm shoving him off of me, and I'm standing up on wobbly legs. His come slides down them, and I want to scrub it from my skin. It's no longer sexy. Now, it's just a reminder of how vulnerable I was with him just moments ago. How he's been lying to me.

"What the fuck, Whit?"

He turns to look at me, shame on his face, his eyes glassy and despondent.

"I'm sorry, Caleb."

"You were cheating on your fiancé with me?" I run a hand through my hair and then mutter, "Oh fuck. This is so bad."

He sits on the bed, pulling a sheet over his waist, and I stare down at my own flaccid cock.

"Who is he?" I ask, thrusting my legs into my boxers, needing armor for this conversation.

"It's not a man."

"You're shitting me."

"It's a woman."

I laugh angrily at that. "Stop fucking with me."

"I'm not."

I tug on my hair roughly. "Are you for reals right now? What is this shit show, Whit? Why the hell are you engaged to a woman? You're gay!"

He swallows roughly, and he clutches the sheets tightly.

"It's all a formality. It means nothing."

"Is that who you've been texting?" I ask. I cannot believe this. Can't wrap my head around it. He's engaged to a woman. *To a woman.*

"Yes. We're getting married in May."

"In May?" I'm shouting now, unable to help it. He's tearing apart my world, ripping my chest open. I'm bleeding out on the fucking floor. "That's in like four months, Whit. What were you going to do? Fuck me until you were headed down the aisle?"

He bites down on his bottom lip and shakes his head. "I didn't know what I was doing with you. I...I don't want to do this. To get married to her."

I'm pacing now. "Then don't do it, for fuck's sake."

He lifts his head, a tear streaking down his cheek, and it takes everything within me not to softly wipe it away.

"I can't. I have so much riding on this."

"So much so that you'd marry a *woman* to get it?"

Whit swallows, another tear moving down his cheek. He swipes at it and nods.

"Give it up then! Give it up, Whit. Your happiness is more important than money."

He inhales shakily and then meets my gaze. "I was fine with it. Fine with it until I met you. Why did I have to meet you?"

His voice is so soft that my heart breaks straight down the middle. But I straighten my shoulders and face him.

"So let me get this right. You're marrying a *woman* to get the money from your trust. Is marrying her one of the other stipulations on top of becoming a lawyer."

He nods, his eyes on the floor.

"So, I'm guessing your parents don't like that you're gay."

He shakes his head. "You don't understand. It was so easy

for you to come out, to be with me, but that was not my experience. They hated that my inclinations went in a different direction. It wasn't acceptable to them, so they tried to beat it out of me. When that didn't work, they starved me. When that didn't work, they found a way to manipulate me into being the obedient son they always wanted."

I see red, and I have to clench my fists at my side, so I don't punch a hole in the wall.

"So...you'd go the rest of your life repressed and married to someone you don't love, for money?"

He swallows and tips his head down, his chin hitting his chest.

"I suffered my entire life for it, Caleb. Bled for it. Starved for it. I don't know how to give it up now."

I grind my teeth together and grit out, "Just because you suffered for it doesn't mean you should hold onto it."

He lifts his gaze, and those watering eyes meet mine. He holds his arms out toward me, those long, jagged scars staring straight at me.

"Don't I, though? I survived all those times for what?"

For me, I think, but don't say it. Just swallow the words down. I know I won't like the response from him.

My voice cracks. "Why didn't you just tell me?"

Whit moves his eyes from mine and stares at the floor. "Because I was selfish. Because I wanted this with you. Even if it was just for a short time."

I pull at my hair, and a tear streaks down my cheek. "But that wasn't fair to me, Whit! I'm half in love with you now!"

His head whips up, "What?"

"You heard me, and you know it. Deep down. You always knew. I was open with you, and you used me. You knew you'd wreck me, and you did it anyway."

"I know," he whispers, more tears streaming down his face.

I want to rage, scream, punch holes in things, and at the same time pull him into my arms and cradle him to me. Fuck, this guy makes me crazy.

"Why are you telling me this now? Why not wait until May when you end up getting married?"

"Because she's coming to visit."

I clutch the back of my neck and squeeze my eyes shut. And then something occurs to me.

"Do you fuck her? Kiss her, huh?"

Oh god, the thought of that leaves me breathless, and I have to clutch onto my knees.

"Never," he whispers. "I've never...We're not in love. We don't even know each other. Not really."

"Then why do it? Don't fucking do it, Whit! Choose me!"

Whit shakes his head. "I can't. It's already set in motion. There's nothing to be done."

"Of course there is! There's always a choice, but you can't see it through all the shit in front of you. You can leave. Say *fuck you* to your parents and leave."

"I'm not strong enough."

"I can be strong for you," I say. "Don't be a coward. Don't let them win."

Whit doesn't reply, and I have my answer. He doesn't want me to be there for him. He wants to go through with this because money is more important to him than I am.

I guess this was just casual for him after all. I gave him my heart, and he destroyed it. Knowingly.

"I can't do this," I say and walk out of the room.

Whit scrambles out of bed and chases me, grabbing onto my arm.

"Please stay, Caleb," he chokes out, his voice rough and broken.

"And what, Whit? Watch you get married to a fucking woman in a few months. Fuck that."

I wrench my arm from his grip and grab the duffle bag he bought me. I don't even want it anymore. Ripping it open, I grab a pair of pants, tug them on, and then slip on my shoes. I pull my jacket over my naked torso and pull my ballcap low over my forehead.

"I'm staying somewhere else tonight."

Whit exhales shakily, his face wet, those tears dripping onto his lips. The lips I'd just kissed moments before.

"Please don't go," he whispers, and I can't help it. I reach out and cup his face. God, my heart hurts. I can't fucking *breathe*.

"Will you be safe if I leave?" Because even though I'm pissed, betrayed, and my entire life is falling apart around me, I don't want him harming himself.

He chokes on a sob and leans into my palm. His tears fall onto my fingers, burning me.

"Will you. Be safe?" I ask, my voice cold. Colder than it should be. I never want to speak to Whit like this again. I should be making him laugh. Smile. Not cry.

Fuck him for making me do this.

Whit nods, and then my hand is gone, and I'm wrenching the door open.

"Wait," he calls out, and I pause, looking over my shoulder. "Does this..." he inhales shakily, "...does this mean we're over?"

God, my crushed heart. I rub my eyes.

"Yeah, man. We're through."

And then I turn my back on him and walk away.

CHAPTER SIXTEEN

WHIT

If I thought the brutal beatings by my parents were terrible, the days I spent locked away, starved, and miserable. If I thought the excruciating pain I felt after slicing my wrists open was painful, nothing compares to how I feel now.

I'm a shell of a person, a ghost moving from one end of the apartment to the other. Nothing has any meaning. Nothing matters. Life, as I know it, isn't worth living.

I miss him.

Miss him.

Two days ago, Mal showed up, his eyes cold and wary. He looked at me like I was scum, like I wasn't fit to even look in Caleb's direction. Then he shook his head and silently packed Caleb's things in boxes and carried them away. He took him away. Stole him from me.

In a moment of clarity, I took one of Caleb's shirts and

tucked it beneath my pillow so I could breathe him in at night.

I found it only makes it worse.

My days are spent just sitting, staring at the wall, not showering, not eating, and wasting away. Classes are forgotten, emails unanswered. All I can do is replay every wrong decision I ever made since meeting Caleb. Every. Single. One.

Emily should be arriving soon, but I can't manage it. Don't want to see her. She's a reminder of everything I don't want. A reminder of how I let this all get so out of control.

I resent her, and she's done nothing wrong but agree to this scheme in the first place.

A day later, I had another moment of clarity and called her and asked her to lie. To say she visited, and I bribe her with a trip far, far away from me.

She agreed because she doesn't care about me. She's in this for the same reasons I am.

Money.

My parents are paying her handsomely for this sham of a marriage. To make their gay son "straight."

The phone rings and rings, but I ignore it. They keep calling, but my parents can go fuck themselves. They've left messages, but I delete them. The only person I want to hear from is Caleb, and he's yet to reach out. He doesn't want me, though. Not after what I did.

Pushing myself up, I move to the kitchen and stare at the knives.

Perhaps I should just end it. Put myself out of this misery. I move toward them, running my finger over the hilt of one. I unsheathe it and then stare at the sharp point.

To let myself bleed out. Let myself *go*. I can't stand this suffering.

But then I remember Caleb, how I've broken him, but ending it...he'd never forgive himself. He'd shoulder the blame. It would ruin him. I can't do that to him. So, I slowly put the knife back.

I can make it another day without doing *that*. I can.

I will.

I think.

It's been five days since he left, and I can't breathe. Each hour bleeds into another, each day the same as the one before it. My phone's died, and I don't bother to charge it. He hasn't called or texted anyway. What's the point of keeping it on when the one person that matters has left me? I have no one else I want to hear from.

I'm going to miss my finals, and I don't care. Nothing matters. What is the point of life when there's no one in it to love me? No one's ever loved me enough to stay, and the one that did, I drove away with my lies.

A knock on the door has me glancing at it, but I don't move.

Whoever is there can go fuck themselves.

"Open up, asshole," Sem grumbles from the other side, and I inhale sharply. Sem reminds me of Caleb, and thinking of Caleb makes me want to rip into my skin and bleed all over the floor. I've barely managed to keep it together the past few days. I don't need this.

Go the fuck away!

"You asked for it," Sem says roughly, and then I hear scratching, and the front door pops open. Sem steps inside. Seeing him, how similar he is to Caleb, steals the breath from my body.

Sem looks around with a scowl on his face. "Smells like shit in here, man."

He's right. It does. Because I'm unwashed and I haven't cleaned.

And I don't care.

I could die tomorrow, and I wouldn't even care.

I stare up at him from the couch but remain silent. I have nothing to say. Can't speak anyways. Too many memories of Caleb filtering through my mind right now.

Sem finally turns his eyes to me. "Wondering why I'm here?"

When I don't respond, he sighs. "Caleb wanted me to check on you."

My heart clenches in my chest, and I pant. So much fucking pain. Can't breathe.

Sem moves to stand in front of me, and he crouches down, his eyes meeting mine. "Wanted me to check your arms and legs, man."

I clench my jaw, breathing heavily through my nose, and look away. Can't look too long at those blue eyes. So much like *his*.

"Shit," Sem mutters, and then he stands up. He glances around the apartment, shaking his head, and then he's gone, the door clicking shut behind him. And I'm all alone. Again. I'll always be alone.

I didn't have to be. But I chose this, didn't I?

He'd said he loved me. Or was I just imagining that? But he still must care because he sent someone to check in on me. He has to still feel something for me. Right?

A tear slips down my cheek, and suddenly I'm sobbing, my entire body shaking. It's messy and ugly, but I can't stop the flood. Just clutch at my chest, hold onto my stomach as I curl up on the couch, and ride through it.

When my tears finally stop, when my body is drained, and when I finally manage to swallow the hollow moans wrenched from my soul, I hear another gentle knock on the door. And when I don't answer, don't call for anyone to come in, the handle turns.

And he's here.

He's here.

He's the sunshine obliterating my shadows.

"Whit," Caleb inhales softly, his voice the gentlest of balms on my bruised heart.

I glance up at him from where I'm cradling myself on the couch, and even though I want to move, I'm afraid that he'll disappear if I do.

So, I just let him approach me, his eyes moving around the apartment, taking in the wreck that's my life now.

And I'm ashamed. For so many reasons.

"Whit," he says, his voice cracking.

He kneels in front of me, his hands on his thighs, and I meet his eyes. He looks tired, with purple rings under his blue eyes, but he looks so good. So damn good.

I lick my cracked lips and exhale shakily.

"Sem said you wouldn't let him see," he says, his fists clutched on his thighs. "Can I?"

I blink up at him, and when I don't respond, he reaches over and pulls my shirt sleeves up. His breath comes out on a shaky exhale at finding nothing there.

He has no idea how hard that was. I did it for him.

I did it for you.

"I need to check your legs now," he says, and then he gently tugs my pants down, exposing my thighs. He's careful not to touch my skin, and I notice it. Notice how disgusted he must be with me. I'm rotting from the inside out.

His eyes sweep over my scars, but when he discovers nothing new, he pulls my pants back up, rubbing a hand over his face in relief.

"Good. That's good."

I watch him, drinking him up. God. I need him.

How can I live without him?

He looks around the apartment and then stands, moving to pick up the trash littering the counters, and I watch him do it. Watch as he runs the dishwasher, wipes down the counters, and then runs a load of laundry.

I'm gasping for breath now, still lying on the couch, tears streaming down my face. How is there anything left inside of me? I'm empty. Hollow.

Caleb stops in front of me, and he crouches down next to me, his fists clutched tightly as if he's preventing himself from reaching out and touching me.

Don't blame him. I wouldn't touch me either.

"Let's clean you up."

He helps me sit up, and I lean into his touch, though it's fleeting and cold.

Then he tugs me into him, walking me to the shower. I sag against the wall as he turns on the water and tests it.

How can this man even care about me after everything I've done?

He hands me a toothbrush, and I weakly scrub at my teeth before swallowing the paste, not even bothering to spit it out.

He watches me and then steps toward me, helping me undress, first my shirt and then my pants. When I'm completely nude, I'm shaking so badly that my teeth clatter noisily in the quiet room.

"Whit," he says gently, his hands clutching my arms. "You've lost weight. Are you eating?"

I lick at my lips, and fresh tears leak from my eyes.

His face crumples, and his nostrils flare, those fingers digging into my skin.

"You need to shower. You'll feel better. You always felt better after."

I shake my head once and lean into him. His hands tense against me, and then he's pulling me into him, cradling me to his muscular chest, and I clutch onto him, ugly, wretched sobs escaping my trembling lips.

"Whit," he whispers, running his hands through my dirty hair, but he doesn't care. My mess never bothered him.

And I let him hold me, soaking his shirt with my tears.

I miss him.

When my sobs turn to hiccups, he cradles my face in his hands and moves away from me. But I lean toward him, needing him to hold me. Just for a minute longer. A second. I'll take whatever he'll give me.

Then he's undressing, pulling his clothes off, and I can't tear my eyes away. He's more beautiful than I remember.

"Let's wash you," he says softly and leads me into the shower. Warm water soaks my skin, but all I can feel is the way he washes me reverently. Like he still wants me. Like he misses me too. I turn my face into his chest and let my lips slip across his collarbone.

He exhales shakily, his cock hardening between us. For the first time this week, I feel alive.

I push into it, but he pulls his hips back. "Don't," he says, and I feel ashamed.

He's right. What am I doing?

"Rinse," he says, tilting my head back, and I do as he asks, those thick, strong fingers stroking through my hair.

And when he's done, my body finally clean, he looks at me and wets his lips.

"God, Whit," he mutters, and I blink up at him, clutching him.

I can't let go just yet. I need more time.

"Please," I say. My first word in days, and I'm begging.

But I don't care. I'll grovel if it means I can keep him.

"Baby," he murmurs, and then his thumb is smoothing across my bottom lip, and I tremble against him.

"I miss you," he says, and I close my eyes, my tears mixing with the water cascading down me.

When I don't respond, Caleb starts to move away from me, and I grab onto him, finding my strength after days of doing nothing.

"Come home," I say, clutching onto him, pressing myself into him.

I'm desperate.

"I can't."

My breath stutters, and I hold onto his hair roughly, tilting his face toward mine, and I see how his dark pupils widen at that.

"Stay," I say, my lips so close to his, and he shakes his head, swallowing roughly.

"Can't."

I brush my lips against his, and he moans brokenly at the contact, and then our mouths collide, like two comets meeting in space, and my entire body explodes from the feel of him. From the taste of him. My teeth knock against his as we tilt our heads and try and consume each other. I need more, more.

It's not enough.

I press him into the shower wall and tangle my tongue with his, my cock hardening between us. He groans beneath me, and I gasp as he bites down roughly on my bottom lip before licking the sting away. His fingers thread through my hair, pulling me to him. I'm not going to stop him. He can do whatever he wants to me. I'd even let him fuck me. If that's what he wanted. If that's what got him to stay.

This is the first time I've felt anything since he left. I'm helpless to do anything but continue.

He fucks my mouth with his tongue, plundering it, ravishing it, and I let him hold my head roughly while he does what he wants with me. I'll let him do anything. Anything. Just need him. Need him.

And then he wrenches his face away from mine, and his breath stutters, his chest heaving.

"No," he says, and those strong fingers loosen against me, freeing my head from his grasp, moving me gently away. "No, Whit."

I bite my swollen lip to hold back a whimper as he turns off the water and steps out of the shower, grabbing a towel and wrapping it around my trembling body. Then he pulls on his clothes. His cock is still hard, and he tucks himself away, his hands shaking slightly.

He still wants me.

"That shouldn't have happened," he says. "I'm sorry. Did I...did I hurt you?"

He glances at my swollen lip, and I shake my head.

He lets out a relieved breath. "Good. Let's get you dressed."

I let him take the towel from me and dry my still wet legs,

and then he's helping me into clean underwear, and he's pulling a shirt over my head.

"Better."

I just stand there, my hands hanging loosely by my sides, as he rubs at his chest.

"Hate seeing you like this, Whit," he finally says, his voice breaking.

"Then come home," I manage to croak out.

His eyes close, and he turns his face from me. "I can't be here when I know you're getting married. I can't do that to myself."

When his eyes open, he looks at me, "Are you still going through with it?"

"I don't know," I whisper, and he moves toward me, his knuckles brushing my cheek.

"Charge your phone, please."

I blink up at him, leaning into his hand.

Don't go!

"Take care, Whit."

And then he's gone.

CHAPTER SEVENTEEN

The days turn into weeks, and I find myself worried about Whit. My thoughts are consumed by him. But I can't go back. Can't see him again, or I'll do something I'll regret. Like, let him fuck me. Kissing him was painful enough. I've tried to repress that memory of his body against mine, his tongue in my mouth, but it keeps popping up, taunting me. He felt so good in my arms.

But he also *looked* broken in those moments. So fragile. Those dark eyes watching me. Hopeless. He was like a shell of the man I once loved.

My heart clenches in my chest, and I rub at it.

There have been so many times I've almost gone back, turned around, and said, who cares if he's marrying someone else. The pain I feel is unbearable. I secretly just want one more day with Whit, one more week. I'll take anything I can get, even though I know he's not choosing me in the end. But Mal won't let me go. Neither will Bree.

They're right.

I deserve better.

So instead of running back to Whit, I force myself to plod along, finishing up my classes and packing my bags to head home for winter break.

I haven't heard from Whit since that day. I'd told him to charge his phone, but I haven't reached out to ensure he did as I asked. My aunt keeps me updated, though. She calls and texts daily. She's worried about him after I told her that he has a history of self-harm. But he doesn't answer her calls either.

So Sem stalks him.

He reports back and tells me he's okay. I have to be alright with that, with not really knowing how he's doing. Has he hurt himself since I last checked? Is he taking care of himself? Is he attending his classes?

God, why does this hurt so much? I've never cared about someone like this before.

Christmas approaches, and with it comes memories of my mom. And of Whit. I find myself languid and listless through it all. Smiles are forced. I feign excitement for simple things. I feel like the world is tilting sideways. Nothing makes sense anymore.

My aunt watches me warily, and my uncle hugs me more often. Luke has slept in bed with me every night since arriving home, his snores dispelling the emptiness I feel.

I wake up crying. Chasing dreams of Whit. Luke never knows what to do when that happens, so he just awkwardly pats me on the head and falls back asleep.

Whit would hold me. He'd run those fingers through my hair.

I miss him.

On New Year's Eve, I break down.

I drink too much and text him.

Me: Hi

I don't get a response, which just pushes me over the edge. He's probably with his fiancé. Planning his wedding. Sem told me where he went for the holidays. He snooped around the apartment and saw the plane tickets. He's in New York with his family. With his awful parents who don't know what an amazing man he is. I hate them. If I ever meet them, I will murder them. My cousins will help me bury the bodies. I have it all planned out.

Me: Are you safe?

No response. It's hours and then days, and my message stays on *read*.

So, he got the message but chose not to respond. Maybe he's finally over me. Maybe he's come to terms with marrying someone else, and I'm just a distant memory.

God, the thought of him with that woman makes me sick. The idea of him forgetting about me is almost debilitating.

When the break finally ends, I come back to campus. And despite trying not to, I find myself constantly looking for Whit. But I never see him. Magnus confirms that he hasn't seen him either.

He's a ghost. Did he only exist in my head? Was this all a fucking dream?

"Are you sure you don't hate me?" Magnus asks nervously, his neck craning up to meet my gaze.

Shortly after leaving campus, Magnus told me he knew about the engagement. He'd happened upon the information by accident but was sworn to secrecy.

"No. I mean, I was, but I get it. No need for all of us to be miserable," I say and pat the top of his head.

He bristles, and I manage a small, forced smile for him.

He's wearing a polka dot long-sleeve shirt, purple pants, and a pair of wing-tipped shoes. He looks adorable, like a pet.

"Why do you all insist on patting me on the head," he mutters, and I pat his head again. He deserves it, the lying little shit.

"Let's go in before people wonder why we're late," I say.

Mag nods and opens the door for me.

"No need to keep kissing my ass, Mag. I forgive you for betraying me," I say, and he blushes in annoyance.

"You made it!" Bev says, pulling me into a hug as soon as I step inside. People I recognize mill around, chatting. Streamers hang from the ceiling. It's the annual New Years' LGBTQIA get-together, and I couldn't *not* come. Magnus practically dragged me here.

"Have you heard from him?" Bev asks, her eyes worried.

I shake my head, my stomach clenching. The last time I was here, Whit was with me. They know. They all know what happened. That we broke up, that he didn't choose me.

Sad, pitying eyes stare back at me, and I smile slightly. No one wants to see a broken man. They'd never know what to do with me if I really let it show how broken up I am about this.

"Stop looking at me like that. I'm fine," I tell Bev and then say it louder so everyone else can hear.

But the truth is, I'm not fine. I'm a fucking liar.

I sling my arm over Magnus' shoulders and pull him forward. He stumbles a little under the weight of me leaning against him.

"Little weakling," I say, and he scowls up at me.

"I'm not weak. I'm just normal-sized. Unlike you, weirdo."

I snort and dip my shoulder down, and swing him over my shoulder. "You're pint-sized."

"Put me down," he squirms, and I tickle his side until he's squealing with laughter. The sound makes me smile genuinely for the first time in weeks.

"Never," I say and tickle him some more.

When we finally make it to the other side of the room, Magnus is begging to be let go, so I take pity on him and let him slide down my front.

But he clutches on and clings to me like a monkey, his legs wrapped around me and his ankles hooked against my lower back.

"What are you doing?" I ask, my eyebrows drawn together as he attaches himself to me like Velcro.

"I'm going to smother you," Magnus says, his eyes flashing with annoyance.

I poke at his side, and he only clutches on tighter.

This asshole.

The more I try and remove him, the tighter he gets. He's like a jumping cactus. I can't get rid of him.

"Get off me," I say with a loud laugh.

"Shouldn't have thrown me over your shoulder and tickled me. And I am not pint-sized," he growls like a tiny kitten and then increases his grip on me.

I dig my fingers into his sides, but he continues to stick. I finally give up and sag against a wall, him still wrapped around me.

"Okay, I give up," I mutter, out of breath. This little shit is determined.

"You surrender?" he asks, leaning his face back and looking at me.

I narrow my eyes at him, and he pats my cheek. "Was good to hear you laugh again, big man."

"Was good to do it," I admit, and Magnus slides down my body.

And once his feet hit the ground, I feel it.

Feel him.

Turning slowly, I see Whit standing across the room, his hands clenched by his sides, his mouth parted slightly as if breathless. He looks good, thinner than usual, the cheekbones in his face more prominent, and a purple hue under his eyes. But he still looks like a dream. Why is he here? He hates these things.

And then I realize.

He saw me with Magnus. He must think....

"Oh shit," I mutter and then begin to move. My legs tremble so hard that I trip slightly, knocking over a chair, trying to catch him. But he's too quick. He's out the door and into the cold night before I can even reach him.

Don't fucking run, asshole!

"Whit!" I call out, cursing myself for letting Magnus get the better of me. For wrapping himself around me. What must Whit think, seeing us like that?

"Whit!" I'm bellowing like a mad man, running at full speed to catch up to him. People stop and stare, but I don't care. I just need to get to him. To make him understand.

It's only when I finally reach out and grasp onto his arm that he stops. He's panting, his cheeks flushed, his hair tousled.

"I shouldn't have come," he blurts, his fingers clutching his stomach. "Go back to Magnus. I..." his words trail off, and he swipes at his eyes. "You looked happy. You should just go back. I'm fine. I'll be fine."

"Fuck that. You might be fine, but I've been miserable," I blurt. So much for playing hard to get. That was never my thing anyway. "Magnus was just being an annoying little shit. It meant nothing."

"He wants you."

"No, he doesn't. He's just being...Magnus."

Whit blinks rapidly and then turns to walk away. Again.

"Don't go," I say, grasping onto him, holding him in place.

It's been too long. Too long, and I'm so weak. I can't let him go again. I just need a few minutes with him. To just gaze at him.

"You really should go back in there. To him. He's..." he swallows roughly. "He's perfect for you."

I reach up and grab at my hair and tug on it. This *infuriating man*.

"I'm not with Magnus!" I nearly shout. "I'm not interested in anyone but you! I don't *want* anyone but you! Get that through your stupid, smart head!"

Whit watches me, those dark eyes assessing the truth of my statement, and then he exhales shakily.

"Are you...are you sure?"

"Of course, I'm fucking sure, Whit. I want you! YOU!"

He's silent for a moment and then, "Oh. Okay."

"Okay? That's it? That's all I get after everything? No, absolutely not, man. You need to give me more. Why did you show up tonight? You *hate* these things. Why are you here?"

He watches me, silent, and then, "I came to find you."

Yes. Yes, Fuck yes.

"Why?" I ask, my voice hoarse, my heart beating so hard I can hear it in my ears.

Whit plays with the end of his coat, his fingers tugging a thread free and wrapping it around his thumb. "I gave it up. All of it."

I nearly slump to the ground with relief. "You did?"

"Yeah."

Oh shit, I can't breathe. I'm having a heart attack. "You're...oh fuck...you're not getting married anymore?"

"No."

"Why? Why did you do it?" I ask, needing to hear it. After everything that happened, I need to know.

"For you," he whispers, those dark eyes meeting mine. "I can't live without you, it seems."

I reach for him, pulling him into my chest, and he crushes himself into me, his face pressed against my cheek. And I bury my face into his neck and inhale.

Still smells so damn good.

"I should think about this. After you lied to me and put me through hell," I mutter, my lips skimming his skin. He tastes just like I remember.

"You should," he says with a broken huff. "Take all the time you need. I'll...I'll wait for you."

We stand there, wrapped around each other, and then I press a soft kiss to his neck.

"Fuck this. Fuck waiting. I've been miserable for weeks. Take me home," I say.

Whit shakes his head. "You should take all the time you need...."

"Shut up, Whit," I grumble. "Shut it. If you don't take me home and fuck me, I will throw you over my shoulder and carry you home. Then I will be the one tying you to the bed."

Whit swallows roughly and links his fingers through mine, tugging me forward.

"You sure?" he asks as he drags me along.

"A thousand percent."

When we arrive at the apartment, we crash through it, all

limbs and tongues and teeth as we fight to consume one another. It's been so long. He tastes so good. Feels just right.

"Now, need you now," I say, stripping off my clothes and stumbling into the bedroom.

And then we're naked, grinding against each other, hands everywhere, mapping out our bodies, feeling where one ends, and the other begins.

"Hurry," I plead, and Whit pushes me down onto the mattress.

I hold onto my thighs, exposing myself to him. Then his fingers are inside of me, pushing, crooking, fucking me until I'm nearly coming from the feel of it.

"Been so long, baby," I say, and he pulls his fingers out of me and pauses. His eyes hooded, flashing.

"Do I need a condom?" he asks softly.

And I nearly laugh because, fuck this. Like I'd let another man fuck me.

"I haven't been with anyone but you."

He inhales deeply and then says, "Same."

Then he's over me, his hands by my head, his hips pushing forward, and I take all of him in one swift push.

The two of us groan at the feeling. He stretches me so wide and I accept all of him.

And then he's kissing me, our tongues tangling as he tunnels in and out of me.

"Caleb," he whispers. "I missed you."

"Missed you more," I say, gasping as he angles his hips just right. He knows me, knows me so well. The headboard hits as he slams into me, the bed creaking, but all I can hear is Whit above me. Panting. Moaning. Saying *my* name. A few minutes later, I gasp and come onto my chest, unashamed that I found my release so quickly. Because he's here with me, and that's all that matters.

"Caleb," Whit groans, and I feel his body tensing as warmth floods me. And it's over. But already I'm already to go again.

"Shameless," Whit says, catching sight of my already growing cock.

"It's been deprived," I tell him, and he rolls his eyes.

He wipes me clean and lowers himself onto me, but it doesn't feel right, so I roll him onto his back and stretch across him.

"Better," I mutter and tuck my face into his neck.

We lay like that, my heart slowly stitching itself back together as he rubs his fingers across my skin. I could stay like this forever.

"Can I ask you something?"

"Anything?"

"How much was in that trust, babe?" I ask, tracing the line of his collarbone.

"Millions."

I look up at him, and he meets my gaze. "Shit. Will you resent me for it? Ten years down the road? When you're stuck with poor ol' me?"

He shakes his head adamantly. "Never. You are worth so much more than money."

My heart melts, and I press a kiss to his chin.

"I love you," I say, and Whit's eyes widen.

He exhales shakily. "What?"

It's my turn to roll my eyes. "You heard me. I. Love. You."

"You do?"

"Yeah."

"Why?"

This guy.

I scoot up a little and press a kiss to his lips.

"Because you're strong and smart, and you put up with my family. Because you deserve it after everything, you deserve to be loved. Because I just do, Whit. I've been in love with you for ages."

He blinks rapidly at me like he can't comprehend what I'm saying.

"Did I break you?" I ask, pressing my fingers to the pulse on his neck. His heartbeat is strong and fast under my fingertips.

"No..." he wets his lips and then threads his hands into my hair. "I love you too."

And my heart soars. It's literally taken flight, and I've died and gone to heaven. How is this my life?

"I have something for you, actually," he says, and then he leans up and reaches into the end table near his bed. "Close your eyes."

I do, my heart thundering in my chest.

"Open them," he whispers.

And on his chest, I see a small black box.

"What's this?" I whisper, my body trembling.

"Open it."

I swallow roughly and meet his gaze before moving to open it.

Inside is a titanium ring.

"Whit," I say, my eyes stinging with unshed tears.

"I bought this for you before Thanksgiving. But I never got a chance to give it to you. You don't need to wear it. But it's yours. If you want it."

"Can I try it on?" I ask, and when he nods, I slip the ring right onto my ring finger. It fits perfectly. Because, of course, it does. This is Whit we're talking about. I'm sure he painstakingly chose this for me. It makes it all the more special.

"I love it," I say and then move the box out of the way and rest my head back on his chest, hearing his heart thump wildly in his chest.

"Should I buy you a ring now?" I ask, examining the band encircling my finger. It's dark, nearly black, and shines in the faint glow of the moonlight piercing the blinds of our room.

"If you want."

I twirl the ring. "Does this mean we're really engaged this time?"

He tugs on my hair, and I lift my gaze up to his.

"It was that easy?" he asks, confused about how I can just accept it and move on so quickly from everything that happened. Everything he put me through.

"Should I play harder to get? Anne says I'm a pushover."

He narrows his eyes at me. "No. Not with me."

"Good because for you, I'm a total pushover. Get used to it."

Whit blinks rapidly and then shakes his head. "How did I get so lucky?"

I kiss the tip of his nose, his cheeks, and then his lips.

And, of course, it ends up like it always does. Me begging for it.

I end up impaled on him, riding him like my life depends on it, my ringed finger clutching his chest as I come.

EPILOGUE

ONE YEAR LATER

"That took way too long," I groan, shrugging off my tux and throwing it on the ground.

Whit eyes it, then picks it up and sets it on a chair.

"It was our wedding reception," he says, and I roll my eyes and pull him into me. We'd decided on a winter wedding, much to my aunt's delight. And it was perfect. But I was done and ready to get on with the night.

"I just wanted them all to go away so I could get you alone. You made me wait two whole days before I could see you. Torture, babe. Pure torture."

Whit smiles softly at me, not at all remorseful. "I wanted to see your expression as you walked down the aisle."

"And did you get what you wanted?" I ask, linking our fingers together and pressing a kiss to the matching ring now adorning his finger.

"You looked at me like you always do," he says, and I smile smugly at him.

"Told you," I say, tilting my head and giving him a filthy kiss. "I will always look at you like that. Get used to it. Don't know why you thought it would be any different on our wedding day."

Whit huffs as I pull his hand to my crotch.

"Alright, I can't take it anymore. Undress before I rip that suit off you," I say, much too eager, but I don't care how he perceives me at this moment. I'm needy as fuck. Serves him right for making me wait.

Whit shakes his head. "How about *you* undress and wait on the bed."

"Nah," I reply, but Whit shoots me a severe look and then disappears into the bathroom.

"Asshole," I mutter as I strip so quickly that I stumble and fall against the table. A lamp falls onto the ground, and Whit says sternly through the bathroom shut door, "Do not break anything, your body parts included. It will ruin the night."

I snort and flop onto the bed, my cock aching and straining toward his voice. That stern lilt does things to me.

Shocker.

As the time ticks by, one minute, two minutes. Now five minutes and, he still doesn't appear. I sit up and shout, "You're killing me here, Whit! It's been a whole fucking day, and I'm literally dying. My balls are way too blue. I think it's becoming a condition."

I hear a snort, but he continues to ignore me. A few minutes later, he appears completely naked, his hard cock bobbing in front of him, and I just want to swallow him whole.

"God, finally," I say, stroking myself as he crawls onto the bed.

I start to pull up my legs, but he places his hands on them and pushes them down beside me.

"What's your plan?" I say, much too excited to think rationally. I just want him inside me.

And then he's straddling me, and my eyes widen.

"Wh—?"

My throat constricts as he positions his ass above my cock. Oh, holy shit. I'm dead.

"Whit," I breathe. "What are you doing?"

"Giving you your wedding present," he says and sinks down an inch onto me, and my eyes roll back in my head, my hands clutching his hips.

"You don't have to. I don't need this..."

"Want to feel you inside me," he hisses and then sinks a little lower.

I'm trying to stay still, not move because I don't want to hurt him, but it's impossible because it feels so good.

"Shit," I mutter, wiggling beneath him as he lowers himself further onto me.

"I've been practicing, but you're so big," Whit said, bouncing a little on top of me, and I nearly come right then.

"Don't hurt yourself," I say, and then he sinks all the way down as if to prove a point. The little shit.

The two of us breathe heavily, his body impaled on me. My cock inside of him for the first time.

My hand reaches up, and I run it across his chest.

"Why are you doing this?" I ask, cupping the back of his neck and bringing his face to mine.

He presses a soft kiss to my lips. "I wanted you to be my first."

And just like that, this guy cracks my heart open all over again.

"I love you."

"Love you more."

And then he's moving, and I want to do everything at once. Touch, thrust, kiss, but I end up just lying there, my hands scrambling to hold onto him as he rides me like he's done this his entire life.

And, of course, I come first, emptying myself into his ass. He follows me shortly after, shooting all over my stomach and hitting my chin and mouth with his release.

I lick my lips, and he huffs, wiping me clean with his thumb. He presses that finger into my mouth, so I can taste him.

"You're a mess," he says as he does it, watching me suck his release off his skin.

When my entire chest is wiped clean, I arch my back. I'm still inside of him, and he hisses at the feeling.

"That was amazing."

"I'm glad you liked it."

I wiggle beneath him again. "Did *you* like it?"

He presses his forehead to mine. "Of course. It was with you."

"Are you too sore?"

"I think I'm okay," he says, clenching himself around me.

"Oh god," I moan. "Just give me like ten more minutes and I'll be ready to go again."

Whit huffs and then shifts off of me.

"Shower first."

God.

This guy.

EPILOGUE

FIVE YEARS LATER

We made it. Even when it seemed impossible.
　　I graduated with my B.S. in Business Administration and took over my uncle's scrapyard near campus. At the same time, Whit went on to take his LSATs and was accepted into a university near my aunt and uncle's house.

I worked my ass off the next few years to put him through law school, using the money from my mom's life insurance to afford a small studio apartment near his graduate school so he could focus on classes and not have to work. It wasn't easy all the time. We ate in most nights, rarely going out. Sometimes bills didn't get paid right away. Credit card debt was racked up during emergencies. Our free time was spent with my family or lounging inside our studio apartment, making out, fucking, or cuddling.

Needless to say, it's been the best five years of my life, even when it was tough.

"You ready for your first day tomorrow?" I ask Whit, who is laying out his recently pressed suit. Tidy as ever.

He glances over at me and nods. "I am."

"Did I tell you how much I liked your office?" I smirk at him. "You have a very nice desk. Very sturdy."

Whit narrows his eyes at me but adjusts himself all the same. He's remembering when we moved everything into his brand new office space two days ago after hours. He ended up fucking me on that sturdy desk. Did unspeakably filthy things to me.

I made such a mess all over.

"You left a stain."

I beam at him. "Not my fault you got me all excited. You know how I get."

He scoffs and then lays out his tie. I want to fuck him on that suit. Wrinkle it a little.

Two weeks ago, Whit was hired by a law firm to work in international law. He plans on using his degree to help queer individuals living under persecution in other countries.

I'm so damn proud of him. I could burst with it. It's a shame his parents aren't around to see how amazing he is. Neither of them have bothered to contact their only son. Too bad for them and good riddance. And to be honest, Whit doesn't seem too bothered by their absence. My aunt has stepped into the role of mother hen and Whit basks in the love she shows him.

"You're asking for it," he says, and I palm the zipper of my jeans.

"Duh."

He stalks toward me, intent clear in his eyes.

A groan slips out of me. "Oh god."

"Don't you ever get tired of it," he asks, always so flabbergasted that I'm raring to go at all hours. I mean, my sex drive has only increased with age.

"It's you, Whit. Don't know why you can't get that through your super smart brain. I'm obsessed with you."

He reaches up and presses his palm to the back of my head, and pulls me forward.

"I love you."

"I know. I love you too," I say, licking my lips.

"Kneel," he says, and I do.

AFTERWORD

Want to know what Caleb and Whit did for their honeymoon? Find out here!

ACKNOWLEDGMENTS

Thank you to my editor Angela O'Connell who reached out after reading Whit and offered to help me edit my book. We all know it needed help!

And to everyone who read and promoted this book. I sent this out into the world thinking no one would read it. So, thank you for giving an unknown author a chance.

ABOUT THE AUTHOR

Cora Rose loves any kind of romance and consumes way too many books each year. She currently lives in the U.S. and spends her days daydreaming about the characters inside her head.

f

ALSO BY CORA ROSE

The Unexpected Series

Whit

Sem

Emery

Luke

Lex

Colin

Diablo

The Inevitable Series

Until Him

Always Him

Standalone

Waiting for You

Unlucky 13

Exception

Printed in Dunstable, United Kingdom